THE COSMIC LOOTERS

By
EDMOND HAMILTON

I0616683

ARMCHAIR FICTION
PO Box 4369, Medford, Oregon 97504

*For more information about Armchair Books and products, visit our
website at...*

www.armchairfiction.com

Or email us at...

armchairfiction@yahoo.com

BESIEGED BY INTERPLANETARY HIGHWAYMEN

After being violently awakened in the middle of the night by a beautiful, black-haired woman from outer space, Wyatt was informed of an imminent attack upon his world. But Wyatt knew his government wouldn't believe it—he didn't believe it. So who was this strange woman and what were her real motivations? After hitching a ride in her spacecraft, Wyatt found himself hurtling through the void to the Alpha Centauri system—all in his stocking feet! He was soon witness to a large-scale planetary attack—a vicious raid for plunder—on a slightly less advanced, but no less civilized planet than his home planet, Earth.

So with the fate of Earth hanging in the balance, Wyatt plotted a course for the races of two worlds to finally put an end to the empirical conquests of the Cosmic Looters.

FOR A SECOND COMPLETE NOVEL, TURN TO PAGE 89

CAST OF CHARACTERS

DUNCAN WYATT
This communications man was brave, tenacious, and liked to hitch rides with good-looking female aliens.

CAPTAIN BRINNA HALPHARD
She was an officer in an alien task force set to plunder Earth, but her blind ambition wanted much more than just being an officer.

CAPTAIN MAKVERN
A staff captain of Varsek's task force, his loyalty was to his people, but not necessarily to his commander.

VARSEK
He was basically a paranoid, sadistic thief who operated on a grand scale, plundering planets and hurting those who defied him.

THE SECOND PARTY
They'd been in space for a long time—too long. All they wanted to do was stop looting and return home to their loved ones.

A.C. BURDICK
A typical cowboy, looking for a good fight, but tangling with an alien task force got him a lot more than he bargained for.

THURNE OF OBRAN
Native to the fourth planet in the Alpha Centauri system and a king's messenger—he was ready to fight beside his people.

CHAPTER ONE

DUNCAN WYATT SPRANG up, grabbed his gun and started toward the door before he had his eyes properly open. His ears were ringing with the explosive roar that had awakened him and the pre-fab shack still quivered in the shock wave.

He thought the Third World War had started.

He crouched in the doorway and peered out onto the mesa. The unorthodox shape of the experimental ultra-tight-beam transmitter loomed over him, black against the star-blazing New Mexican sky, bearing a red star of its own to warn low-flying planes. He was all alone here. His partner, Bannister, had flown out to the Coast to oversee the making of new components for a projected improvement in design. Wyatt had never felt lonely before, even in the total solitude of the mesa top with nothing around it but the vast impersonals of sky and desert, sun and wind. Now he did feel lonely, and scared. He wondered where the bomb had dropped.

He couldn't see anything, so he went out and around the corner of the shack, keeping low and sticking tight to the wall.

Now he could see a larger area of the mesa, softly but almost adequately lighted by the billion stars above the crystal-clear air.

He saw what it was that had fallen out of the sky.

It wasn't a bomb. It was a—plane? Call it a plane. Call it a rotary-thrust flying wing. Call it anything you want to, it was there, round and glimmering faintly against the drab rock.

The boom and shock that had shaken him out of his bunk must have been the result of the thing pulling out of a steep dive at super-sonic speed.

He should have been relieved that this was so. Somehow Wyatt was not. He had a feeling. It was such a crazy feeling that he could not believe it, but he couldn't get rid of it either.

He stood still in the shadow by the corner of the shack and waited to see what would happen next.

A light came on with blinding suddenness, shining from the center of the queer plane. It showed up every pebble and stunted bush, every grain of the rock, the sun-bitten pre-fab wall, himself in his sock feet and rumpled khakis, standing stiffly with the gun in his hand.

A portion of the black outer rim of the round plane dropped down, unfolding into a stair.

Wyatt shouted, "What is it? Who are you?" His voice was thin and small in that vastness of windy air. "I have a gun," he shouted. "Come out slowly, with your hands up!"

The words sounded ridiculous even while he was saying them. But he had to put up some kind of a front, simply because he was scared. If he didn't he would have had to turn and run away.

It was the damned round queer-looking plane. He was in a cold shaking sweat waiting to see what came out of it.

When he did see he didn't believe it.

She stood in the aperture at the top of the narrow metal stair. Her hands were raised just a little, so that he might be sure there was no weapon in them. He thought she was smiling slightly. She had black hair, black as the blackest shadow you could imagine, shorn close around her head. She was dressed in black—soft boots, closefitting pants, wide belt with holster, severely plain shirt with a splotch of gold on the front of each shoulder. Somehow he sensed that the gold splotches were insignia, not decorations. He also sensed—

from something about the way she stood, the way she looked at him, the hard, disciplined strength that underlay the splendid lines of her body—that this woman was not like any of the women he had ever known, and that probably the Third World War might have been easier to cope with.

She said, "There is no need to be afraid."

Her English sounded as though she had learned it by mathematical formula, and in a hurry.

Wyatt said untruthfully, "I'm not afraid. Just cautious." He walked out closer to the disc-shaped plane. The mesa rock was icy under his socks, the wind was icy down his back, and there was a chill inside him that was purely personal.

"Where do you come from?" he asked. "What do you want?"

SHE DROPPED her hands and came quickly down the stairs, apparently satisfied that he was not going to shoot her.

"I haven't much time," she said. Her eyes were the color of pure turquoise, startlingly bright, curiously tilted. She gave a swift glance at the sky and then spoke urgently to Wyatt.

"Try to understand, to believe. Your world is going to be attacked. Not tonight, but within a short time. I want you to take a warning to your government, so that we may be prepared when the attack comes."

"I see," said Wyatt. He had a wild desire to laugh. He saw himself going to Washington and telling various personages at the White House and the Pentagon that a beautiful girl landed in a funny round ship and told him the Earth was going to be attacked and so they should call out the armed forces to be ready.

"They'd shoot me first," he muttered, "and then throw me in a padded cell." He stepped closer to the girl. Her face was handsome, perfectly human and perfectly alien at one and the same time. It was not a soft face. It was used to decision and command. The red mouth, he thought, would never pout or be petulant, but it could easily be cruel. "What's going to attack Earth? Who are you?"

She said impatiently, "It does not matter who I am, except that I'm in a position to know what I'm saying. Listen. There is a huge interstellar task force out there, working its way through this sector of the galaxy, plundering as it goes. These fringe areas are too far away from our center of power at Uryx—a star-system you never heard of here—to make permanent conquest practical, so all we are interested in is loot. Our advance scouts go far ahead of the main body. We scouts have been here before. *I've* been here before. Now I'm warning you. The main force will be at Alpha Centauri when I return to it. When it is finished there, Earth is next."

"I don't believe you," Wyatt said. But in spite of himself, he did.

He was close to the foot of the stair now, close enough almost to touch the tall, slim girl with the black hair blowing around her forehead and the brilliant, wary eyes. The strange ship loomed above them both. Wyatt looked at it and shivered and gnawed his lip.

"Why are you warning me?" he said suddenly. "You're part of the force. Why do you want to betray it?"

"I have my reasons," she said, "and they are good ones. But you wouldn't understand them. In any case, the warning is true. Don't question it."

She started to withdraw from him, up the metal steps.

"Wait," said Wyatt. "Nobody on earth would listen to me if I told them that story. They'd only think I was crazy. Listen, if you really want to have your warning taken seriously you'll have to go to Washington yourself."

"That's impossible," she said curtly.

Again she started up the steps and again he stopped her.

"No," he said, and now he knew that he must not let her get away. As wildly improbable, not to say insane, as this whole business was, she was real and her ship was real, and wiser men than he should be handed the responsibility of dealing with that reality.

"You and I together couldn't convince anybody by just talking," he said. "The only thing that could is your ship. *That* was never made on Earth and they would know that. They could test it, examine it, prove it isn't a fake, a hoax of any kind, and that's going to be hard—you haven't any idea how hard."

HE STEPPED onto the lowest step of the stair. "You've got to fly this thing to Washington."

"I told you that's impossible," she said. "I've given you the warning; you'll have to do what you can with it. Stand clear!"

She turned her back on him and sprang lightly through the aperture into the ship.

Wyatt did not stop to think. He rushed up the stair after her and it began to draw itself up as he did so folding him under, so that he thought he was going to have to jump clear or be crushed. There was a whine of power from inside. Damn her, thought Wyatt, she doesn't care if she kills me. He scrambled frantically up the tilting, flattening rungs and caught the edge of the aperture and kicked himself forward through it.

The panel that was sliding in to seal the opening caught him halfway and held him in an agonizing grip. He cried out with pain and the fear of being cut in two. He could see into the round cockpit now, with the black-uniformed woman stopped in the act of sitting down at the controls, her startled face turned toward him.

Then her expression became one of intense annoyance. Her hand moved toward the weapon holstered at her waist. In the same instant a warning bell started to ring and the sliding panel re-opened automatically. Wyatt lurched the rest of the way through, sick and dizzy but knowing that this was no time to indulge his symptoms. He was afraid to fire the gun that he still held clutched tightly in his hand, even as a gesture of intimidation. The cockpit was small and faced in metal. A ricocheting bullet could kill either or both of them, or seriously damage the control panel so that the craft could not fly.

So he threw the gun instead. It whizzed past her head close enough to touch her hair, and in the second she was busy ducking it he had crossed the tiny metal floor and grappled with her.

She did not scream or claw his face or tear at his hair or do any of the things women customarily did. She fought, and she was strong as spring steel. He held her wrist so that she could not get at the weapon in her belt, and her free fist came up under his chin and made him see stars. Then her knee got him in the pit of the belly.

All Wyatt's ideas of chivalry deserted him. He let go of her wrist and gambled that he could knock her out before she could get the weapon, whatever it was, out of its holster.

He won, but by a shamefully tiny margin. She sagged down and he snatched the weapon himself and then retrieved his gun and stood panting, feeling very shaky at the knees.

She shook her head, grunted, looked up at him with blazing eyes, and started up all ready to come back and kill him.

He pointed her own weapon and his gun at her, using both hands.

"Mine will kill," he said. "I don't know what yours will do, but you know." He motioned to the pilot's seat. "Get in there. We're flying to Washington."

She gave him a wicked little smile with the sharp edge of her teeth and did as he told her.

CHAPTER TWO

THERE WERE PLACES for four beside the pilot spaced around the circular cockpit. Wyatt strapped himself into the seat nearest the girl. He imagined the take-off would be something special, and he was braced for it, but even the almost instantaneous transition from a state of sitting still on the ground to one of shooting straight up into the sky at a hell of a rate was hard to take. He jammed the gun into her back between the shoulders and said,

"Not too high. We're not going to Alpha Centauri."

"There are commercial air lanes," she said irritably, "and military air bases and radar installations, and ground-to-air missiles. Even in this ship I couldn't guarantee to elude every one of them."

Wyatt considered that, uneasily aware that his gun was now largely a bluff. He was not likely to use it on her, unless he wanted to come down a lot faster than he went up, and she would know that. He said, "All right, get up over the obstacles, but don't try anything too clever, I'm a pretty good pilot and I could gamble on flying this thing myself."

That was a flat lie, but he thought it might be worth telling.

The girl did not seem to be interested one way or another. The craft continued to go straight up, whistling shrilly as it went, and then it swerved around with surprising gentleness and headed east, Wyatt looked out the small double-sealed window beside him.

The stars blinded him. They had ceased to twinkle, and they had grown huge, and they had multiplied. The sky was no longer flat but deep and endless, so that even as countless many stars as there were did not crowd it. Far below there was a dark wrinkled rind like the edge of a round cheese, and Wyatt knew that it was the Earth.

It was the most magnificent sight he had ever seen, and he wished intensely that he was not seeing it. It was the final touch of insane reality that made the whole wild nightmare consistent.

"I was just lying there minding my own business," Wyatt said bitterly, turning away from the window. "Why did you have to pick on me?"

"You were obviously a technician, and it would require a technician to grasp what I had to tell you. The others seem not to believe even when they see."

"Others?" asked Wyatt startled by a new thought.

"Of course. How do you suppose we plan our attacks? How do you suppose we learn the things we must know, including enough of the language to be able to Communicate with the people after the invasion? In the normal course of events I would have considered you an especially valuable find. The accessible ones have all been herders of animals or fishermen or primitive tribesmen or poor wanderers, who could not tell us much beyond their own language and their own calling."

"You mean," said Wyatt, "that if you hadn't decided to give me the warning instead, you'd have kidnapped me? Taken me—" he nodded at the window, "—out there? Or tried to?"

"Of course."

"Well," said Wyatt. "I'll be damned."

He was enraged, and more alarmed than ever. "Don't forget for a second that I've got this gun in your back."

"I'm not likely to," she said in a curiously calm voice: "How are you called?"

He told her.

"I am Brinna Halphard—Brinna the Dark, I think you would say."

It seemed a little ridiculous to say. How do you do? Wyatt grunted uneasily and asked, "Why the sudden friendliness?"

"I'm a soldier, and I know it is impossible to win every skirmish. I've learned to make the best of things."

"That's fine," said Wyatt, not trusting her for a minute. But he was curious. "Are all women soldiers where you come from?"

"As many as wish to be. There is no difference made between the sexes, only between individuals according to their abilities. There are many women in the task force—pilots, technicians, officers, gunners, ordinary troops."

"Nobody thinks a thing of it?"

"Why should they?"

Wyatt could not really think of any good reason, except that on Earth they did.

Brinna reached for a panel at her right side and started to open it.

Instantly Wyatt was alert, "What are you doing there?"

"You want to go to Washington. Unless you can tell me the exact coordinates yourself, I must have the computer work out a course."

"Okay," said Wyatt. "Open the panel, but slowly."

Behind it there was only a remarkable compact receptor-effector unit. "You see?" she said. "Now if you will allow me—"

He allowed her. He asked, "Do you have a chart designation for Washington already in that thing?"

"For everywhere in your world," said Brinna. *"Naturally."*

A CHILL went crawling down Wyatt's back. Some of the larger implications of the situation were beginning to catch up with him.

Enemies had entered the skies of Earth, spying, charting. Enemies from another star, so far away that Earth had never heard of it. Earthmen had been kidnapped, the names of cities had been written down, plans had been made. And somewhere out there, in the immense black and fire-blazing gulf that surrounded Earth—not any longer as a protective barrier but as a pathway for invasion—an alien fleet proceeded on its way.

Wyatt stared in horror out the window and wondered how, even if all Earth's defenses were mustered, she could fight off an attack by an enemy so superior in technology that interstellar flight was a commonplace.

"Brinna," he said, "what—" He started to turn his head toward her and out of the tail of his eye he saw her hand move on the controls but it was already too late to do anything. The plane went out from under him sideways and the window tried to push itself through his head. Then he was thrown the other way with a violence that nearly snapped his neck. The seat belt cut into him and his arms flew out wildly. The gun was pulled from his hand as by a powerful magnet. He yelled involuntarily and then for the second time direction was reversed and his head slammed into the window again and all the stars went out.

When he came to he had no weapon at all and his hands were securely fastened to the back of the seat with his own belt. His head ached abominably. "That was a dirty trick," he said. "Now I see why you made that first turn so gentle— so I wouldn't know how fast this thing could maneuver at right angles."

Brinna said, "Would you have expected me to give you a performance sheet?"

"All right," he said sourly, hating her, hating the feeling of helplessness and disadvantage, raging at the combination of circumstances that had chosen him to grapple with a situation that no one man could possibly have handled. "Where are we going now?"

"Back to where I found you. You'll have to get to Washington with the warning some other way."

Wyatt groaned. "What do I have to do to make you understand? Nobody will believe a word I say."

"It's your world," she said. "I can do no more than tell you what will happen."

"You mean you *won't* do any more," he said furiously. "What's your game, anyway? If you really cared whether Earth is attacked or not you'd make sure—"

A pair of little blue lights began to flash alternately at the left of the control panel, accompanied by a shrill buzzing.

Brinna started. She said something in her own language that sounded like a curse.

"What's the matter?" Wyatt asked.

"Trouble. Oh, not with the ship, that's only the communicator." She put out her hand and at the same time she gave him a hard glare. "Just keep quiet. Don't say anything at all, or you may only make things worse for, yourself."

She flipped a switch. The flashing and buzzing stopped and a man's face appeared in a tiny screen. Wyatt could not see it too clearly from his angle, but it seemed a not unlikeable face of which the chief characteristics were strength and a sort of inner weariness. The man spoke to Brinna and she answered him, and Wyatt could not understand a word of what they said.

Some part of the conversation seemed to concern Wyatt himself. He became more and more frantically uneasy. When the contact was broken and the screen was blank again, he leaned forward against his bonds and demanded, "What's all that about?"

Brinna nodded briefly toward the window. "Look out there." Her brows were drawn down into a black angry bar and she seemed to be thinking hard. Wyatt looked out the small window.

A SECOND DISC-SHAPED craft had joined them. It was about four hundred feet away, keeping pace. Even while he looked at it the craft tilted, showing a glowing pink center surrounded by the black outer ring, and appeared to shoot away into the starry void.

Brinna followed it.

Wyatt said, "Hey. You said you were going to put me off on the mesa—"

She shook her head. "Not now. That's Makvern out there, the good gray Makvern who would be suspicious of his own father. He knows you're aboard. There is only one place I can take you." She pointed expressively. "Out. If I tried to drop back down to Earth now I'd be in front of a court-martial before breakfast."

She turned to face him. It seemed that she had done her thinking, compensating for the sudden change in direction that Makvern's appearance had necessitated.

"Listen," she said. "I'm the only hope you have of getting back to Earth before the attack. If you tell anyone that I tried to pass on a warning, that one hope will be gone, do you understand me?"

"Perfectly," Wyatt said. He had been doing some thinking too. "I am also your only hope of getting a warning to Earth before the invasion, which you badly want to do not because you give a tinker's damn what happens to Earth, but because of the effect you think it will have on some deal of your own. So I guess in a sense we're partners, then?"

"You could say that." Her eyes were as bright and hard as two chips of blue stone. She was as handsome a girl as Wyatt had ever seen, and she scared the devil out of him. "Partners. Yes. But whatever my motives may be they do not concern you, or Earth. And if I do not succeed with my plan this time—" She shrugged. "There will be other worlds."

Wyatt said shrewdly, "They might not be as well able to fight back as Earth, though. We don't quite have space flight yet, but we do have nuclear weapons. Enough to give even your force a real jar. And that's what you want, isn't it?"

Her face changed slightly. He thought she almost smiled, in a wry unhumorous way.

"You're far too clever," she said. "Don't let your cleverness betray you."

"I'll watch it," he said, not feeling clever at all, feeling sick and agonized as the last thin rim of Earth dropped away out of sight and all of a sudden he knew that he was in space.

For one wild moment he thought. This whole thing is a dream, it happened too fast and it's all too crazy to be real, and pretty soon I'll wake up. But he knew it was not a dream. He was here, awake and substantial, and he was a captive, going with bound hands into an unknown void.

And going fast.

CHAPTER THREE

IT HAD BEEN NIGHT, and suddenly it was day.

There was no twilight zone, no period of transition. The craft shot out of the Earth's shadow into the full blaze of the sun, and it was like somebody turning on all the lights in the world in the middle of a dark room.

Wyatt flinched and turned his head away. When he dared to look again there was a filter lens over the port. Actually it must have slid into place at once, or the raw glare would have blinded him. And now space seemed to be brimming over with light, all the blackness hidden beyond that golden blaze.

He could see Makvern's craft, still in position ahead and to one side, its polished rim flashing and glittering. It seemed to skim through the ocean of light like a fleeting shadow, and Wyatt found himself mesmerized by the illusion that he, too, was being buoyed up and whirled along, a chip on the floods of heaven.

Brinna hunched brooding over her controls and never gave it all a second look. Wyatt realized that of course this was an old story to her. She must have seen suns all over the galaxy and consider them no more interesting than street lamps.

It was not an old story to Wyatt. He was still frightened to death of being where he was, but even the fear was getting lost in the overwhelming wonder and magnificence of it. He craned his neck around to peer at the actual sun itself, but that was behind them and the ports on that side of the cockpit were blacked out completely. All he could see were shaking veils of fire that sprang out suddenly to cover half his field of vision and then fell back, streaming in golden streams. He thought these must be solar prominences, or part of the corona. The golden flood of light spread out and out and he could not see any end to it, though he knew there must be one. Rushing obliquely ahead of the craft was a thin black knife-edged blade cutting sharp across the radiance, and he knew that that was their own shadow.

There was the light, and Makvern's craft, and the shadow, and nothing else. Then a white curved thing like a gnawed bone slid into view, and he knew it was the edge of the Moon.

They headed toward it. For the first time Wyatt had something by which to estimate their speed. Whatever it was in miles per hour, it was too damned fast. The Moon fairly sprang at them. He could see craters opening and weird jagged mountains shooting up, exactly like pictures of growing plants taken with a strobe camera. The flinty peaks glinted like rows of teeth. Wyatt's heart came up in his throat. He understood that Makvern and Brinna must know what they were doing, and he was determined not to yell, but he found himself trying to push his feet through the floor in an involuntary gesture of putting on brakes.

The two craft tilted and swung across the face of the Moon—it was only the airlessness of space and the brilliance of the reflecting sunlight, Wyatt knew that made the surface seem close enough to reach out and pick up the perfectly defined chunks of broken pumice as they passed. Plains, craters pinnacles and ranges, blinding white or etched with inky shadow, flashed beneath them and then they were on top of the terminus and over it—and it was night again, black, black, black and hung with stars.

Wyatt shook himself, feeling dazed. It was like a plunge into deep water, stunning. The filter shield slid automatically away from the window. He looked out at the hind side of the

Moon, glimmering mysteriously in the eternal starshine, and was not very surprised to see that it looked very much like the familiar face.

Once more the two craft tilted and swung, and Wyatt saw the ship.

IT HUNG MOTIONLESS between the Moon and the stars, an enormous cylindrical shape catching dull glints on its flanks and its blunt nose. He could only guess its size by the area of stars it blotted out, and even that was only a guess. It was big. Big enough.

It was not showing any lights at first, but then one came on, laying a hard white path across the empty blackness. Makvern's craft found the path and raced along it, slowing as it went, and presently vanished.

"What is it?" asked Wyatt, and Brinna said,

"Scout tender. You didn't think we were going all the way to Alpha Centauri in these skimmers, did you?"

Wyatt said, "I hadn't really thought about it, one way or the other."

Alpha Centauri, he thought. My God.

Brinna put the skimmer, as she called it, into the lighted guide path.

"You're likely to have a fairly rough time of it," she said. "They will question you. They're not brutes, but they're thorough. I won't be able to do anything about that. But hang on, and I'll arrange your escape as soon as I can."

"Thank *you,*" said Wyatt bitterly.

"If," said Brinna with equal bitterness, "you hadn't been in such a blazing hurry to make me go to Washington, you wouldn't be here. So don't blame me for all your troubles."

The skimmer slowed, climbing up the beam of light.

A resurgence of panic took hold of Wyatt. "Why Alpha Centauri? Why do I have to go there?"

"Two reasons. We work well ahead, always planning the next campaign before we finish the last one. I told you they'll question you. In the normal course of events you would be shown the Centauri campaign so that you could get a clear idea of just how we work, and then you would be used to persuade your people not to resist."

"But you'll arrange my escape before that."

"I'll do what I can," she snapped, "as long as you keep your mouth shut. Now we're going in, and from here on you're just another captive."

Wyatt looked at her. He didn't trust her promise, not at all. He thought he had better never trust this dark girl too far.

The skimmer rose up into a great hatch. Wyatt heard a thunderous click transmitted through the air in the cockpit and felt a strong jar as what he thought must be a magnetic grapple took hold. Beyond the window now he saw a brightly lighted space that looked as big as Grand Central, equipped with great incomprehensible pieces of machinery. None of them looked like any propulsion or communication machines he knew. How did a faster-than-light ship communicate, anyway? An idea came to him.

Small figures moved out there. He recognized them as men wearing spacesuits. The suits were astonishingly like those being tested by the Air Force for high-altitude flying. He thought the A.F. boys would be glad to know their designs were good.

The skimmer was dormant, being lifted and handled by forces outside. Brinna said, "We have to wait for pressure to build up."

The huge hatch doors beneath had closed. Presently Wyatt heard sounds faintly from outside the skimmer, chiefly a throbbing noise like the beating of a gigantic heart which he thought must be the air pumps.

He nursed the idea that had come to him. He didn't think it was a very good idea but it was the only one he had, and he had to do something, try somehow, to get a warning to Earth. He could not just wait for Brinna to help him escape; it might never be possible—even if she wasn't double crossing him as she was obviously double-crossing someone else. He'd try his own way.

Soon a light showed on the Control board and Brinna pushed a lever under it.

She got up. "All right," she said. "You go ahead of me."

Wyatt rose, his hands still tied. He passed through the aperture and onto the narrow stair which had unfolded from the rim. There was a platform under the bottom rung and he stepped onto it. Brinna came behind him. The skimmer hung suspended from a grapple on an overhead track. Makvern's craft was just beyond it on a similar grapple. At the end of the track was a mobile rack with three skimmers already in it and two empty slots. Three other racks held fifteen more, stacked up like pies in a bakery.

THE MEN IN SPACESUITS—some of them were women—were taking off their helmets. They were looking at Wyatt, interested but not unduly so. Makvern was walking toward them. He also was looking at Wyatt. His eyes were dark and his skin was leathery with exposure to many suns. His hair was rough and wiry, iron gray. His shoulders were wide and his body was hard and narrow and his legs were long, Wyatt thought if he had not met Makvern in another time and place he might have liked him. As it was, he hated him.

Makvern nodded to Brinna. He wore the same black uniform, but the insigne on his shirt was different and contained a ruby stud. He watched Wyatt as another man untied his hands.

"A technician, eh?" he said. Speaking English no better than Brinna did, but perfectly intelligibly, "Good work, Captain. We have needed one badly."

"Thank you," said Brinna. "I hope he'll be useful."

Makvern said to Wyatt, "What is your field?"

"Communications," said Wyatt. "And I can tell you right now that I don't know anything more about weapons and defense than anybody who can read the daily papers, and that I won't be useful at all."

Makvern said, "I see Brinna explained to you why you were being brought here."

"She did. Fully."

"Well," said Makvern. "Come along."

He walked away and Brinna motioned for Wyatt to follow and he did, padding in his sock feet over the deck. It was a hell of a thing, he thought, to be on his way to Alpha Centauri without any shoes.

But his hands were free now. They were so sure he couldn't escape, inside their ship. Well, he couldn't. But maybe he could do something else. He looked at Makvern as they walked along the huge room.

"Star ships," Wyatt said. "Faster than light. How the devil can you communicate at speeds and distances like that?"

Makvern smiled slightly. "That's right; you said you're a communications man. Well, there are ways. There are beams you never heard of."

"I'd like to see an outfit that can send a signal faster than light," Wyatt grunted.

Makvern looked at him thoughtfully. "Why not? We'll be going right past the communic room."

Brinna looked as though she wanted to say something, but she didn't, and they went on out of the hold and through a neat functional labyrinth of corridors.

"Here we are," said Makvern and opened a bulkhead door.

Wyatt sprang forward, low and fast, like a football player making a desperate tackle. His shoulder struck Makvern in the small of the back, his arms clasped him tight around the waist, and his weight bore him forward and down, through the door into the communications room. They hit the deck together, Wyatt on top, Makvern grunting heavily from the impact. Two men inside the room sprang up from their places in alarm. Wyatt turned his head and saw Brinna in the doorway and kicked the door shut in her face. There was no way to lock it. He scrambled to his feet, wild with the need for haste, and he realized then that Makvern was not moving. He must have hit his head on the deck when he fell. Wyatt dragged him against the door to block it, and by that time one of the two men had turned back to his instruments and was shouting into what Wyatt assumed to be the ship's intercom.

The other man was almost on top of him.

Wyatt could not possibly avoid that rush. The man was big and he was young and strong and he pinned Wyatt against the wall and pounded at him. Wyatt did not worry about prize-ring rules. He lowered his head and butted, hard. The man staggered back and Wyatt gave him a clip on the jaw to help him down and then made a rush of his own, at the man who was busily arousing the whole ship.

This man was not a pugnacious type. He looked at Wyatt with large horrified eyes and flung up his hands in a vague gesture of striking but Wyatt's fist took him solidly in the face and he whimpered and turned around and folded over his own knees.

The communic room was now quiet, except for a series of noises outside the door. Wyatt stood panting, looking at the maze of equipment.

Right here within reach was the means of warning Earth. The radio system on this ship must be strong enough to blanket every receiver on the planet. All he had to do was figure out how to use it.

He swore in an agony of frustration. Nothing was marked right, nothing was as he knew it. It was all there, and it was totally useless.

He reached down and took hold of the man who was crouched on the deck near him. He dragged him upright. He shook him.

"Listen," he said. "Listen, you're going to get this thing working. Understand?"

The man shook his head dazedly from side to side and said something in his own language.

Wyatt's grip became cruel. "You're going to send a message to Earth," he said, and then Makvern spoke quietly behind him.

"He can't understand you, Wyatt. Let him go."

WYATT SPUN AROUND, still holding the man. Makvern had got up. He was standing beside the door with a weapon in his hand. The door was now open and Brinna was standing in it, her thumbs hooked in her belt, watching. Men were arriving behind her in the corridor.

Wyatt said, "If you shoot me you'll get your own man too." He shifted his grip, dragging the man closer to the control panel. Feeling even while he was speaking the absolute hopelessness of this last ditch play, he said,

"Tell him what I want or I'll smash your communication system so thoroughly—"

"It was a good try, Wyatt," said Makvern, not without a certain admiration, and pressed a stud on his weapon.

Wyatt never knew what hit him.

When he awoke he was lying in a bunk in a small metal cabin. Close beside his head there swung a curious helmet-like device linked by cables to a squat cabinet.

Makvern was standing looking down at him. He looked alert and wary and his hand rested casually on his holstered side-arm.

"How are you feeling now?" said Makvern.

Wyatt started a sour reply, and then he froze in an incredulous astonishment.

Makvern had not spoken in English. He had spoken in a totally strange language—and yet he, Wyatt, had understood him!

"What—how—" Wyatt began.

Makvern smiled. "How do you know the language of Uryx, our language, all of a sudden? Simple. Learning-tapes."

He gestured toward the helmet and the cabinet. Wyatt gaped like a yokel. It was too uncanny. Hearing words he'd never consciously heard before, and yet understanding them—

He articulated with difficulty. "Learning-tapes?"

Makvern sat down. "You've been under a seda-ray for some days, Wyatt. In fact, we're nearly to our rendezvous with the fleet, off Alpha Centauri."

So time had passed? That wasn't surprising. But this other thing—

Makvern went on. "Don't you yet have it on your Earth, the technique of teaching arbitrary knowledge to a subject in his sleep?"

Wyatt began to get it now. "You mean, a recorded voice repeating facts over and over in a sleeping man's ear? Yes. We have that—but it's not good enough to teach a man a whole new language in sleep."

"With us," said Makvern, "it is good enough. We always use it, once we pick up the vocabulary and grammar from our first captives. Makes it easier to question them. Instead of all our intelligence officers, technicians and so on having to learn the captive's language, we give him *our* language."

It was still too much for Wyatt to take in. He lay looking at Makvern, and after a moment he said,

"You seem like a decent guy, not a butcher or a greedy Conqueror type. Maybe you can tell me what gives your people the idea they've a right to go around acting like a bunch of goddamned bandits."

MAKVERN SMILED faintly. "Probably," he said, "because that's exactly what we are. Uryx is still a young empire. I imagine you have learned on Earth how empires grow—starting from a small weak poverty-ridden state fighting for its existence and becoming, by the process of eating its neighbors, a tremendous power able to conquer everything in sight. When it does this it wants to gorge itself on all the things it never had before."

He made a sweeping gesture. "Wealth, beauty, techniques, cultures, knowledge, everything under a thousand suns that can enrich or entertain us. We are still in this stage of acquisitiveness."

Wyatt grunted. "That all sounds very philosophic, but it still doesn't make you anything but bandits."

"When we join the main fleet," said Makvern, refusing to be angered, "you can take that up with Varsek."

"Varsek?"

"Commander in Chief of the Task Force. The—ah—Boss, I think you would say."

"I'll be glad to take it up with him," Wyatt said. "And if he thinks he's going to get any help from me, he's wrong."

He looked up at Makvern and he said suddenly, "You deliberately gave me a chance at that communic room, didn't you?"

"Did I?"

"Yes. You didn't have to show it to me; you must have known what was in my mind. But you had no intention of letting me get a message off to Earth. You shammed unconsciousness till it looked like I might make it, and then you came to and stopped me."

"Why would I do a thing like that?" Makvern asked calmly.

"Why, indeed? That's what I'm asking."

Makvern said, "Perhaps I was testing you to find out something, Wyatt. Let me ask you a question in return. Why did you let Brinna capture you so easily?"

"What do you mean, easily?"

"You had a weapon. Yet you didn't use it on Brinna. Why?"

Wyatt became instantly wary and on guard. Makvern, then, suspected the arrangement between Brinna and himself, suspected Brinna of a double-cross? He'd better be careful.

He said, "What's this about Brinna? To me, she's just a female wildcat that dropped out of the sky."

"She is what you would call very high brass," Makvern said. "A high officer of the Task Force. Completely trusted by Commander Varsek."

Had Makvern faintly emphasized the word "trusted?" Wyatt wasn't sure. He was only sure now that some devil's broth of intrigue went on in the immense Task Force that followed its looting voyage through the galactic suns, and that he, Wyatt, was less than the smallest pawn in the hidden game.

"I wouldn't," said Makvern, "think too much of Brinna. She's beautiful, I know. But she's in love."

Oddly, Wyatt felt a pang to hear that. "In love? With whom?"

"With power," Makvern said grimly, and then the next moment the light in the cabin went blue and there was a vertiginous shock that made Wyatt feel as though he was falling, falling, everything gone from around him, plunging through abysses of darkness—

A whining sound went up to a shriek and passed beyond hearing, and then the lights burned white again and the dizziness in his head passed.

"What the devil—" he began huskily.

Makvern stood up. "We just went out of overdrive. We've reached the Task Force. Come on, Wyatt—for you, this is it."

CHAPTER FOUR

HERE IN THE WINDOWED bridge, the background was all stars.

Clouds of stars, rivers of them, chains and globes of them, and drawn across them here and there like curtains of the most glorious fire ever imagined were the shining nebulae. They were all colors. Red, blue, smoky yellow, green, diamond white. Some of them, Wyatt realized, were not stars at all but galaxies, scattered out in careless millions through the apparently infinite universe. To an earthbound, skybound man like himself, this was almost too much to take. Look at ten billion stars and a million galaxies and all the empty space between for them to roam around in, and realize that this is the universe, you are in the middle of it, not standing on the edge looking up the way you do on Earth but right in the middle of it, the nothingness and allness of it without end, amen. If you have no religion you get one in a hurry, because obviously only God could have made this.

Wyatt was dimly aware that someone—Makvern—was talking to him. Alpha Centauri. A hand pointed, guiding him back from the infinite to the particular.

Ahead, still very far away but close enough to stand out from among the more distant stars like a beacon lamp was a yellow sun.

"There's a companion," Makvern said, "but it's insignificant and did not prevent the formation of a stable planetary system around the primary. Alpha Centauri has eight planets—it's very much like your own Sol. The two inner planets are too hot, and the outer ones are too cold, but the third and fourth support life. The third is closer to the sun than Earth and is still in a comparatively primitive stage of evolution. We can pick up minerals there but nothing else. The fourth world is our target."

Wyatt shut his eyes against the blaze of suns and nebulae and wheeling galaxies and tried to concentrate on Alpha Centauri, its fourth planet, and himself.

"Where's your fleet?" he asked, and opened his eyes again. looking closer at hand instead of trying to see the end of creation.

Once more Makvern pointed.

Once more Wyatt was stunned, this time in a much more personal way. Suns and galaxies were beyond him; the incredible handiwork of God, but men had built these ships. And the one was almost as overwhelming a thing as the other.

It was the hell and all of a fleet.

It too was a long way off, though not anything like as far as Alpha Centauri. Makvern explained that they did not attempt any very close maneuvering in hyper-drive, where you counted your fractional seconds of error in multiples of parsecs. The main task force would approach the system of Alpha Centauri at planetary speeds and deploy according to the master attack plan already decided upon while the fleet had been busy plundering the hapless worlds of the star-system before this one. The Scout ship was now on an intersecting course.

Wyatt watched this convergence with a mounting awe and an increasing conviction that no matter how many warnings he might bring to Earth it would not do them one bit of good.

He had thought the scout tender was huge when he first saw it hanging beyond the dark side of the Moon. The closer he got to the fleet the smaller the tender seemed to him and the smaller he felt himself, until he thought that this must be pretty much like a minnow's eye view of a school of whales passing in all their majesty, accompanied on the flanks by the swift sinister forms of great sharks. The analogy was obvious but not a bad one, Wyatt thought. The phalanx of huge dark shapes swam in space as in black water, touched with vagrant gleams of light that might have been phosphorescence instead of starshine. The hugest of them—the heavy support craft, the troop transports, the supply ships, and the swag-bellied monstrosities that Brinna said were used to store and carry loot—travelled together in a wedge-shaped formation, with the flagship at the apex. Ahead and on both wings were the smaller, faster destroyer-type craft heavily armed but maneuverable. These were the spearhead of any attack, and the defenders of the fleet from any hostile action in space. Behind came a shoal of smaller craft like the tender, the inglorious but indispensable workhorses of the fleet.

CLEAR ACROSS THE galaxy these ships had come, built and manned by humans. Conceived in their brains and controlled by their hands. It seemed a pity their purpose could not have been more noble.

The Task Force swept closer and closer, rolled over the tender like a mighty wave, engulfed it, and carried it along in its resistless rush toward Alpha Centauri.

A communicator at the back of the bridge, which had been rattling away in the course of routine technicalities, suddenly changed its tone. "Clear channels," said a brisk important voice. "Clear channels for Number One." The operator at Fleet Control whose image had appeared on the screen promptly pulled the switch on himself. Involuntarily everyone in the bridge room snapped to attention, even Makvern and Brinna.

Swiftly, under her breath, Brinna said, "What does he want that couldn't wait for our regular report?"

She looked worried. Guilty conscience, Wyatt thought. But Makvern's conscience was clear, at least where Wyatt was concerned, and he looked worried too. Almost, you might say, apprehensive.

When he turned to face the screen there was no sign of this in his face, nothing but the properly alert expression of a staff officer about to speak to his chief.

A smartly turned out operator, owner of the officious voice, appeared in the screen. "ST-6," he said. "ST-6, this is Number One calling. Number One, calling for Staff Captain Makvern."

Makvern stepped forward into the pick-up area. "Captain Makvern here."

"Stand by, sir. Commander Varsek is ready to speak to you."

Makvern stood by. He seemed perfectly at ease. Brinna's mouth was drawn tight and her eyes were narrowed. Wyatt started to say something and she shook her head at him fiercely. He shut up. The bridge waited silently as though the Supreme Being was about to step into it.

The operator had vanished from the screen. It remained blank for a moment or two. Then it brightened again and Commander Varsek was mirrored in it.

He nodded to Makvern, who saluted. He was sitting behind a big desk covered with charts, papers, microfilm spools, a couple of viewers, and various communic media. In contrast to the immaculate turn-out of his operator—and everybody else that Wyatt had so far seen—Varsek's uniform shirt was open down the front, his sleeves were rolled up, and the shirt itself looked as though he had been digging ditches in it. He gave the impression of a man enormously embroiled in work, the two-hours-of-sleep-a-night, coffee-and-

Benzedrine-and-I-thrive-on-it type that automatically makes everybody else feel like a lazy slob. All this part of him Wyatt found only mildly irritating. It was Varsek's face and what he sensed behind it that made Wyatt feel he could really hate this man.

Varsek was a big lean man, and his face was big and lean, with a lot of bone in it and no softness anywhere, and no warmth, and no friendliness. He smiled, and the smile was a lie. Wyatt thought all the rest of it was a lie too, or at least a deliberate pose. Only his eyes were true. They looked at Makvern, and then at Brinna, and then for quite a long moment at Wyatt, and they were rapacious and hungry, cold and cruel, highly intelligent, and disconcertingly demonstrative of a mind capable of handling nearly anything.

"This is your captive, is it?" he said. "Good. He looks more intelligent than any I've seen yet." He turned his attention back to Makvern. "I've sent a skimmer for you. You too, Brinna."

Makvern said, in an almost too carefully expressionless voice, "We were about to report to the flagship."

"This is important, Makvern. Can't wait. I've got Loran aboard, very sick, about dying I'd say. I want you and Brinna here." His gaze flicked again to Wyatt. "Bring him along. It may help him to understand us better."

"Yes, sir," said Makvern.

Varsek nodded and the screen went dead.

Somebody said, "Skimmer's coming into the airlock now, sir."

Makvern turned around and looked at Brinna. His face was absolutely white. So was hers. White, frightened, and bitterly angry.

"Who is Loran?" asked Wyatt.

"One of our under officers," Makvern said, too quietly. "Come on, we mustn't keep them waiting."

They left the bridge and went, not below to the main launching hold, but aft to a small lock. On the way Wyatt asked,

"Can you tell me what's going on?"

"For your own sake," said Makvern, "no."

They got into the skimmer and the pilot took it away and they sat stiff and silent like three people going to a wake. And Wyatt had an idea he was about to get a little closer to the truth of whatever forces were operating behind the scenes here. He needed to know, needed it desperately. He was prepared to sell or double-cross anybody including himself in order to get a warning to Earth in time, but before he could do that he had to know who was buying, and what, and for how much.

The skimmer passed swiftly through the fleet, past the great dull-gleaming hulls tarnished by a thousand atmospheres, pitted and scarred by the cosmic dust and drift of half a galaxy.

The black enormous form of the flagship loomed ahead, blotting out the stars. The skimmer was gathered into it. A minute later, as they stood close together at the ladder head, Makvern whispered in English,

"This is going to be ugly. Keep out of it, you understand? No matter what!"

CHAPTER FIVE

THE MAN WAS obviously sick, probably dying, painfully, spasmodically, and not from natural causes.

He was a fairly young man, younger than Makvern, older than Brinna. He was strapped onto a kind of flat cradle made of a plastic mesh, and this was suspended in a circular pit, not very deep. Above the man, almost but not quite in contact with his body, was a double row of crystal rods, their bottom ends close together, their top ends spread to form a V. They were served by power leads that went away somewhere to the sides of the pit. Every so often, in answer to a signal, power was fed into the double-rods, a rapid flicker of bluish light ran up and down through them, and the man below them writhed and sobbed in a grotesque and hideous agony.

Varsek gave the signals. He was sitting on a seat above the shallow pit, where he could look down comfortably into. Loran's face while he talked to him. There was a ring of seats around the pit. Wyatt sat in one. So did Makvern, and Brinna, and several other officers Wyatt did not know. The pit was situated in the center of a quite small room with soundproof walls and a single door, very thick and having a lock on the inside. The room was deep in the most secret bowels of the flagship.

The crystal tubes were dead now. Loran rolled his head from side to side and moaned. He had bitten his lips and tongue, and he was bleeding slightly from the nose. Varsek watched him. There was not a sound in the room other than Loran's moaning. Nobody moved. Nobody met anyone else's eye. Nobody spoke. There might have been a concourse of waxen dummies above the pit.

Except for Varsek. He spoke. He called Loran by name, several times, with a dispassionate persistence, until he answered. Then Varsek said.

"Who is the leader of the Second Party?"

He had asked that question fifty, a hundred times before, in exactly that tone of voice.

And Loran answered, as he had fifty or a hundred times before, "There is no Second Party." Only his voice was weaker every time he said it.

And Wyatt was sicker. He clenched his hands and shut his jaw tight. There was nothing he could do. He kept telling himself that; There was nothing he could do.

Varsek said, "It's no use to lie to me, Loran. There is a Second Party. Every ship in the fleet including this one has some officers and some men who are not loyal to me—who are in fact dedicated to the task of taking the fleet away from me. This I know Loran, I have absolute proof. I'm only asking you who the leader is."

"There is no Second Party."

"Is he one of my staff officers, Loran?"

"There is no—"

"Which one?" And he named them through one at a time, including Makvern and Brinna, everyone that was there, and they sat in the bright light with blank faces and fear in their eyes.

Loran said, "There is no Second Party."

"Let's be realistic about this," Varsek said. "Your friends, the men you're so nobly protecting, can't help you now. I'm the only one who can. I can have you up out of there in a minute, with the best medical attention and everything you need to fix you up. All you have to do is answer my questions. That's your duty, isn't it, Loran? didn't you swear an oath of loyalty to Uryx and the government of Uryx, and to me as the duly appointed servant of that government?"

No answer.

"You're a young man, Loran. I don't imagine you love the idea of death. Why leap at it? Tell me the names of the disloyal officers you know, and you can live."

Loran said distinctly, "Go to hell."

Varsek gave the signal again.

The banked rods pulsed and flickered, and whatever nerve-searing, flesh-torturing force was in them went to work on Loran.

WYATT GOT UP. He called Varsek the dirtiest name he could think of, in a kind of choked and half-articulate voice, and then he started for him. It was obviously a silly thing to do, but he wasn't really thinking about it. He just had a simple desire to stop Varsek from doing what he was doing.

Several of the officers—Makvern was one of them— caught him before he had taken two steps. Varsek glanced around. He smiled briefly. "I thought you looked like a brave man," he said. "Brave men are usually stubborn. That's why you're here, to see what happens to brave stubborn men."

"There are a lot of them on Earth," said Wyatt fiercely. "They haven't broken for other dirty little tyrants and they won't break for you. Remember that."

Makvern snarled in his ear, "Shut up for God's sake. And sit down." His face was rigidly controlled but in his eyes, deep down, there was a wildness of hate and fury that startled Wyatt into obedience. He allowed himself to be forced back toward his seat. And then Brinna stepped forward and said to Varsek,

"It might be safer, sir, if I put him with the other prisoners now."

Varsek considered that, totally undisturbed by the deathly sounds from the pit. He studied Brinna, who was looking rigidly past his head at the opposite wall. He studied Makvern, who was now as blank as a stone, so that Wyatt wondered if he had really seen what he thought he had seen in Makvern's eyes. He studied the others, who showed varying degrees of unhappiness, and then he said to Brinna,

"You look ill, Captain. How would you expect to command a battle fleet if you can't stand to see one man die?"

Brinna's body was absolutely rigid. She said, "Are you accusing me of plotting with the Second Party to take command? If so, I request a formal—"

Varsek shook his head. "No accusation, Brinna. Merely a statement. I know how it eats on your soul that you probably never will command a fleet just on account of your sex." He grinned at her. "Sex isn't the whole story, Brinna. I'm merely pointing that out to you. Ability and toughness have something to do with it too. Isn't that so, Makvern?"

"I suppose so, sir."

The man in the pit howled like a tortured animal. Varsek pushed a button impatiently and the rods stopped flickering and the howling ceased.

"Very well," said Varsek, turning away, "take your delicate stomach away from here. And maybe you can put your sex to some use with the prisoner. Try it, anyway. The rest of you stay here."

Brinna saluted, turned smartly on her heel, snapped, "Follow me," at Wyatt, and marched toward the door. Wyatt glanced at Makvern, who refused to look at him, and went after Brinna.

He was thankful to get out of the room. Sick and raging himself, he did not feel like talking and Brinna's face discouraged him anyway. The way her boot-heels rang on the iron floor he thought that she was wishing Varsek's head under every one. Finally, when they had left even the level of the pit-room behind and were walking together along an upper corridor with nobody else in sight, he did speak.

"Are you plotting with the Second Party, Brinna?" he asked.

"No," she said savagely. "I am not. I hate everything they stand for."

"But you are plotting against Varsek?"

She stopped and looked at him with eyes as lambent as those of an angry cat.

"If you have thoughts of helping your own cause by going to Varsek about me, forget them. In the first place, Varsek helps nobody. In the second place, I can have you silenced before you could ever get to him."

"No," said Wyatt slowly, "I wasn't thinking of going to Varsek. But what he said about you is true. You do want the command. You figured that Earth, armed and prepared, would give Varsek such a setback that you might be able to oust him and take over."

"Do you blame me?" whispered Brinna. "He's a swine. A cruel, treacherous, sadistic swine. You saw him. No wonder there's a Second Party."

"How big is it, Brinna?"

"Big enough to worry Varsek. Loran is the third poor devil he's tortured to death trying to find out who's in it. He hasn't managed it yet, but he will. And then—" She made an expressive gesture of slashing.

"You said you hated everything the Second Party stands for. What does it stand for?"

"Peace," said Brinna, as though it was a shameful word. "They want to take the Task Force home and force the government to stop this galaxy-wide swing of Conquest."

"And you don't want peace?"

"I'm a soldier. What use would I be at peace?" Her face was hard, shining, exalted with ambition. "Not while I'm still young and unsatisfied, anyway. Listen, Wyatt. I told you women are not segregated and discriminated against in our society and that's true—except for top positions of Power in politics and the military. Even there it's never stated openly. But somehow or other the women candidates never quite make it. I'm going to be the first one to break that custom. I am going to command this Task Force."

SHE PUT HER HAND on his arm, speaking rapidly, with urgent force. "I'm not alone, Wyatt. I have a powerful group behind me. Varsek isn't popular with the officers. The men love him because he wins battles and looks the other way when they abuse the native women, but they don't have to deal with him. All we need is an excuse—a demonstration that Varsek has blundered badly—and we can step in. *I* can step in. Earth could give us that excuse, if your people put up enough of a surprise fight. So you see our interests do run together."

"That far, they do," said Wyatt. "But afterward?"

"What do you mean, afterward?"

"After you take over. What happens to Earth then?" He shook her hand away. "Don't treat me like a fool, Brinna. You don't take over from Varsek on the grounds that he's failed and then admit that you too are licked by the same situation."

Her eyes had narrowed and the anger-light was in them again. "So?"

"So you will then proceed to smash my world. You have to, to prove you're more capable than Varsek. Otherwise, somebody will oust *you.*"

"I warned you before not to let your cleverness betray you," she said. "Let's be realistic about this. Earth is our next target, she's going to be hit warning or no warning, and she's going to be beaten. Now, do you imagine Earth can get better and more merciful treatment from Varsek, or from me?"

"When you put it that way," Wyatt said thoughtfully, "I can see a preference. All right, Brinna. When do you think you can arrange the escape?"

"The only chance will be some time during the attack on Alpha Centauri. I'll get word to you as soon as the arrangements are made, but don't get impatient. You heard Varsek. I'll have to move very cautiously."

"And what happens to me in the meantime?"

"You'll be questioned. Oh, not like that. Varsek reserves the pit for special cases. By our Intelligence group, by subterfuge—the captives' quarters are thoroughly monitored and don't forget it—and by Varsek himself, probably. Don't antagonize him, Wyatt, or you could find yourself in the pit at that."

They had come to a transverse corridor, and now Brinna gave him a warning glance and said in a sharp impersonal tone, "That way." Her hand was on the butt of her stunner.

Wyatt turned obediently, into the transverse corridor. A guard who had been lounging midway of it snapped to attention. He was stationed beside a door, Brinna marched Wyatt up to him and said, "Another one for the tank," and the guard said, "Yes, sir." He did a complicated series of things with his hands, apparently activating power sources that released various locks, and the door opened.

"Inside," the guard said to Wyatt, and jerked his thumb.

With no further word to Brinna, Wyatt stepped through the door.

It closed behind him with the sound of a bank vault shutting for the night.

The room he stood in was fairly large and it had bunks all around the walls. About sixteen bunks, Wyatt thought, and there were about a dozen men sitting on the edges of them, or sitting around a table bolted to the floor in the center of the room. They were all looking at him. They were the damnedest collection of humanity, or whatever you wanted to call it, that Wyatt had ever come across. He remembered Brinna's complaint that the accessible people, the ones easily picked up without giving any wide-spread alarm, usually lived in isolated regions and were without much in the way of technical knowledge.

He could see the problem, all right. Of the five Earthmen there, one was an Arab in a dirty burnoose, one looked like a young Apache Indian in old farm clothes, and one, at a guess, came from Chinese Turkestan and smelled of camels. The other two were closer to home. One was medium-tall and stocky, with a thick chest and thin strong legs. He wore faded Levis: and high-heeled boots and his face was burned brick-red to the middle of his forehead. Above that his skin was as white as a baby's. A Stetson hat hung on a peg over his bunk. The fifth man, who sat beside him, was cut out of the same cloth, but somehow with a difference. Wyatt was puzzled for a minute, and then he remembered once seeing an Australian movie with a long lean leathery actor named Chips Rafferty in it playing a stockman, and he thought he had the answer.

The other six men in the room were not from Earth.

The other six men in the room were not human.

Not as Wyatt was used to thinking of human, homo sapiens, tracing a well-fossilized descent back through the various anthropus forms and ultimately to the primal ancestor. These six walked erect and had facile hands and humanoid bodies and strikingly handsome faces, but whatever their primal ancestor had been it had not been like man's. It had left them an odd legacy of body hair that could not be called anything else but fur, and their skulls were curiously elongated rather than domed, and their fingertips still had their ancient claws, retracing catlike into the flesh. Catlike, Wyatt thought, was a very good word for them—and yet not quite Earthly—catlike. The ears were a little too round, the eyes a bit too large and dark and capable of warmth. They wore garments of fine cloth in bright shades to set off their individual color, and in size and facial conformation they were as different from each other as the Earthmen were.

They looked at Wyatt, sitting in two double rows on the edges of their bunks. The Earthmen looked at Wyatt. And in no eye, human or humanoid, was there a spark of friendliness.

Wyatt said, "Hello."

There was no answer. The stocky man and the long lean one got up, and each one hitched up his pants and left the thumbs of his hands sticking negligently in the waistband.

"Look," said Wyatt, annoyed, "I didn't come here because I wanted to, but I haven't got smallpox or whooping cough, and I haven't wronged anyone's sister."

The two men began to walk slowly forward. The young Apache rose and came after them, a dark gleam flickering deep in his eyes. The Arab rose, and then the Turcoman, and then the six lithe furry men came dropping one by one from the edges of their bunks and all of them moved toward Wyatt, not speaking.

A cold qualm of fear contracted his heart. He set his back against the door and braced himself.

"What is this?" he said. "What are you doing? I'm an Earthman, a captive like you. Why—"

"You're no Earthman," said the stocky southwesterner, in a very cold, mild voice. "You're another goddamn lousy spy."

They came at him all together in a swift purposeful rush.

CHAPTER SIX

INSTEAD OF COWERING against the door or trying to get out, as they expected him to do, Wyatt sprang straight for the man in the Levis. He was easy to get at because he was leading the others by a pace or so. Wyatt hit him.

"Spy, am I?" he snarled. He was mad. The rush closed around him but he hung onto the man, who snorted and grappled with him, and they toppled over thrashing and kicking among the legs of the others. "I'll show you who's a spy," he said. The tall man he took to be an Australian bent over and started to pull at him, and he kicked him furiously on the shins. "One at a time, boy. Keep your paws off." He rolled with his enemy, pounding on a cast-iron body and getting knocked dizzy himself in return. He began to swear. He had never been much for swearing, but the injustice of this attack inspired him beyond his talents. He went on pounding and cursing until after a while he realized that his target was no longer in range and that he was alone in a small circle, surrounded by the others who were looking down at him. He crouched there, blinking, and saw the man in the Levis wiping blood off his mouth with the back of his hand and studying him speculatively.

"So I'm a so-and-so saddle tramp, am I?" he said.

"Yes, and a damn dumb one," said Wyatt bitterly. He got up, bunching his fists.

"Real fast now," said the stockman, "who was it died at the Alamo?"

"Davy Crockett," said Wyatt. "King of the wild frontier. Also William Barret Travis and Jim Bowie and a lot of other good men who never had songs written about them. Come on, let's finish this."

"No," said the other man, stepping back. "I don't reckon anybody but an Earthman could swear like that without stuttering, nor want to fight like that. What would you say, Bill?"

The Australian said he agreed.

"My name's A. C. Burdick," said the stockman, holding out his hand, "and I'm a long way from home. Sorry about jumping you like that, but we've had three guys in a row claiming to be captives like us, only they weren't, and we're getting sick of it."

Still glowering, Wyatt shook hands with him, and then with the Australian. The Arab and the Turcoman muttered and returned sulkily to their places, apparently disappointed that there had been no bloodshed. The Apache youth stood and regarded Wyatt with an unwinking stare from under his greasy hat brim.

"This here is No-Name," said Burdick, grinning. "He was sleeping out in the hills when he was picked up—you know, some of them still find out their warrior-name by getting it in a dream the old way. He figures this is all part of the dream and is waiting till he wakes up."

Wyatt nodded to No-Name, who inclined his head briefly and went back to his bunk where he sat cross-legged, patiently brooding.

Burdick shifted from his native tongue to the language of Uryx and said, "These gentlemen are from Alpha Centauri Four."

The furred slender men clasped their hands and raised them to their breasts. One of them, who was jet black and dressed in a scarlet tunic, said in the same tongue.

"I am Thurne of Obran, a king's messenger. I was taken as I crossed a plain, carrying a message between kings. Now there will be war for all."

The others nodded sadly. Wyatt, all his anger forgotten now, said, "Yes, and for my world too."

"Well," said Burdick, "come in and make yourself at home."

THE TIME that followed then was something of a nightmare to Wyatt, not too protracted but intense. It was a strain watching his tongue when he talked with the others, knowing that every word he said was being listened to outside. The Arab, the Turcoman, and No-Name awaited whatever thing might happen with their several brands of fatalism but Burdick and the Australian had a clearer understanding of the situation and were frantic to do something about it. He would have liked to offer them a word of hope, but he did not dare to For the Alpha Centaurians, Wyatt knew, there was no hope, and they knew it too. With each passing hour, as the fleet roared on its way, Wyatt wished more earnestly for something evil and permanent to happen to Varsek.

It didn't. The only thing that happened was that Wyatt was hauled out away from the others at frequent intervals and questioned, questioned, questioned until he was too dazed and tired to form words any more. He tried not to tell them anything at all, but they were experts, and he suspected that they learned almost as much, if not more, from what he refused to tell them as from what he did. His only comfort was that he had no knowledge of armaments or defense beyond what any ordinary citizen might read in the papers, and which Fleet Intelligence had doubtless also read.

He sweated through it the best way he could and waited for word from Brinna.

It did not come.

Makvern came instead. He said, "Varsek wants to see you."

Wyatt went with him and they walked briskly through the corridors.

"What does he want with me?" Wyatt asked.

"You'll have to ask him," Makvern said.

"Did Loran die?"

"Yes. He died."

"Did he talk?"

"No."

"Then the Second Party's still safe."

"For the time being," said Makvern. "Only for the time being." He would not turn to look at Wyatt. His profile was as expressionless as a king's head on a coin.

Wyatt hesitated while he took three steps, knowing that if he guessed wrong he would almost certainly wind up in the pit, and that Earth quite certainly would be worse off than ever. Then, considering what he had to gain if he guessed right, he plunged.

"The Second Party," he said, "could take over if Varsek had a serious setback at Earth. Then they could take the Task Force and go home. They could start exporting some things from Uryx, like peace and stable government, instead of importing nothing but loot."

Makvern continued to walk briskly, looking neither to the right nor to the left.

"How would you propose that Earth could give Varsek a setback?" he asked.

"Get some of us back to Earth before the fleet, to give warning."

"That kind of talk," said Makvern evenly, "could get you and possibly a number of other people killed, I suggest that you stop it."

His tone was hard, perfectly cold and inflexible. Wyatt's heart sank. He had guessed wrong and Makvern was not one of the underground. And yet he had been so sure, the way Makvern had looked when Loran was suffering in the pit—

An orderly passed them into a huge room that was obviously used as an outer office, full of communic equipment, recorders, electronic files, and busy men. A second orderly opened the inner door for them, and Wyatt found himself looking at Varsek as he had first seen him on the communic screen, sitting behind the big crowded desk with his shirt open and his sleeves rolled up, the picture of demon energy.

HE NODDED and Makvern stepped back a little, leaving Wyatt alone, as it were, before Varsek. Varsek picked up a report and shook it at him.

"This is from Intelligence," he said. "It's not satisfactory. You're not cooperating, Wyatt."

"Would you expect me to?" said Wyatt.

"I expect you not to be a fool," said Varsek. "Look, I'm going to loot your planet. You know that, don't you? All right. Now if I know where things are I won't have to smash a lot of other things trying to find them, will I? And if there's no attempt at resistance, then nobody will get hurt, will they?" He threw the report. "You're not helping Earth, you're making it harder."

"I told everybody in the beginning," said Wyatt sullenly, "that I don't know anything more than they can find out themselves from reading a popular magazine."

"You're a native. You know more about it than we could ever find out in the time we have, and you have a scientific background. You must know approximately where the largest uranium deposits are, for instance, and the main sources of radioactive isotopes. Yet you refuse to verify our information, or correct it if it's wrong."

"That's right," said Wyatt. "I do refuse."

"Brave and stubborn," Varsek said. "Well. I know how stubborn you are. I could find out very quickly about the bravery."

"In the pit?"

Varsek nodded. "What would you say, Makvern?"

"It's up to you, sir," Makvern said, shrugging.

"No opinion at all?"

"None."

"That's not like you, Makvern."

"It's impossible to have any opinion of value concerning the advisability of—ah—questioning a man I don't know at all. I have no idea of his limits. If they're easily reached, fine. If not, he's likely to die before you know it."

"True," said Varsek. "True. And he's the best bet to transmit a convincing message to Earth when the time comes, assuring them of the futility of resistance." He leaned back in his chair and scratched his chest reflectively, studying Wyatt with his bright cold eyes, and Wyatt had an uneasy feeling that Varsek was thinking rapidly of a great number of things only remotely connected with him except that they might have an indirect bearing on his life or death.

"Well," said Varsek finally, "there's always time for the pit later on. We'll follow the customary procedure. Arrange for Wyatt and the other Earthmen to have a good clear view of what happens when we hit Alpha Centauri Four, which will be—" He frowned at a desk chrono, "—in approximately five hours. I want you to watch carefully, Wyatt. This world isn't as mechanized as parts of yours and it doesn't have nuclear power, but it's civilized. Remember that. And remember that your nuclear weapons wouldn't be much more effective against us than their explosive devises."

He jerked his thumb at Makvern. "Get him out of here now. I've got half the planning still to do for this campaign, without worrying about the next one."

He became furiously busy. Makvern ushered Wyatt out and down the corridors again. This time Wyatt did not speak at all, and neither did Makvern. They parted at the door of the prisoners' quarters.

THE FIVE HOURS seemed more like five centuries. The only chance for an escape, Brinna had said, would be during the confusion of the attack. He didn't know whether she had been able to arrange it at all, and if she had, whether he might have made Makvern suspicious and ruined the whole thing by his attempt to make a better deal for Earth through the Second Party. He chewed his knuckles and sweated and thought wild thoughts about escaping somehow on his own hook, but he couldn't plan anything with Burdick and the Australian because it would be overheard, or seen.

The other Earthmen were all restless and upset, as though they sensed a coming crisis. The Alpha Centaurians waited quietly, by contrast. Only their eyes shone with a terrible light. By God, thought Wyatt furiously, I'll kill Varsek with my own hands if I have to, I swear it. It was a childish thing to say even to himself, and he knew it. But he had never meant anything so much.

The Task Force hurtled on, a school of killer whales racing toward an unsuspecting victim.

The door opened and Brinna stood there. There were guards behind her.

"Come," she said. "All of you."

She stood aside while the captives filed out. As Wyatt passed her she gave him one quick fleeting glance. Hope sprang up in him. She had arranged something, and whatever it was he and the other prisoners would see that it worked.

They were marched through the corridors under guard and into a contact lock, where a small craft clung like a remora under the chin of the flagship. Here they were separated into two different groups. The Alpha Centaurians were the first ones to be sent down. Wyatt heard a clashing of metal, and then the Earthmen were ordered down and placed in a semicircular room which was half of an observation turret. The Alpha Centaurians were in the other half," fully visible but securely barred off by a partition of metal rods.

Similar rods slid down behind the Earthmen into Slots in the deck, Wyatt stayed beside the doorway. He heard Brinna dismiss the guards... Their feet clanged on the ladder, going up. Brinna came along the corridor and stopped on the other side of the bars. She was blazing with excitement, triumph, hate, a lot of things that had been bottled up in her and which she was daring now to show.

"It's all arranged," she said, speaking very rapidly but in a low voice. "All but two of the crew are my men. When we're clear of the ship, pass the word quietly to be ready when I—"

She broke off, whirling around, her face suddenly alarmed. Someone was coming down the ladder from the flagship.

It was Makvern, coming fast, and he held a stunner in his hand.

Brinna controlled herself admirably. She said, "Is there some trouble, Makvern? The prisoners are all secure—"

"I'm sure they are," said Makvern. He reached the foot of the ladder and an officer appeared as though he had been waiting for him. Makvern nodded sharply and almost at once the warning bells were ringing and the hatch was sliding shut. A moment later Wyatt felt the jar as contact was broken and the small craft fell free on its own power.

Makvern stood looking at Brinna and Wyatt. "I imagine," he said to Wyatt, "that she was telling you most of the men aboard belong to her. She was just a little bit mistaken. All of them belong to me."

CHAPTER SEVEN

BRINNA'S FACE was now absolutely white, with her red mouth showing on it like a smear of blood. She dropped her hand to the grip of her own stunner.

She almost made it but not quite. Makvern hit her full on with a crackling charge and she fell and lay still and senseless.

Makvern sighed. "Poor Brinna. This is like snatching food from someone that's starving—I almost regret it—"

"I'll bet you do," said Wyatt. If he could have got his hands between the rods and around Makvern's throat he would have killed him, Burdick and Bill Whitfield, the Australian, had joined him now, and Whitfield asked, "What's up?"

"Nothing," said Wyatt with intense bitterness. "Not a damn thing, thanks to me. I had to get smart."

He felt sick with the knowledge of his own folly. He had taken the chance on Makvern in the hope of sparing Earth any attack at all, and this was what had come of it. He and Brinna would now go together to the pit, and what would happen to Earth would happen.

He pushed Burdick aside and went across the narrow room to the curving glassite-paneled wall on the other side and stood there. The others left him alone.

He heard movement and voices in the corridor, but he paid no attention to them. Nothing was important now. He looked out into space, lighted with the baleful light of the twin suns, and saw the whole great Task Force spread between him and the stars overhead, the destroyers coursing ahead of the main body, all their hulls glittering bright, beautiful, swift, deadly, a brazen spear for the slaying of planets.

The small craft in which he and the others were imprisoned was dropping below the fleet. It was extremely difficult to judge speeds here where there was nothing to go by but the stars, but Wyatt thought the Task Force must have been decelerating for some time as it approached its target, and that the small craft was moving considerably faster than the main body. He watched, simply because the ships were before his eyes, and he began to realize that this little ship was leading all the others down to battle.

"Like a damn Judas goat," he muttered, and Burdick spoke from beside him.

"They took that lady officer away," he said. "I reckon she's in trouble?"

Wyatt said, "The worst. She was going to help us escape."

Burdick said shrewdly, "Bill and me figured it was something like that. Too bad it went wrong."

Wyatt explained why it had gone wrong, "I should have been content with what I had. But I thought if—oh, what the devil's the use of hashing it over!" He looked at the steel rods that separated them from the Alpha Centaurians. "If we could just get those bars out of the way, get all together, the twelve of us—we might still do something. This is a small ship. It can't carry much of a crew, probably not more than five or six beside Makvern. If we could rush them and take the ship, we might be able to force them to fly it to Earth—"

Moonshine. Fool's talk, the babble of desperation. On the other hand, what did they have to lose?

Their lives, of course. But that would have to be up to the individual. As far as Wyatt was concerned, the pit was no beautiful prospect.

And if they succeeded—if—

"Well," said Whitfield, "let's get cracking." He crooked his finger at the Arab, the Turcoman, and No-Name.

In the spaceship, with the incredible panorama of space and the racing war fleet beyond the observation panels, the six Earthmen held a conference, speaking to each other not in their own diverse tongues but in the language of Uryx, a place they had never seen and had not even known existed until suddenly it had become the most important thing in their lives.

The conference was brief. When it was over Wyatt and Burdick went to the wall of rods and talked to the Alpha Centaurians.

THURNE OF OBRAN spoke for them all. "We will fight," he said. "We will fight gladly." He turned and pointed, his eyes blazing with a feral light that made him look more like a black panther than a human man. Wyatt followed his gesture and saw a misty blue planet rushing toward them in the golden glare of the primary.

Burdick said matter-of-factly, "Before we do any fighting we got to get out of here, so we better start looking for holes."

They looked. They had no way of knowing whether they were being watched as they had been on the flagship, but they had to risk that. They tested every rod and searched in vain for a weak spot. They tried by main force and by cleverness and there was no way. And the blue misty planet rushed closer and spread into a vast globe, and the blue color faded into greens and browns and ochres, splotched with the harsher blue of water. A high-pitched shrieking began and grew in intensity. The blaze of the sun was softened and the stars were blotted out. Clouds whipped and rolled and were gone, and the wild downward rush stopped. The ship hung in a greenish sky, and there was a yellow desert of sand and tumbled rock below. Cutting through the desert was a gorge with a river in the bottom of it, and where the river left the gorge at the edge of the desert was a green and most beautiful land full of little streamlets and flashing lakes, with queer-colored orchards and many-colored fields. And in the middle of the land there was a city.

"Obran," Thurne said.

Wyatt took the rods in his hands and strained until the veins swelled to bursting on his forehead and his face was crimson.

He could not budge them, but the other rods that barred the corridor suddenly slid up out of the way and Makvern stood there with another officer behind him.

Makvern said, "Wyatt—"

But Wyatt had already spun around and launched himself like a charging bull at Makvern.

He hit him and knocked him back into the other officer. There was a moment of wild confusion, while Burdick and Whitfield and the others piled through the door and into the fray, Wyatt was only clearly aware of one thing and that was that he had Makvern down and that he was going to kill him and it was all very pleasant. Then Whitfield was hauling at him and saying something about needing this one later on and Wyatt allowed himself to be hauled away, and the fight was over. This much of it, at least.

Burdick pulled Makvern to his feet and held him with one arm doubled behind his back. The Turcoman was methodically strangling the other officer and Wyatt went over and made him stop, explaining that the man might be necessary for flying the ship. Then he turned back to Makvern, who was shaking his head hard to clear it.

"Take their stunners and keep watch," Wyatt said to Burdick and Whitfield. "No-Name, you hold him. Good, don't be afraid to hurt him a little—remember Cochise." He spoke then to Makvern, "How do I raise that partition?"

The Alpha Centaurians were all squeezed against it, trying to see what was going on.

Makvern said, "I'll raise it myself in a minute, God, Wyatt, don't you ever think before you jump?"

"I've thought," Wyatt said. "Plenty. Where's that control? And where's Brinna?"

He nodded to No-Name, who exerted pressure. Makvern began to look really angry. He snapped.

"Will you stop bawling at me and listen? I'm on your side. I'm the man Loran died for. I *am* the leader of the Second Party!"

The other officer, who had finally recovered his voice a little after the Turcoman's mauling, croaked out. "You won't be the leader of anything for long if we don't get that broadcast going. The flagship has already checked us once. If Varsek doesn't find you anywhere else in the fleet and we don't behave just the way we ought to—"

MAKVERN GLARED at Wyatt. "Well? Do you still want to go to Earth, or would you prefer to accompany Brinna and me to the pit?"

Wyatt said to No-Name, "Let him go."

"Thanks," said Makvern sourly. "This shows signs of becoming a habit. I would have liked to tell you earlier that plans were already laid, but I didn't think it was wise. Varsek is unpredictable. He might have sent you to the pit—"

"Yes," said Wyatt. "You were a big help there. No opinion. You might at least have said no."

"If I had, you'd have been there in five minutes. Anyway, I've been teetering on the brink of that pit for weeks. All I wanted to do was hold out until now."

"So, you let Brinna go ahead with this on her own hook, to kind of cover for you?"

"Yes. It kept her busy, and kept Varsek puzzled about me. It worked out well. Most of Brinna's men are really Second Party men, though it's going to be a shock to her to find that out. We were taking no chance of exchanging Varsek for another ambition-hungry chief, even if this one is female and handsome."

He had moved into the observation cell and was talking as much to the Alpha Centaurians as to Wyatt and the Earthmen.

"Your idea of warning Earth and using a setback there to put us in power—the same thing Brinna had in mind—wasn't a bad one, except that we can't wait that long. Varsek is alarmed. He's willing to torture the whole fleet if he has to to root us out. We would have liked to put this off until we were just a little stronger. The fleet has been away from home a long time now and discontent is growing among the men—we could have capitalized on that. But we have no choice. If we don't move now we'll be destroyed, inevitably. So we're making our break at Alpha Centauri."

"How?" asked Wyatt.

"A full-scale revolt is out. Things will go well here, not much effective resistance and a lot of loot. Men don't oust a leader under those circumstances. We can't hope to take over the whole fleet. After the ships have landed and the ground phase of the attack is under way, we'll separate ourselves from the main force and take over as many of the destroyers as we can man. Anybody that wants to can come with us—in the heat of a successful battle, I'm afraid that won't be many. After that—" Makvern shrugged. "There are too many variables. I don't know."

"Can you help my world?" asked Thurne. "My city?"

Makvern said sadly, "I won't lie to you. No. Except in that Varsek will have fewer men and ships, we can't help. We're not strong enough."

"And you would not fight against your own comrades, anyway," said Thurne.

"Not under these circumstances, no. That would be too much of a stab in the back and we'd lose all chance of ever winning them over. About all I can offer you, Thurne, is the hope of vengeance and the promise that if we do win we'll make what restitution we can."

"And what about us?" asked Wyatt. "What about Earth?"

"We'll send you there. If Varsek is sufficiently shaken up there may not be any need for a warning. If not—well, his force will be that much the weaker."

Wyatt looked at the others and said, "That's fair enough."

Makvern turned to the Alpha Centaurians, who had been talking among themselves.

"Varsek is already hunting for me through the fleet. He's been told that I'm not here but if anything about the required routine of this ship is wrong he'll send a force at once to search it and that will be about the end of me and the revolt both. What do you say, Thurne? Can I raise the bars as between comrades, or must I treat you still as captives?"

Thurne said, "Raise them. We will do what we can against Varsek."

"Good," said Makvern. "Good!" He called to the other officer and the steel rods slid up out of sight. "Now we must hurry. Thurne, you were given some instructions quite a while ago. Follow them. I know they're distasteful to a brave man, but you'll be doing your people no disservice. To urge them to fight against us would be suicidal."

"Nevertheless," said Thurne, "they will fight."

MAKVERN SIGHED. "That's usually the case. Make the speech anyway. That's what we're here for. We're leading the whole fleet, remember, out in front where everybody can see us."

He showed the reluctant Alpha Centaurian where to stand, on a lens-like circle of crystal in the deck, with a similar one over his head. Almost at once both lenses brightened, so that Thurne stood encased in a pillar of light.

"But," said Wyatt, "there are no radios down there, no receivers. His culture hasn't built them yet. How are you going to broadcast?"

Makvern motioned him and the other Earthmen to the observation panels on their side of the cell. "Watch," he said. "That's what you're supposed to do anyway. The value of example. The prospective victim is softened up by seeing what happens to his predecessor."

He started away. "I've watched enough of these things, world after world. They make me sick. I have things to do now. Listen for the intercom and be ready to jump when I tell you."

He went out. Thurne stood stiffly in his pillar of light. The ship dropped lower over the city of Obran. And now the ships of the Task Force had begun to come into view in the higher air.

A metallic voice said, "Begin the talk, Thurne."

Burdick said suddenly, "I'll be damned. Look there."

In the clear air above the city, ahead of and below the ship, stood a gigantic three-dimensional image of Thurne, perhaps thirty feet high, moving slowly as the ship moved, his insubstantial feet brushing the tops of the queer ornate towers. And now Thurne was talking. Faintly through the hull came an echoing vibration from outside, and Wyatt knew that Thurne's voice, as greatly amplified as the prismatic projection of his personal image, was booming out over

Obran. Down in the streets, in the sunlight, between the tall buildings and in the parks and along the rows of little mud-brick houses, people were running out to stare up in fear and amazement.

Thurne was speaking to his people in his own tongue so that Wyatt could not understand the words, but from his tone and the snarling glint of bared teeth he was not preaching submission as whole-heartedly as he might have done. Probably the Task Force was used to that. They could not control their captives absolutely on these propaganda broadcasts. They gave them the chance, and probably it paid off in enough surrenders to make it worthwhile. With more primitive people than Thurne's, the appearance of a giant in the sky over their heads would be enough in itself to make them collapse in utter panic.

Down below in the sunlit streets the people began to run here and there, and a haze of dust arose and shimmered. From the towers and the high walls a million carven faces looked out unmoved, the faces of a million dancing stone gods and goddesses.

The fleet came down in a whistling rush among the orchards and fields, burning and crushing where ever they landed in a great circle around the city. The people ran. They had no nuclear weapons, no ground-to-air missiles, no planes. They ran and there was no place to run to They were already trapped.

Poor devils, thought Wyatt, and imagined what New York or Washington would be like under similar conditions, with a gigantic image of himself striding the sky and bellowing at them to surrender. The success of Makvern's revolt and the creation of a wide split in the fleet itself were now his only hope that that might not happen.

"I thought," said Burdick, "that Thurne was so sure they'd fight."

"They will," said Wyatt. "Look. The panic's already quieting." The women and children had disappeared from the streets now. Groups of men still ran but their running was purposeful. Suddenly from various places around the outskirts of the city puffs of smoke burst out and Whitfield said.

"Little cannon, by God!"

The pillar of light flicked off. The image of Thurne disappeared from the sky. Makvern's voice came over the intercom. There was an iron note in it.

"We've been ordered to land at once beside the flagship. Obviously we can't. And if you look up you'll see trouble on the way."

They looked. Two small fast craft, light-armed but plenty heavy enough for the propaganda ship, were headed in their direction.

"They will attempt to force that landing on us, and I can't fight them in this tub. I propose to land at once. It may be rough, so take what precautions you can. Wyatt, there's a supply of stunners here. Come and get them."

Wyatt found his way to the bridge. A case of side-arms, apparently fresh out of stores, had been smuggled there and hidden alike from Varsek's men and Brinna. Makvern's face was wire-drawn with tension and excitement. He showed Wyatt the case and then handed him a three-pronged key.

"She's in the skipper's cabin—it's the only one that's locked. Don't give her arms or a chance to make trouble. Apart from that I leave her up to you."

Wyatt said, "Thanks."

Makvern went out, hurrying.

They smashed open the case and served the stunners out, but Wyatt didn't wait for that. He grabbed one for himself and then went hunting for the skipper's cabin. He could hear a mounting tumult from the bridgeroom. The ship was low, skimming the housetops, lurching this way and that so roughly that it was hard to stand up. The two pursuing ships were closing fast.

He heard Brinna before he found her. She was shouting through the door, demanding to be freed. Wyatt struggled with the unfamiliar lock. The ship rocked wildly. There was a roar and a crack like the grandfather of all lightning bolts. Blue fire sheeted from the metal inner surfaces. Half stunned, he saw the door come open under his hand and then Brinna seemed to leap through the air at him, her eyes wide and her arms outstretched. She hit him, but he was already flying backward himself as the ship went out from under him and they fell together against a wall that had suddenly become a deck. There was a very great noise and a sound of things moving and somehow the branches of a tree had appeared, stuck through the broken port of the skipper's cabin which was now directly overhead.

CHAPTER EIGHT

IT TOOK WYATT quite a long minute to realize that he was still alive and not even badly hurt. He didn't know about Brinna, but when he pushed her off him, he was relieved to see her move. He scrambled to his feet and helped her up. Makvern came from the direction of the bridge. He shouted and made urgent motions. He was bleeding from a cut on the cheek and his shirt was torn. Wyatt pushed Brinna toward him and clambered over the buckled walls to the observation chamber.

Burdick and Whitfield and the Apache were already crawling toward him. The Turcoman came after them, but the Arab was dead, lying in a corner with his head twisted under him. The Alpha Centaurians had taken less damage on their side. Three of them were hurt but they were all able to move. Wyatt shouted at them to come out and made his way back to where Makvern and the officers from the bridge had got the hatch open. In a minute he had dropped out of it perhaps eight feet to the ground, in a tangle of broken trees, and the others were coming one by one after him. The two ships, one of which had brought them down, had shot over them and away, presumably to turn and make another pass.

Or maybe there was no need for another pass.

They had crashed at the edge of the city, just missing a row of mud-brick houses shaped like ovens with round brick roofs. Beyond, the ships of the Task Force stood like ominous towers in the green fields, discharging their ground attack vehicles.

Wyatt had heard about these but he had never seen any. Every destroyer carried a number of them to clear the way for troops, in the manner of tank units, only these were not in any way like tanks. They consisted of a monstrous red globe mounted on four jointed legs which were about four times a man's height so that the globes stood high off the ground. There was a small propeller mount underneath so that the globes could become amphibious at need. They were horrible-looking things to come stalking at you over the flat fields, and they were stalking pretty fast. Some twenty yards away to the right a battery of three small shiny cannon popped and banged, served by furry men whose courage was only exceeded by the futility of what they did.

Makvern was talking. He was fierce and alert, a man caught in a tight spot and determined to get out of it.

"Our men are to gather in the northwest sector of the perimeter. We'll try to fight our way to them. This sector here is designated as northeast and we're pretty close to the middle of it, so it could be worse. Stick together and let's go fast."

Brinna said quite coolly, "Watch it, they're coming within range."

They began to run, away from the wrecked ship and toward the row of houses, bunched together and looking warily over their shoulders. One of the globes in particular seemed to have decided to follow them—probably it had been ordered to after the ship crashed. Now Wyatt could see a circle of round shuttered ports around its top, and one of them had opened. A large sort of gun or projector was rising from the hole on a flexible mount, bobbing about in an inquisitive fashion like the head of a bird on a long neck. Suddenly it made a point directly at them and a brilliant white beam shot toward them. They leaped for cover between the houses, but the beam was short. Where it hit the ground it erupted into a shower of green sparks.

"Heavy-duty stunner," Makvern said. "When one of those hits you, you stay down till the battle's over."

They ran again, ducking and dodging between the queer round-roofed houses.

"Don't they kill?" Wyatt asked.

"Not often. The very old, little children, invalids. It's humane, as weapons go."

Another white beam sizzled down close behind Whitfield, bursting green where it hit. The red globe towered over them against the sky, grotesquely like a huge round-bodied quadruped with a ludicrously small head on that bobbing little neck.

"I don't reckon," said Burdick, "that we're going to outrun that for long."

THURNE TURNED a slitted panther look on the globe and said, "I can lead you by safer ways, if you can run very swiftly ahead of it for a little time."

"We can run," said Makvern.

They ran, Wyatt, Burdick and Whitfield all had ideas about giving Brinna a hand, only to find that she was going fleet as a deer with long clean strides. They ran their hearts into their throats and the breath clear out of them and they made it into a long colonnade that covered the walk beside a great building covered with the rows of sculptured dancing gods that seemed to delight Thurne's people. In the broad street men were dragging more of the queer little cannon into place. Their body-fur was dark and mottled with sweat. Several of them left the cannon and came leaping toward Makvern's party, their teeth and claws bared, but Thurne shouted at them in his own tongue and they stopped reluctantly. The five who had been captive with Thurne now ran to join the men with the cannon, which were already hurling shot at the stalking globe and not hurting it at all. Thurne pointed to a wide low door and said, "In here."

They crowded through. Over his shoulder, in the brilliant sunlight outside, Wyatt saw green fire in the street. The cannoneers fell down and the little guns were silent.

Inside it was quite dark by contrast, a great vaulted place so crowded with carvings and shadows that for a minute or two he couldn't tell if anything alive was in there or not. Then he got the sounds, the breathing and stirring, the whimpering of small creatures, the whisperings. His eyes adjusted to the dim light and he saw that the place was full of women and children huddled along the walls on either side and in the alcoves which he supposed were shrines because they had big ornate statues in them and little lamps. The children, especially the very young ones, looked like oversized kittens.

Makvern said, "See those statues, and the gilding of the vault? All gold, and the stones are real too, every one of them. A poor place to seek sanctuary from looters."

The hot feral eyes of the women made Wyatt shiver. All along the way they would rise and come out with a white gleaming of claws and teeth. If it had not been for Thurne they would have been torn to pieces in seconds, Wyatt was glad when they reached the other end of the building and emerged again into sunlight and the sharp sounds of battle.

The red globes were stalking everywhere now, their monstrous forms visible over the roofs of houses or between the towers of the larger buildings. The defenders were being struck down or driven back into the heart of the city, and troops of Uryx were already in the outlying streets, beginning the systematic business of sacking Obran.

A globe had just passed by in the street, leaving in its wake a litter of stunned forms that looked sufficiently like corpses, but the troops had not yet come in sight. There was another huge carved building across the way. They raced toward it, and the men who were operating the departing globe did not see them in time to fire.

This building was better lighted inside, although it had just as much carving, gilding and statuary as the last one. This was obviously a hospital. Some of the patients began to scream at the sight of the strangers and attendants ran to bar the way. Once more Thurne's authority got them through—almost. This time, as they reached the doorway at the far end, a party of Varsek's troops came in.

There were eight or nine of them with stunners in their hands. They were expecting trouble but nothing more than they could easily handle, and the first thing they saw about the group inside was the uniforms of Makvern and his officers. The leader actually saluted, and while he was doing it he saw the Earthmen all armed, and the Alpha Centaurian armed, and he said in sudden alarm to his party.

"Look out, these are the people—"

He didn't get any farther. Makvern's stunner knocked him down and then Wyatt began firing and so did the others. There was a brief but violent crackling of beams, and when it was all over seven of the fleet party were down and two had made it out the door. Whitfield and No-Name and two of the officers had gone down.

So had Thurne.

From here on they were on their own.

"Well," said Makvern grimly, "let's get them up and out of here."

WYATT HEAVED No-Name onto his shoulders and Burdick carried Whitfield, his long legs dragging. They left Thurne where he was, with his own people. Burdened and staggering, they started out the door. And now Brinna said.

"You'd better give me a weapon."

Makvern shook his head.

"I don't see what you're afraid of," she said. "I know you won't kill me and I know Varsek would. He wouldn't believe any story I could tell him now."

Makvern hesitated and then said, "All right. Take one of theirs."

She picked up a stunner and they all went out together, cautiously, into the bright sun.

Here they were near one corner of a broad square. A globe was marching toward them on its jointed stilt-legs, coming up the street to their right, with men on foot following behind it. There were overturned cannon and fallen men near the corner, where the beams had hit, and other men were running away across the square, their faces wild with fury and fear and helplessness.

Makvern pointed to the mouth of a street diagonally across from them. "Make for that. Our ships should not be far beyond here now, if—"

Wyatt thought he was going to say *if the Second Party has been successful.* But he didn't. It was hardly worth bringing that up, not now.

They ran out across the square, heavy and slow with their burdens.

Once again they were lucky. They made the transit past the corner before the men in the globe could fire at them, and then the buildings protected them. A haze of dust and smoke hung in the air. The queer high-piled towers and the crowded masses of carving seemed to waver like things seen through water. The gods and goddesses almost seemed to move, dancing and smiling with fierce, grotesque dignity.

Some of the Alpha Centaurians who had been running away saw them and turned back.

They had weapons like very primitive pistols, and they had long sharp knives. The ones with pistols paused to load them. The others charged. And from the street behind came the measured clanging tread of the globe.

Wyatt fired. Nobody stopped running, they didn't dare to, because the globe was a worse enemy than these furry men. They fired as they went and some of the Alpha Centaurians fell under the stun rays and the rest turned back, waiting for the others who were loading their pistols. Wyatt panted and labored on under the weight of the Apache. The mouth of the street was not far away now, Brinna and those of the men who were not burdened had lagged behind to cover the others. Their stunners crackled. Another one or two of the furry men went down, and then there was a series of sharper crackling sounds and one of the officers stopped and looked down in astonishment at the hole in his middle, from which blood had begun to flow. A ball hit close to Wyatt's feet and skipped away over the stones. Others rattled off the walk.

Makvern yelled to them to hurry, sweeping the Alpha Centaurians with a continuous flare from his stunner. Brinna was helping the wounded man, half carrying him and firing steadily with her free arm. Wyatt softened toward her immensely in that moment.

The street mouth swallowed them. In almost the same instant the walking globe rounded the corner. Its heavy beams took care of the Alpha Centaurians, which was a favor to Makvern's party that was more or less forced upon it. It would be after them too, probably, but in the meantime the street ahead of them was clear and there was a bend in it that would give them protection.

They staggered on, in the dust and the hot sun. They rounded the bend and Wyatt saw a short row of little houses and over them the tall distant forms of ships.

He thought for a minute that they were safe, that they had made it. And then he saw the uniformed troops running up the street toward them, utterly cutting them off.

CHAPTER NINE

MAKVERN SAID sharply, "Hold your fire. They're ours."

It was a minute before Wyatt took that in, and by that time someone had lifted the ten-ton weight of No-Name off his back and he was being hurried along the street and out across the fields toward the ships. There was some fighting still going on—the Second Party men had attacked the skeleton crews left behind after the troops disembarked, and a few of them were still holding out.

"We'll have them mopped up soon," a young officer panted, running beside Makvern. He looked as though he had had a rough time. "God, I'm glad you got through, sir! We were trying to find you—"

"How well did we do?" asked Makvern.

"We've got about one third of the fleet. I was hoping—"

"Yes," said Makvern. "So was I. Well, a third is better than a quarter, or a tenth."

"It's hardly a victory, though," said the young officer flatly. He pointed off across the fields in the distance. "Look there, sir. Varsek's starting to pull some of the men back to their ships. He can catch us dead on the ground."

"Send an order to prepare for take-off at once," said Makvern. "Is this the command ship? Good. Get everybody here aboard, see that the wounded are cared for. I'll want—" he reeled off a string of names—"on the bridge immediately—"

Things were already moving fast. Now they raced, under the whiplash of Makvern's orders. Nobody stopped Wyatt, so he followed Makvern to the bridge. Even he could see the danger. If Varsek's heavy-armed units were manned in time to get above them they would be stopped before they started.

Makvern got his ships off the ground.

They roared screaming into the sky, and before they were clear of the atmosphere Varsek's face was mirrored in the communic screen.

It was a face flinty and implacable with anger, not the wild kind that soon burns out but a deeper-colder thing that would last until the men he considered to be his enemies were no longer any threat to him or anyone else.

"Did you think you could go home to Uryx now?" he asked, looking at Makvern with his cold eyes. "You may be free of the fleet but you're not free of me. If you go home I'll have you all tried for desertion, I'm still your chief, Makvern, and I have powerful friends."

"Who profit from the loot," said Makvern. "Yes, I know that. It was my thought that we could force a few changes at Uryx too, before it stinks too high of corruption."

Varsek laughed. "With the whole fleet, you might do that. With your handful—no." He leaned closer into the pick-up field so that he seemed to be coming right through the screen. "Listen, Makvern. You've made your move and failed. You can't fight me and you can't go home and you can't even run for long. You haven't enough supply ships. You haven't enough fuel or food. You'll have to start looting yourself or try stealing from me, and sooner or later I'll catch up with you and annihilate you."

"Annihilate," said Makvern slowly. "That's a big, cruel word. I wonder how your men will feel about it. We've been comrades for a long time and our quarrel is with you, not with them. Perhaps a lot of them are as sick of this life as we are and would like to get home to the families they haven't seen in years. We didn't harm any of them when we took these ships, and we'll welcome any of them who want to join us, now or later. We'll be around for a while."

WYATT KNEW that Makvern was not talking to Varsek alone, but to all the men who would be listening to the communics all over the fleet. He was a good talker, but it didn't look to Wyatt as though talking was going to do him much good.

"If that is intended as a challenge," Varsek said, "I'll accept it. My plans will not be changed. As soon as we finish here we go on to Earth, and after that to whatever system offers the best pickings. I'm in no hurry, Makvern. I can go on indefinitely. Hang on my flank and hope for deserters as long as you want to sooner or later—" He brought his hand down in a slashing gesture. "—I'll destroy you."

His gaze slid past Makvern to Wyatt.

"I warned you twice," he said, "about the fate of brave stubborn men. Whether you stay with Makvern or go back to Earth I'll find you. And I'll give Earth some special attention because of you, we do have weapons that will kill at need." Once more he smiled, and now his gaze included both Wyatt and Makvern. "I know that Earth will be warned. I accept that, too."

"You might lose a lot of men," Wyatt said. "We're not quite as primitive as the Alpha Centaurians."

"You have nuclear weapons," said Varsek, "but no way to get them up to us in space. And people usually hesitate to drop bombs on their own cities, to destroy an invader who is only temporarily there. So your warning does not frighten me."

"We have tactical weapons, too," said Wyatt. "Or didn't you tell your men about those?"

"My men are soldiers," said Varsek, "not babies. Go home, Wyatt. Spread the alarm. And take Brinna with you.

That was her plan, wasn't it—warn Earth and thus unseat me." His voice rose and it was as though he was shouting a warning to the whole fleet. "No one can unseat me! This is my Task Force, I command it, and I will command it, until such time as my superiors call me home."

"That will be never," said Makvern wearily, "as long as you keep the loot ships pouring into Uryx to make them rich."

He broke the contact—probably the first time anyone had cut Varsek off first. He turned to Wyatt and his officers.

"Much of what he says is true. We are short of food and fuel. Both of those we can get at Earth, but it will have to be peaceably. I propose that we offer ourselves to help in her defense—that we force a showdown with Varsek by placing our ships between him and Earth. If we're to be destroyed, it might as well be now as later, when we'll be even weaker and less able to fight."

He looked with a terrible grim look at Wyatt and said, *'We can carry nuclear weapons into space.*"

Brief minutes later, Makvern's little fleet, all fast destroyers and a few light supply ships that could outdistance the slower-moving Task Force, went into hyper-drive, headed for Earth.

And now the customary business of landing on a target world was played in reverse. They did not have a propaganda ship, but as soon as they reached the outer limits of Earth's atmosphere Wyatt began to broadcast, blanketing the Western Hemisphere with the ship's powerful transmitter. He sent the same message over and over again, beginning with, *We come in peace* and going on with a summary of the situation, begging the powers that were not to attack them when they landed. He had Burdick and the Australian speak, and No-Name, and even the Turcoman. He had Makvern speak.

But when an answer did come it was from the government radio in Washington forbidding them to land until the United Nations had been consulted and preliminary talks had been had with Makvern via shortwave, with proper assurances of their intentions. Then Bannister got a message through from the big transmitter on the mesa, starting with, "What the hell happened to you, you can't be telling the truth!" Wyatt assured him he was, and Bannister said, "Then for God's sake don't land. Everybody's in a panic. They're evacuating Washington and setting up gun-emplacements on every corner, and the crackpots are having a field day. Wait until they all calm down!"

"We've been trying to make them understand," said Wyatt, "that we can't wait. There's a fleet coming right on our heels and if arrangements aren't made right now it'll be too late for all of us."

"Well," said Bannister, sadly and without hope, "good luck."

They went about their landing.

MAKVERN'S COMMAND ship came down in one of Washington's parks. They had decided that Makvern and Wyatt, with one man to operate the thing, would leave the cruiser in one of the stalking-globes. There was not room enough in it for Burdick and the other Earthmen.

Brinna had maintained a brooding silence all the way, but she broke it now by saying bitterly to Wyatt,

"You know your people out there are panicky about this sudden eruption from space—they'll destroy you before you can talk to them."

"I'll have to take the chance," Wyatt said.

"Just as you had to force me to take you to Washington—how long ago?" said Brinna. She added with sudden fierceness, "God defend us from having to do with fools!"

Wyatt grinned. "Are you angry because your schemes are ruined, or because I'm in danger?" Before she could make wrathful reply, he kissed her and pushed her out of his way, and went after Makvern.

They got into the red globe, and stalked out of the cruiser. They needed the globe, not for attack but for their own defense. Above them in the sky a squadron of skimmers wheeled, easily eluding the slower and clumsier jets of Earth, and keeping at such a low altitude that the planes hesitated to fire on them for fear of hitting their own men on the ground.

The red globe stalked ponderously into Washington.

Bannister had told the truth. The city was deserted except for soldiers. Watching the 360 degree screen inside the globe, Wyatt saw men in olive drab fire at them and he heard the vicious battle of bullets against their armor plate. Makvern had assured him it was proof against practically anything short of atomic projectiles, but when the anti-tank guns and the flame-throwers appeared Wyatt began to get nervous and was glad when Makvern decided not to take any chances. He ordered one of the heavy stunners unlimbered and asked for support from the skimmers. Then he turned the radio over to Wyatt.

The screens now showed bursts of green fire all around where the stun rays were striking. The gun crews were being struck down, the soldiers with rifles stunned or driven back. An area of quiet was laid down around the globe, travelling with it as it moved, constantly being pushed ahead by the white beams of the stunners.

Wyatt talked tensely on the radio. "You force us to defend ourselves but you will find that these men are not dead or harmed in any way, only stunned. We beg the President and Congress to give us a hearing—"

No answer. Wyatt mopped sweat from his forehead, and talked on.

"You are faced with an enemy more terrible than any you ever dreamed of, approaching you through interstellar space at many times the speed of light. You see what we can do, but this is only a fraction of *their* power. Your only hope is to accept our offer of help, plan with us how to stop the Task Force before it ever lands. Or you'll have hundreds of these red globes stalking the countryside, and hundreds of ships against which your planes will be useless as they are right now against the skimmers."

No answer.

Makvern said to Wyatt, "We have to stop somewhere. This is your country—what do you suggest?"

Wyatt looked at the screen. They were in front of the Supreme Court building. Soldiers were firing at them from the approaches, the steps, the portico. Some of them had already been stunned and were lying on the pavement. While he watched a white beam shot out from the globe's projector and burst in green fire among a group on the steps. Wyatt's patience, worn thin by long anxiety, suddenly snapped.

"This place is as good as any," he told Makvern, and then he shouted into the radio, "All right, damn it, I'm an American citizen and I came here in good faith. I haven't committed any crime, and I don't see why I should have to hide and cower in the streets of my own capital, which were paid for out of my taxes. So I'm getting out of this globe, unarmed, and if any damned fool shoots me down he can take it up with his conscience later on."

He got up and snapped at Makvern. "Open the hatch. And pull that stunner in."

"Brinna was right, they're panicky," Makvern said. "They'll kill you. Wait a bit."

Wyatt swore. "We *can't* wait, it's now or nothing! They'll stay panicky until they actually see that I am an Earthman and not a bug-eyed monster lying to them over the radio. Then we may get somewhere with them."

Makvern hesitated a moment and then pressed a button. The hatch opened and a thin ladder extended itself.

Wyatt went down it.

He went down slowly, and it was a warm day in Washington but he was as cold as mid-December. The sweat of fear was clammy on him and his legs shook. The soldiers in the immediate vicinity were all unconscious or had taken cover, but more would undoubtedly come. He hoped their field command posts would relay his radio message to the men with the guns.

He reached the foot of the ladder and stood there.

There was a great silence. Then a soldier with a rifle edged cautiously around one of the pillars of the portico.

Wyatt watched him, thinking *He will raise that gun and fire and that will be the end of it.*

The man's voice reached him, thin with distance and surprise, "Hey, it's a man. It's human. It ain't no monster after all—"

From inside the open hatch of the globe Wyatt heard a radio-transmitted voice speaking,

"If you will withdraw your—er—aircraft a sign of good faith, our representatives will come to—"

Wyatt didn't hear the rest of it too clearly. He was struggling with the reaction of relief. Not only for Earth, but for himself.

AFTER THAT it was not so difficult. Once the high brass was convinced of the danger, and of Makvern's sincerity, things got done in spite of red tape and provincial stubbornness. The testimony of Burdick and Whitfield, the Apache and the Turcoman, helped immensely.

Makvern's ships were allowed to refuel and take on supplies. They took to space again, but without any nuclear weapons aboard. "Those are my own people," Makvern said. "I can't use that against them."

The air forces of the world were deployed as a second line of defense, coordinated with ground-to-air missile batteries and with squadrons carrying air-to-air missiles. On the ground, the armies readied themselves.

Varsek's fleet came, a great dark arrow of ships into the light of the Sun.

Once more Wyatt was aboard Makvern's command ship, on the bridge. He was acting with others of the regular armed forces of several nations, as liaison officer. He watched the dramatic wedge of ships approach, catching fire on their sun sides as they drew closer until their brazen glitter was painful to the eye. And his heart sank. What Varsek had said was true. Nothing could stand against that fleet.

As though to emphasize that point, Varsek's face appeared in the communic screen.

"So you decided to face me here," he said. "Good. Oh, very good!"

"Perhaps," said Makvern. "Perhaps not. Earth has been warned, Varsek, and now I'm warning you and every man in the fleet. She has powerful armaments, including hydrogen devices, and she is prepared to use them. She can kill a great many of you before she's beaten."

"And who warned Earth?" said Varsek. Both men, Wyatt knew, were speaking to the fleet as much as to each other. "You, Makvern. A traitor's act. Every life we lose here will be your responsibility!"

"Not at all," said Makvern quietly. "You know what the situation is. All you have to do now to avoid any casualties is to withdraw the fleet from Earth without attacking."

"Turn tail and run?" said Varsek. "You should know me better."

Suddenly Makvern's voice blazed fierce, white-hot with old rage. "I know you, Varsek! You'll sacrifice every man in the fleet before you'll admit you've been bested. Remember that, you men, when he's ordering you into battle! Try to figure out what real reason you have for attacking and then see whether you think it's worth dying for! If you don't—"

Varsek's great voice drowned him out. "This is a general order to the Task Force. Battle stations, all personnel. Executive officers of destroyer squadrons Three, Four and Five will proceed with landing operations according to plan."

"You heard your commander," Makvern flared. "Go down and die for him, for his ambition and the fat pockets of his friends, if you want to. If you don't, take your ships out of formation and join us. Then we can all go home. Then—"

"Destroyer Squadrons One and Two," Varsek's voice rolled inexorably on, "will attack the enemy ships at once, proceeding at individual discretion. You will use Type Two armaments—*these traitors must be destroyed!*"

This time it was Varsek who broke the contact with Makvern, and it was as though by that gesture he declared them all dead.

"Well?" said Wyatt tensely.

"God knows," said Makvern. He began to rap out orders, preparing to fight his ships as well as he could.

Wyatt withdrew into a corner out of the way and found Brinna there. She was regarding the preparations inboard and the movements of the fleet with an expert, eager, frustrated gaze. The realization of the defeat of her ambitious plans changed her, Wyatt thought, very little.

"If *I* had the command here—" she said, between her teeth.

"I don't think you could swing the men in the fleet, if you had," he said. "Maybe even Makvern hasn't swung them—"

It didn't look as though he had. The Task Force was breaking up in orderly segments, the heavy attack craft wheeling into position behind their destroyer screens, ready for the screaming plunge downward into the sky. And now from their stations at either side of the forward point of the fleet the two destroyer squadrons leaped toward Makvern's ships.

"Type Two armaments," said Wyatt, "are the lethal ones, I take it. No polite stunning of the victim, just good honest annihilation."

Brinna nodded, her hand closing unconsciously on his.

Makvern was hunched like a bulldog in the forepart of the bridge, rapping orders.

"Hang on," said Brinna. "We move."

THEY DID MOVE, roaring straight up in an effort to get above the oncoming destroyers, Wyatt could see other ships going up with them, while still others dropped and circled. They were trying some kind of a boxing-in maneuver, but the destroyer squadrons were old hands at this game too. They counter-moved with lightning speed. Wyatt did not see any projectile pass through space, but suddenly there was a silent blossoming of fire like the birth of a small sun and one of Makvern's ships ceased to exist in the time it took Wyatt to blink.

"I believe," said Brinna in a steady voice, "that's the first time I have ever seen Type Two projectiles in use except on a test range."

There was a kind of a stunned silence on the bridge. Then once more the ship was in tangential motion, and somebody began to shout, "Look at their formations! Some of Varsek's ships are pulling out—"

"Fire!" said Makvern, and the ship shuddered twice. White stunning beams lanced out and struck a dark iron flank with green fire and sent it staggering away. Wyatt assumed that these beams were powerful enough to knock out not only men but delicate electrical equipment as well.

"They are pulling out," said Brinna. "Breaking up. Look!"

He could see that the orderly formations of Varsek's fleet had become suddenly ragged, some of the ships frankly deserting the ranks and others lagging as though they were hesitant.

"It was the projectile," Brinna said. "Seeing one of their own ships full of men they knew destroyed that way—I think it must have shocked them all as it did me."

The face of a man appeared on the screen, white and strained. "Makvern," he said. "You know me—Shannar, commanding the First Squadron. I'm pulling out—this is murder—"

Varsek's face appeared, superimposed over Shannar's in a ghastly double image.

"Follow your orders! Destroy—"

"The hell with you," said Shannar. "I'm a soldier, not an executioner."

He faded, and a second face appeared through the image of Varsek. "Me, too. After what you've led us into, the Second Squadron is quitting."

Now Varsek's face stood clear in the screen, and outside in space the dark ships wheeled away and joined the number that was gathering behind Makvern's force.

Varsek, his face distorted with a violent fury, cried out, "I *order* the commander of every ship to proceed with his assigned duties! If he refuses, I authorize every officer in the chain of command to take over until one loyal man is found.

I order this! Prepare to land. I'll destroy Makvern myself if none of you have the guts to do it."

And the great bulk of the flagship moved from where it had hung in space and gathered speed, and bore down upon Makvern's command ship like the ultimate hammer of doom.

"He must have packed the flagship with his most trusted officers," Brinna said.

Ignoring every other craft in space, the enormous ship rushed at them.

Makvern spoke into the communic.

"I don't think you quite understand, Varsek. The situation has changed. You are now fairly well isolated. There's been enough killing. Surrender and we'll see that you get a fair trial at Uryx."

"You won't live to go anywhere," Varsek snarled. He began to talk to others who apparently were in the room with him, out of range of the pick-up. "Why the hell doesn't the fleet move? I ordered them. Order them again, and prepare a projectile, Type Two— What are you waiting for?"

"Sir," said a voice, "have you noticed the disposition of the destroyer squadrons?"

"What of them?"

"They're between us and the target. All of them. The commanders request that you surrender. They say there will be no more Type Two's used on men of Uryx."

Varsek spoke into the communic. "Clear the way," he said. "I'll ride over you and smash you. I command this fleet." He pulled his sidearm from its holster and turned around. "As for you—I thought you were loyal to me. I handpicked you, and this is how you repay me! I order you to prepare a projectile—"

A hard matter-of-fact voice said, "You pushed it too far this time, Varsek. You're one man against a fleet. We have been loyal, but you're not the commander any more."

A STUNNER BEAM caught Varsek from the back before he could turn around. He fell below the focus of the screen, and the face of another man replaced his.

The man said, "Varsek has surrendered."

There was a long silence in the command ship. Then the men began to cheer and other voices came over the communics, cheering, and only Makvern turned away so that no one could see his face.

Later, after Makvern had made his speech to the fleet, taking over as commander, he said to Wyatt.

"This is where we part. We go home, to put a stop to this looting and pillaging—it's time Uryx grew up and became an empire to be proud of rather than a nest of outlaws. And you can go home too, knowing that Earth will sleep safe tonight."

Brinna stepped forward. "And what about me?"

"I have that planned," said Makvern sternly. "You'll learn about it in good time."

Wyatt smiled, but did not say anything.

He had no chance to say anything later on, when the ship had landed on the desert near the mesa and Makvern and Brinna had shaken hands with him for the last time, standing on the cool sand in the moonlight at the foot of the ship's ladder. Makvern had moved so quickly while Brinna was occupied with her farewells that she did not realize he was already in the lock and the ladder drawn up until it was too late to follow him. He looked down at her and grinned, and said,

"This seemed to be the best solution to your problem, Brinna. It'll be a long time before Earthmen get into space, and by then you'll be too old to make trouble and I'll be too old to care."

"You mean you're leaving me here?" she shrieked.

"In the care of Wyatt, a brave and stubborn man. Goodbye. And clear away now, we're taking off."

Wyatt hauled the temporarily speechless Brinna to a safe distance. She watched the ship take off into the starry sky and Wyatt did not dare say anything then.

He wasn't at all sure he had made a good bargain. But he was determined to make the best of it.

He started out by kissing her.

After a long enough time, she stopped fighting.

THE END

INTERPLANETARY WARFARE ERUPTS!

There were nine major planets in the Solar System and it was within their boundaries that man first set up interplanetary commerce and began trading with the ancient Martian civilization. And then they discovered a tenth planet—a maverick!

This tenth world, if it had an orbit, had a strange one, for it was heading inwards from interstellar space, heading close to the Earth-Mars spaceways, upsetting astronautic calculations and raising turmoil on the two inhabited worlds. But even so none suspected then just how much trouble this new world would make. For it was WANDL THE INVADER and it was no barren planetoid. It was a manned world, manned by minds and monsters and traveling into our system with a purpose beyond that of astronomical accident!

ABOUT RAY CUMMINGS...

Born in 1887, Ray Cummings acquired insight into the many vast possibilities of future science by a personal association with American genius, Thomas Alva Edison. It was during the 1920's and 1930's that Cummings thrilled millions of his readers with his wonder-filled tales of time and outer space. The infinite and the infinitesimal were all parts of his canvas, and past, present, and future, the interplanetary and the extra-dimensional, all made their initial impact on the reading public through his many stories and novels. When Cummings died early in 1957, the world of modern science-fiction lost one of its genuine founding fathers. For the imagination of this talented writer supplied a great many of the most basic themes upon which the present superstructure of science-fiction is based. Following in the tradition of Jules Verne and H. G. Wells, Cummings successfully bridged the gap between the early dawning of science-fiction in the last decades of the Nineteenth Century and the full flowering of the field in these middle decades of the Twentieth.

WANDL THE INVADER

By
RAY CUMMINGS

ARMCHAIR FICTION
PO Box 4369, Medford, Oregon 97501-0168

*For more information about Armchair Books and products, visit our
website at...*

www.armchairfiction.com

Or email us at...

armchairfiction@yahoo.com

CHAPTER ONE

"It's a planet," I said. "A little world."

"How little?" Venza demanded.

"One-fifth the mass of the Moon. That's what they've calculated now."

"And how far is it away?" Anita asked. "I heard a newscaster say yesterday..."

"Newscasters!" Venza broke in scornfully. "Say, you can take what they tell you about any danger or trouble and cut it in half; and even then you'll be on the gloomy side. See here, Gregg Haljan."

"I'm not giving you newscasters' blare," I retorted. Venza's extravagant vehemence was always refreshing. The Venus girl glared at me. I added: "Anita mentioned newscasters; I didn't."

Anita was in no mood for smiling. "Tell us, Gregg." She sat upright and tense, her chin cupped in her hands. "Tell us."

"For a fact, they don't know much about it yet. You can call it a planet, a wanderer."

"I should say it was a wanderer!" Venza exclaimed. "Coming from heaven knows where beyond the stars, swimming in here like a comet."

"They calculated its distance yesterday at some sixty-five million miles from Earth," I said. "It isn't so far beyond the orbit of Mars, coming diagonally and heading very nearly for the Sun. But it's not a comet."

The thing was indeed inexplicable; for many weeks now, astronomers had been studying it. This was early summer of the year 2070 A.D. All of us had recently returned from those extraordinary events I have already recounted, when we came close to losing Johnny Grantline's radiactum treasure on the Moon, and our lives as well. My ship, the *Planetara*, in the astronomical seasons when the Earth, Mars, and Venus were within comfortable traveling distances of each other, had carried mail and passengers from Greater New York to Ferrok-Shahn, of the Martian Union, and to Grebhar, of the Venus Free State. Now it was wrecked on the Moon.

I had been under navigating officer of the *Planetara*. Upon her, I had met Anita Prince, whose only living relative, her brother, was among those killed in the struggle with the brigands; Anita and I were soon to marry, we hoped.

I was waiting now in Greater New York upon the decision of the Line officials regarding another spaceship. Perhaps I would have command of it, since Captain Carter of the *Planetara* had been killed.

It was a month or so before that adventure, April, 2070, that this mysterious visitor from interstellar space first appeared upon our astronomical horizon. A little thing, at first, a mere unusual dot, a pinpoint on a photo-electric star diagram which should not have been there. It occasioned no comment at the time, save that some thought it might be another planet beyond Pluto; but this was not taken seriously enough to get into the newscasts. None of us had heard about it as late as May, when the *Planetara* set out on what was to be her final voyage.

Presently, it was seen that the object could not be a planet of our solar system; Coming in at tremendous speed, it daily changed its aspect, gathering velocity until soon it was not a dot, but a streak on every diagram-plate.

In a week or so the thing passed from an astronomical curiosity to an item of public news. And now, early in June, when it had cut through the orbit of Jupiter and was approaching that of Mars, fear was growing. The visitor was a menace. No astronomical body could come among us, with a mass as great as a fifth of the Moon, without causing trouble.

The newscasters, with a ready skill for lurid possibilities, were blaring of all sorts of horrible events impending.

I TOLD the girls all I knew of the approaching wanderer. The density was similar to that of Earth. The oncoming velocity and the calculated elements of its orbit now were such that within a few weeks more the new planet would round our Sun and presumably head outward again. It would pass within a few million miles of us, causing a disturbance to Earth's orbit, even a change of the inclination of our axis, affecting our tides and our climate.

"So I've heard," Venza interrupted me. "They say that, and then they stop. Why can't a newscaster tell you what is so mysterious?"

"For a very good reason, Venza: because you can't throw people into a panic. This whole thing, up to today, has been withheld from the public of Earth and Venus. The Martian Union tried to withhold it, but could not. Every heliogram between the worlds is censored."

"And still," said Venza sarcastically, "you don't tell us what is so mysterious about this wanderer."

"For one thing," I said, "it changes its direction. No normal heavenly body does that. They calculated the elements of its orbit last April. They've done it twenty times since, and every time the projected orbit is different. Just a little at first, but last week the accursed thing actually took a sudden turn, as though it were a spaceship."

The girls stared at me. "What does that mean?" Anita asked.

"They're beginning to make wild guesses but we won't go into that."

"What else is mysterious?" Venza demanded.

"The thing isn't normally visible."

Venza shifted her silk-sheathed legs. "Don't talk in code!"

"Not normally visible," I repeated. "A world one-fifth as large as the Moon could be seen plainly by our 'scopes when well beyond Pluto. It's now between Jupiter and Mars, invisible to the naked eye, of course, but still it's not very far away. I've been out there myself. With instruments, we ought to be able to see its surface; see whether it has land and water, inhabitants perhaps. You should be able to distinguish an object on its surface as large as a city, but you can't."

"Why not?" asked Anita. "Are the clouds too thick? What causes it?"

"They don't even know that," I retorted. "There is something abnormal about the light-waves coming from it. Not exactly blurred, but a distortion, a fading. It's some abnormality of the light-waves."

A swift rapping on our door-grid interrupted me, and Snap Dean burst in.

"Hola-lo, everybody! Is it a conference? You look so solemn."

He dashed across the room, kissed Venza, pretended that he was about to kiss Anita, and winked at me. He was a dynamic little fellow, small, wiry, red-headed and freckle-faced, and had been the radio-helio operator of the ill-fated *Planetara*. He was a perfect match for Venza, for all the millions of miles that separated their native lands. Venza, too was small and slim, her manner as readily jocular as his.

"And where have you been?" Venza demanded.

"Me? My private life is my own, so far. We're not married yet, since you insist on us going to Grebhar for the ceremony."

"Do stop it," protested Anita. "We've been talking of..."

"I know very well what you've been talking about. Everybody is. I've got news for you, Gregg." He went abruptly solemn and lowered his voice. "Halsey wants to see us, right away."

I regarded him blankly and my mind swept back. No more than a few short weeks ago Detective-Colonel Halsey of Divisional Headquarters here in Greater New York had sent for us, and we had been precipitated into the Grantline affair. "Halsey!" I burst out.

"Easy, Gregg." Snap cast a vague look around Anita's draped apartment. An open window was beside us, leading to a tiny catwalk balcony. It was moonlit now, and two hundred feet above the pedestrian viaduct.

But Snap continued to frown. "Easy, I tell you. Why shout about Halsey? The air can have ears."

Venza moved and closed and sealed the window.

"What is it?" I asked, more softly.

But Snap was not satisfied. "Anita, do you have a complete isolation barrage for this room?"

"Of course I haven't, Snap."

"Well, Gregg do you have a detector with you?"

I had none. Snap produced his little coil and indicator dial. "It's out of order, but let's see now. Shove over that chair, Gregg."

He disconnected one of the room's tube-lights and contacted with the cathode. It was a makeshift method, but as he dropped to the floor, uncoiling a little length of his wire for an external pick-up, we saw that the thing worked. The pointer on the dial-face was swaying.

"Gregg!" he muttered. "Look at that. Didn't I tell you?"

The pointer quivered in positive reaction. An eavesdropping ray was upon us.

Anita gasped, "I had no idea!"

"No, but I did." Snap added softly. "No one very close."

He and I carried the detector to the length of the hall. The indicator went nearer normal. "It must be the other way," I whispered.

We went to the moonlit balcony. "Way down there on the pedestrian arcade," I said.

"We'll soon fix that," Snap said.

Inside the room, we made connection with a newscaster's blaring voice. Under cover of it we could talk. Snap gathered us close around him.

"Halsey has something important, and it's about this interstellar invader. It all connects. His office paged me on a public mirror. I happened to see it at Park-Circle 40. When I answered it, Halsey's man wanted me to talk in code. I can't talk in code; I have enough to worry about with the interplanetary helios. Then they sent me to an official booth, where I got examined for positive legal identification, and then they put me on the official split-wave length. After all of which precautions I was told to be at Halsey's office tonight at midnight, and told a few other things."

"What?" demanded Venza breathlessly.

"Only hints. Why take chances, by repeating them now?"

"You said he wants me, too?" I put in.

"Yes. You and Venza. We've got to get into his office secretly, by the vacuum cylinders. We're to meet a man from his office at the Eighth Postal switch-station."

"Venza?" Anita said sharply. "What in the universe can he want with Venza? If she's going, I'm going too!"

Snap gazed at her and grinned. "That sounds like a logical deduction. Naturally he must want you; that's why he said Venza."

"I'm going," Anita insisted.

We left half an hour before midnight. The girls were both in gray, with long capes. We took the public monorail into the mid-Manhattan section under the city roof of the business district, and into the Eighth Postal switch-station where the sleek bronze cylinders came tumbling out of the vacuum ports to be re-routed and dispatched again.

A man was on the lookout for us. "Daniel Dean and party?"

"Yes. We were ordered here."

The detective gazed at the girls and at me. "It was three, Dean."

"And now it's four," said Snap cheerfully. "The extra one is Miss Anita Prince. Ever heard of her?"

He had indeed. "All right," he said. "If you and Haljan say so."

We were put into one of the oversized mail cylinders and routed through the tubes like sacks of recorded letters; in ten minutes, with a thump that knocked the breath out of all of us, we were in the switch-rack of Halsey's outer office.

We clambered from the cylinder. Our guide led us down one of the gloomy metal corridors. It echoed with our tread.

A door lifted.

"Daniel Dean and party."

The guard stood aside. "Come in."

The door slid down behind us. We advanced into the small blue-lit apartment, steel-lined like a vault.

CHAPTER TWO

Colonel Halsey sat at his desk, with a few papers before him and a bank of instrument controls at his elbow. He pushed his audiphone and mirror-grid to one side.

"Sit down, please." He gave us each the benefit of a welcoming smile, and his gaze finished upon Anita.

"I came because you sent for Venza," Anita said quickly. "Please, Colonel Halsey, let me stay. I thought, whatever you want her for, you might need me, too."

"Quite so, Miss Prince. Perhaps I shall." It seemed that in his mind were many of the thoughts thronging my own, for he added:

"Haljan, I recall I sent for you like this once before. I hope this may be a more auspicious occasion."

"So do I, sir."

Snap said, "We've been afraid hardly to do more than a whisper. But you're insulated here, and we're mighty curious."

Halsey nodded. "I can talk freely to you, and yet I cannot." His gaze went to Venza. "It is you in whom I am most interested."

"Me? You flatter me, Colonel Halsey." She sat gracefully reclining in the metal chair before his desk, seeming small as a child between its big, broad arms. Her long gray skirt had parted to display her shapely, gray-satined legs. She had thrown off the hood of her cloak. Her thick black hair was coiled in a knot low at the back of her neck; her carmine lips bore an alluring smile. It was all instinctive. To this girl from Venus it came as naturally as she breathed.

Halsey's gray eyes twinkled. "Do not look at me quite like that, Miss Venza, or I shall forget what I have to say. You would get the better of me; I'm glad you're not a criminal."

"So am I," she declared. "What can I do for you, Colonel Halsey?"

His smile faded at once. His glance included us all. "Just this. There is a man here in Greater New York, a Martian whom they call *Set* Molo. He has a younger sister, *Setta* Meka. Have any of you heard of them?"

We had not. Halsey went on, slowly now, apparently choosing his words with the greatest care. "There are things that I can tell you and there are things that I cannot."

"Why not?" asked Venza.

"My dear, for one thing, if you are going to help me you can do it best by not knowing too much. For another, I have my orders; this thing concerns the very highest authorities, not only of the U.S.W., but in Ferrok-Shahn and Grebhar too."

He paused, but none of us spoke. Then Halsey said quietly, "Well, this Martian and his sister are here now in Greater New York. They have some secret. They are engaged in some activity, and I want to find out what it is. I have picked up only little parts of it."

He stopped; and out of the silence Snap said, "If you don't mind, Colonel Halsey, it seems to me you are mostly talking in code."

"I'm not, but I'm trying to tell you as little as possible. You, Miss Venza, need only understand this: the Martian, Molo, must be induced to give you some idea of what he is doing here."

"And I am to induce him?" Venza asked calmly.

"That is my idea." The faint shadow of a smile swept Halsey's thin, intent face. "My dear, you are a girl of Venus. More than that, you have far more than your normal share of wits and brains."

It did not make Venza smile. She sat tense now, with her dark-eyed gaze fastened on Halsey's face. Anita, equally breathless, reached over and gripped her hand.

Then Venza said slowly, "I realize, Colonel Halsey, that this is something vital."

"As vital, my child, as it could be." He drew a long breath. "I want you to understand I am doing my duty. Doing, what seems the best thing, not for you, perhaps, but for the world."

I seemed to see into his mind at that moment. He might have been a father, sending a daughter into danger.

"I need not disguise the danger. I have lost a dozen men." He lighted a cigarette. "I don't seem to be able to frighten you?"

"No," she said. And I heard Anita murmur, "Oh, Venza!"

"But you frighten me," said Snap. "Colonel, look here; you know I'm going to marry this girl very soon."

"Yes, I know. You'll have to consider this a sacrifice, a voluntary descent into danger, for a great cause in a great crisis. You four have just come out of a very considerable danger. We know of what stuff you are made, all of you."

He smiled again. "Perhaps that prominence is unfortunate for you, but let me settle it now. Is there any one of you who will not take my orders and trust my judgement of what is best? And do it, if need be, blindly? Will you offer yourselves to me?"

We gazed at each other. Both the girls instantly murmured, "Yes."

"Yes," I said at last. It was not too hard for me, for I thought I was yielding him Venza, not Anita.

Snap was very pale. He stared from one to the other of us.

"Yes," he said finally. "But Colonel, surely you can tell us more."

Halsey tossed his cigarette away. "I will tell you as much as I think best. These Martians, Molo and his sister, do not know of Venza; at least, I think that they do not. They apparently have not been here very long. How they got here, we don't know. There was no passenger or freight ship. In Ferrok-Shahn, they have a dubious reputation at best; but I won't go into that.

"Venza, I will show you these Martians and the rest depends upon you. There is a mystery; you will find out what it is."

He reached for his inter-office audiphone. "I want to locate the Martian *Set* Molo. Francis, Staff X2, has it in charge."

The audible connection came in a moment. "Francis?"

We could hear the answering microphonic voice, "Yes Colonel."

"Is the fellow in a public place by any chance?"

"In the Red Spark Cafe, Colonel. With his sister and a party."

"Good enough. The Red Spark has an image-finder. Have you visual connection?"

"Yes, the whole room; they have a dozen finders."

"Use a magnifier. Get me the closest view you can."

"It's done, Colonel. I did it just in case you called."

"Connect it."

In a moment our mirror-grid was glowing with the two-foot square image of the interior of the Red Spark Cafe. I knew the place by reputation: a fashionable, more or less disreputable eating, drinking and dancing restaurant, where money and alcholite flowed freely. The patrons were successful criminals of the three worlds, intermingled with thrilled, respectable tourists who hoped they would see something really evil.

The Red Spark was not far from Halsey's office; it was perched high in a break of the city roof, almost directly over Park-Circle 29.

"There he is," said Halsey.

We crowded around his desk. The image showed the interior of a large oval room, balconied and terraced; a dais dance-floor, raised high in the center with three professional couples gyrating there; and beneath them the public dance-grid, slowly rotating on its central axis. A hundred or so couples were dancing. The lower floor was crowded with dining tables; others were upon the little catwalk balconies, and still others in the terraced nooks and side niches, half-enshrouded, half-revealed by colored draperies.

The image now was silent, for Halsey was not bothering with audio connection. But it was a riot of color, flashing colored floodlights bathing the dancers in vivid tints; and there were twinkling spots of colored tube-lights on all the tables. I saw, too, the blank rectangles of darkness against the walls which marked the private dining rooms, insulated against sight and sound. Here one might go for frivolous indiscretion, or for conspiracy, perhaps, and be as secure from interruption as we were, here in Halsey's office.

Venza asked eagerly, "Which is he?"

"Over there on the third terrace to the left. That table. There seem to be six of them in the party."

We heard Francis' voice; he was in Halsey's lower Manhattan office, with this same image before him. "We'll get a closer view."

The table in question was no more than a square inch on our image. We could see an apparently gay party of men and women. One of the couples was gigantic, a Martian man and woman, obviously. The others seemed to be Earth or Venus people.

Francis' voice added: "I've got an audio magnifier on them. Foley's been listening for an hour. Nice, clear English. Much good it does us; this fellow is as cautious as a director of the lower air-lane. Here's your near-look."

Our image shifted to another view. The lens-eye with which we were connected now gave us a view directly over the Martian's table. We were looking down diagonally upon the table, at a distance of no more than ten feet.

There were three Earthwomen in the party. There was nothing peculiar about them. They were rather handsome, dissolute in appearance, all of them obviously befuddled by alcholite. There was a man who could have been Anglo-Saxon. A wastrel, probably, with more money than wit; he wore a black dinner suit edged with white.

Our attention focussed upon the other two. They were tall, as are all Martians. The young woman, *Setta* Meka, seemed perhaps twenty or twenty-five years of age, by Earth reckoning, in stature perhaps very nearly my own height, which is six feet two. It is difficult to tell a Martian's age, but she was very handsome, even by Earth standards; and in Ferrok-Shahn she would be considered a beauty. Her gray-black hair was parted and tied at the back with a plaited metal rope. Her short dark cloak, so luminous a fabric that it caught and reflected the sheen of all the gaudy restaurant lights, was parted, its ends thrown back over her shoulders. Beneath it she wore the characteristic Martian leather jacket, and short, wide leather trousers ornamented with spun metal fringes and tassels. Most Martian women have an amazonian aspect, but I saw now that *Setta* Meka was an exception.

Her brother, who sat beside her, was a full seven feet or more. A hulking sort of fellow, far less spindly than most of his race, he might have come from the polar outposts beyond the Martian Union. He was bare-headed, his gray-black hair clipped close upon a round bullet head, with the familiar Martian round eyes.

I gazed into the face of Molo, as momentarily he turned his head. It was a rough-hewn, strongly masculine face with a hawk-like nose, bushy black brows frowning above deepset round eyes. The face of a keen scoundrel, I could not doubt, though the smooth-plucked gray skin was flushed now with alcholite, and the wide, thin-lipped mouth was leering at the woman across the table from him.

Like his sister, he had thrown back his cloak, disclosing a brawny, powerful figure, leather clad, with a wide belt of dangling ornaments, some of which probably were weapons.

How long we gazed at this silent colored image of the restaurant table I do not know. I was aware of Halsey's quiet voice: "Look him over, Miss Venza. It depends on you."

Another interval passed. It seemed, as we watched, that Molo's interest in his party was very slight. I got the impression, too, that though at first he had seemed to be intoxicated, actually he was not. Nor was his sister. Anxiety seemed upon her; the smile she had for jests seemed forced; and at intervals she would cast a swift, furtive glance across the gay restaurant scene.

More drinks arrived. The Earthpeople at the table here seemed upon the verge of stupor; and suddenly it appeared that Molo had completely lost interest in them. With a gesture to his sister, he abruptly rose from his seat. She joined him. They left the table, and a red-clad floor manager of the restaurant came at their call. Then in a moment they were moving across the room.

Halsey called sharply into his audiphone: "Francis! Hold us to them if you can."

They were standing now by the opened door of one of the Red Spark's private insulated rooms. We caught a glimpse of its interior, a gaily set table with a bank of colored lights over it.

The figure of a man was in there. He was on his feet, as though he had just arrived to meet the Martians here, and a hooded long cloak enveloped him. It may have been a magnetic "invisible" cloak, with the current now off.

We caught only the fleetest of impressions before the insulated door closed and barred our vision. The glimpse was an accident. Molo, taken by surprise at this appearance of his visitor, could hardly have guarded against it. The waiting figure was very tall, some ten feet, and very thin. The hood shrouded his face and head. In his hand he held a large circular box of black shiny leather, of the sort in which women carry wide-brimmed hats. As Molo joined him he put the box gently on the floor. He handled it as though it were extraordinarily heavy; and as he took a step or two, he seemed weighted down. Just as the room door was hastily closing, Meka sliding it from the inside, we caught a fleeting glimpse of horror.

The lid of the hat box had lifted up. Inside was a great round thing of gray-white, a living thing; a distended ball of membrane, with a network of veins and blood-vessels showing beneath the transparent skin.

For the instant we gazed, stricken. The ball was palpitating, breathing! I saw convolutions of inner tissue under the transparent skin of membrane; a little tentacle, like an arm with a flat-webbed hand, was holding up the lid of the box. The lid rose a trifle higher; the colored lights overhead gave us a brief but clear view of it.

The thing in the box was a huge living brain. I saw goggling, protruding eyes; an orifice that could have been a nose, and a gash upended for a vertical mouth. It was a face. And the little tentacle arm holding up the box-lid was joined to where the ear should have been.

Was this something human? A huge distended human brain, with the body withered to that tiny arm?

The palpitating thing sank down in the box and the lid dropped. And upon our horrified gaze the insulated door of the room slid too.

"By the gods!" exclaimed Halsey. "One of them dares come to the Red Spark. Here, almost in public."

So Halsey knew what this meant. His eyes were blazing now; his face was white, with an intensity of emotion that transfigured it.

"Francis, tell Foley I'll be in the manager's office in five minutes."

He snapped off; our image connection with the Red Spark went dead.

"We're going to the Red Spark," he announced. "This changes everything, yet I don't know. Venza, I may need you more than ever, now."

Halsey herded us to the office door. From his desk he had snatched up a few portable instruments, and he flung on a cloak.

It was a brief trip to the Red Spark, on foot through the sub-cellar arcade to where, under Park Circle 29, we went up in a vertical lift to the roof. We were in the side entrance oval of the restaurant in five minutes.

In the dim metal room of Orentino, the Red Spark's manager, a barrage was up and Foley was waiting for us. We could hear it faintly humming. Now we could talk.

Halsey slammed the door down. He said swiftly, "My men caught one of these things this morning. They have it now and I think Molo does not yet know we captured it. A brain; we're convinced it understands English and can talk, but no one has been able to make it talk yet. Foley, order that damned Orentino to de-insulate the room Molo is in. Now, by the gods, we may see and hear something."

The frightened manager of the Red Spark was in the control room. Halsey killed our barrage to let the outside connections get through to us. We all crowded around the mirror-grid which stood on Orentino's desk. Foley gave us connection with the control room. We saw Orentino's face, his eyes nearly popping with fright. "Colonel Halsey, I will do whatever you tell me."

"What room is that Martian occupying?"

"Insulated 39."

"Break off the insulation. Do it slowly and he may not notice. Then give us connection, audio and vision."

"But I have no image-finders in the insulated rooms."

"Cut off the barrage. I'll get connection there."

Foley was already setting up his eavesdropper on the desk. The mirror blurred a little; then it clarified. We had the interior of the secret room, and voices were coming out of Foley's tiny receiver.

The image showed the box on the floor, with its lid down. The tall hooded shape of the stranger stood with Molo and his sister by the table. They were talking in swift, vehement undertones. The language was Martian, a dialect principally used in Ferrok-Shahn. Our equipment brought it in and I could understand it.

Molo was saying: "But you are the fool to have dared to come here!"

"The master knows that there is danger. Something is wrong." The hooded stranger spoke like a foreigner, but not a Martian, nor an Earthman, and not like any person of Venus I had ever heard. It was a strange, indescribable intonation, a flat, hollow voice.

"I say the master is concerned."

"Let him be."

"And he demanded I bring him here to find you. He is displeased that you are here."

What gruesome thing was this? Their glances seemed to go to the box on the floor at their feet, as though the master were in there. But the lid of the box did not rise.

"Well, you have found me," Molo declared impatiently. "When you know me better, always you will find I have my wits. The thing is for tomorrow night, not tonight."

"But that, my master is not sure." The hollow voice was deferential but insistent. "He fears danger; something has gone wrong. He is working on it now, striving to receive the message! There is a message. He knows that much. Perhaps from our world, Wandl, itself."

For a moment Molo had no answer. His sister had not spoken. I noticed that her gaze seemed roving the room.

"What is it I should do?" Molo asked at last.

"Come with us to your home-room."

"But I have everything ready there. The contact is ready for tomorrow night. Your world will control Earth."

"But if it be tonight?"

Again Molo was silent. My breath stopped. On our mirror I saw the stranger's hood part just a little. There seemed to be no face; just the blur of something brownish.

"But if it be tonight?" the voice insisted.

"I will go," Molo said abruptly, "but your coming here was dangerous. Suppose we cannot get out undetected? You know I will never go to where all our instruments are set up and have some damnable spy follow me. Is all going well on Venus and Mars?"

"Yes. My master feels so. He seems to get messages. The contacts will be made simultaneously." A gruesome chuckle. "The capture of these three worlds. We shall have all three enchained at once. Helpless."

The lid of the black box seemed again about to rise when there came a sharp cry from Meka. "This room is not insulated!"

Our eavesdropping was discovered. Beside me, I heard Halsey give a low curse. On our mirror we saw sudden action. The ten-foot, cloaked figure laboriously lifted the black box, and swung with it toward the outer wall of the room. I saw now clearly with what a dragging, heavy tread that giant shape moved, as though it weighed, here on Earth, far more than the normal weight to which it was accustomed.

"Over there!" Molo gasped. "The escape-port; this room has one. Meka, go with him. I will join you. You know where."

Foley cried, "Colonel, I may be able to stop them!"

But Halsey saw on our image that Molo was staying. "Wait. Let them go. If we have the Martian here, that's better."

I saw the room's escape-port swing open as Meka and the hooded shape carrying the box moved for it. The moonlit darkness of the outer catwalk enveloped the disappearing figures.

Molo was left alone. He closed the port swiftly. His detector now was in his hand, but Halsey anticipated him by a second or two. Our listener went dead; our mirror darkened. Doubtless Molo was never sure whether he had been spied on or not.

Halsey was on his feet. "Foley, get out into the main room. Stay with him."

But there was no need to follow Molo. He had sent his visitor and sister out by the escape-port, which was usual enough; now he was back in the main room as though nothing of importance had happened, with an appearance of intoxication about him. He wavered jovially across the room, threading his way through the gay diners, and reached the table where his party still sat carousing.

Again Halsey shut us off.

"He's got a base somewhere in the city; you heard what they said about it. We've got to trick him into going there, unsuspecting."

Halsey seized the audiphone. "Your chance, Venza. It's the only way. Foley, keep away from that Martian. Shut off all contacts. I'll meet you out there in a moment. I'm sending a girl; she'll go after him."

"Now?" Venza asked.

"Yes. It's the only way. Perhaps you can get him drinking. Venza, use all the wiles you possess now."

"No!" gasped Snap. "It's too dangerous!"

Anita was clinging to Venza. "Colonel Halsey, I'm going too."

Halsey stared, then made a swift decision. "Right. That is still better."

I jumped to my feet. "Colonel, I should prefer that one of us men…"

He gripped me by the shoulders. "Gregg Haljan, I take no suggestions from you!" His blazing eyes bored into me. "There isn't a second to lose. Don't you realize this means destruction of our three inhabited planets? I'll sacrifice myself, you, or these girls! Venza, take Anita outside. I'll join you immediately, give you last instructions. Take a portable audiphone with you."

He turned to Snap. "This is the only way. These demons can't be forced. You know that."

The girls were moving toward the door. I met Snap's anguished gaze.

"Gregg, don't let them go!"

"No! No, I won't!"

I made a lunge past Halsey, with Snap after me. Halsey did not move, but one of his rays struck us. With all senses numbed, I felt myself falling.

"Gregg—don't—let them…"

Snap had tumbled upon me. My senses did not quite fade. I was aware of Anita's and Venza's horrified cries, but Halsey pushed them toward the door. It slid up. I vaguely saw the two girls going out with Halsey after them; and the door coming down.

CHAPTER THREE

I have no idea how long it was before Halsey came back. Snap and I were seated on a low metal bench against the wall. The effect of the paralysing ray was wearing off. We were tingling all over, our senses still confused.

Halsey stalked in upon us. "So you are recovered?"

Snap stammered, "We—I say, we're sorry as hell we acted like that."

"I know you are." His voice softened. "If I could have done anything else, believe me, I would have. But I don't think harm will come to them. They're clever."

"Are they outside?" I asked. "Did they find a way of meeting the Martians? How long have you been gone?"

Halsey merely stared at me as though he had no intention of answering. And then the audiphone on the desk buzzed.

"This is Halsey," he said. "Yes, I have them here. Bring them—did you say bring them?"

We could not hear the answering voice, for Halsey had the muffler in contact.

"No, I would prefer not to come. I'm watching something. I'm at the Red Spark Cafe. Well, I'm going back to my office presently to wait there."

He continued in code. Like Snap, I had never had occasion to learn it. The words were a strange sounding staccato gibberish. He ended, "I will send them, Grantline. Very well, I'll tell them to locate him. At once, yes." He closed off the audiphone.

Halsey swung on us. "You're all right now?"

"Yes." I stood up, drawing Snap up with me. "What is wanted of us Colonel?"

"That's better, Gregg." He smiled, but he was still grim. "I wanted you here to wait for this call from the Conclave of Public Safety. It met at midnight. They have ordered both of you there."

"That's a secret meeting, isn't it?" asked Snap. "There was no report of it over the air tonight."

"Yes. Secret." He was leading us to the door. "They won't need you for more than half an hour. When they finish, come back to my office. You can come openly." He stood with his finger on the door lever. "Good-by, lads. Foley will lead you to the service room. You are to take a mail cylinder for Postal Switch-station 20. They'll re-route you from there to the conclave auditorium."

The door slid up. "When you disembark," he added, "Ask for Johnny Grantline. You are to sit with him."

He showed us out and the door slid down before him. We trudged the corridor, and Snap gripped me.

"For myself," he whispered swiftly, "I'll go to the damnable conclave because I'm ordered. But I won't stay there long. Once we get out of it, if I don't route myself back to the Red Spark, I'm a motor-oiler."

I agreed with him. We had a mental picture of Anita and Venza in the Red Spark's public room. Doubtless Orentino had created a way for them to meet Molo. They would sit there in the Red Spark with that drinking party, and in less than an hour we would be back.

But as we crossed diagonally across an end of the main room with Foley leading us, we caught a glimpse of Molo's table. The party was still there, but Molo, Anita, and Venza were gone!

We had no time to get any information. Foley abruptly left us and another man took his place. In the service room a passenger cylinder was waiting. Our guide entered it with us.

At the switch station we had the breath knocked out of us. After another ten minutes in the vacuum tube, we reached our unknown destination. The cylinder-slide opened. We found ourselves with a lone guard; and through a gloomy arcade opening, Johnny Grantline was advancing, to greet us.

"Well, so here you are, Gregg. Hell to pay heaven, going on here. Come on in; I'll tell you."

"We were sent for," Snap said.

"Yes, but they don't want you yet. Come in here."

He waved away the guard and led us through a padded arcade into a low-vaulted audience room, windowless and gloomy. Across it, a doorway panel stood ajar. Grantline peered through it. There was the glow of light from the adjoining room and the distant murmur of many voices.

Grantline closed the door. "Sit down and I'll tell you..."

"Where are we?" I asked.

"The ninth Conclave Hall."

I knew its location: Lower Manhattan, high under the city roof.

Grantline produced little cigarette cylinders. "Steady your nerves, lads; you'll need it."

He grinned at us. The hand with which he lighted my cylinder was steady as a tower-base, but he was excited. I could see it by the glint in his eyes, and hear it in his voice.

"What's going on?" Snap demanded.

"It's about this invading planet. By the gods, when you hear what's really been learned about it!"

"Well, what?" I asked.

He sketched what he had heard this night at the conclave. The mysterious invader was inhabited.

"How do they know that?" Snap put in.

"Wait. I'll tell you the rest of it. The accursed thing changes its orbit. It banks and turns like a spaceship! It stopped out in space; it's poised out there now between Mars and Jupiter. A world about a fifth the size of the Moon, and the beings on it can control its movements. They've brought it in from interstellar space, into our solar system. Evidently the point they've reached now is far as they want to come. They've poised out there, getting ready to attack, not only us, but Mars and Venus simultaneously."

Grantline gazed at us through the smoke of his cigarette. He was much like Snap, small, wiry, brisk of movement and manner, but older. His hair was graying at the temples; his voice carried the authority of one accustomed to commanding men.

"Don't ask me for the technicalities of how they reached these conclusions. I'm no astronomer. I'm only telling you their conclusions and what their discussions have been here for the past hour."

Heaven knows, we had no inclination to dispute him. What we had seen and heard at the Red Spark tallied with his words.

He went on swiftly, "The attack, of whatever nature it may be, is impending at once. Not next month, or next week, but now. Lord, Gregg, I don't blame you for staring like that. You don't know what's been going on for the past two days on Earth, and Venus and Mars. It's all been suppressed. Neither did I, until I heard it here tonight. The U.S.W., the Martian Union, the Venus Free State, are all preparing for war. Every government spaceship on Earth is being commissioned. We're not going to sit around and wait for invaders to land; the war won't be fought on Earth if we can help it."

We stared. Snap asked, "What makes them so sure?"

"That war is coming? Plenty. This new planet has sent out spaceships. The planet itself is hovering sixty million miles away from us, about forty million miles from Mars and close to ninety million from Venus. Perhaps its leaders think that's the most strategic spot.

"Then it sent out spaceships, three of them. One is hovering close to Venus. Another is near Mars, and the third is some 200,000 miles off Earth. Several of our interplanetary freighters are overdue; it seems now that they must have encountered these invading ships and been destroyed.

"Still more, and worse: these three hovering ships have already landed the enemy on Mars and Venus. The helio-reports mention mysterious encounters in Ferrok-Shahn and Grebhar. For three or four days, Mars has been in a panic of apprehension; Venus almost as bad. And some have landed here. Not many, perhaps; but one has been captured. A thing—God, it's almost beyond description."

We could well agree with that, since Snap and I had just seen one.

"They've got it here," Grantline was saying. "They've tried to make it talk. They can't but they're going to try again."

He jumped to his feet and went to the door. "They're bringing it in." Upon his face was a look of awed horror.

We stood crowding the small door-oval. It gave onto a darkened balcony of the conclave hall. The girders of the city roof were over us. There were a few official spectators sitting up here in the dark on the balcony, but none noticed us.

The lower floor of the hall was lighted. Around the polished oblong tables perhaps a hundred scientists and high governmental officials of the three worlds were seated. Near the center of the hall was a small dais-platform. On a table there, someone had just placed a circular black box, similar to the one we had seen previously.

The hall was hushed and tense. On the dais stood a group of Earth officials. One of them spoke. "Here it is, gentlemen. And this time, by God, we'll make it speak."

Grantline whispered, "That's the War Secretary from Greater London."

I recognized him: Brayley, Commander in Chief of the land, air, water and space armies of the United States of the World. He was gigantic in stature, with a great shock of gray-white hair. A commanding figure, if there ever was one.

Beside him, Nippor, the Japanese representative in Greater New York, seemed a pigmy. The acoustics of the silent hall carried his soft voice up to us. "I would be afraid of drugs. Will we use force? It is vital."

"Yes, by God! Anything."

It seemed that everyone in the hall must be shuddering: I could feel it like an aura pounding up at me. Brayley lifted the box-lid, reached in and raised the horrible thing. He held it up, a two-foot ball of palpitating gray-white membrane. Another living brain.

"Now, damn you, you're going to talk to us! Understand that? We're going to make you talk. Get that box out of the way."

They flung the box to the floor, and Brayley placed the brain on the table.

A glare of light, focussed on it, showed beneath the stretched taut membrane the convolutions of the brain, like tangled purple worms. The blood-vessels seemed distended almost to bursting now. The gruesome face, with popping eyes and that gaping mouth, showed a horrible travesty of terror. From where its ears should have been, a crooked little arm of flabby, gray-white flesh came down, one on each side and braced the table. And I saw now that it had a shriveled body, or at least little legs, bent, almost crushed under by its weight.

"Now, damn you," Brayley said, rubbing off his hands on a rough towel, "for the last time: will you talk?"

The goggling eyes held a terrified but baleful gaze upon Brayley's face. Did it understand? The eyes were fronted our way, and suddenly their glance swung up so that I seemed for an instant to see down into them. And it struck me then: this was a thing of greater intelligence than my own. A humanoid, with brain so developed that through myriad generations the body was shriveled, almost gone. A mind was housed here, an intelligence housed in this monstrous brain.

Were these the beings of the new planet which had come to attack us? But how could this helpless creature, incapable of almost everything, obviously, save thought, do the work of its world?

Then I recalled again that insulated room of the Red Spark Cafe: the thin, ten-foot hooded shape which was carrying the box. Was that, perhaps, an opposite type of being with the brain submerged, dwarfed, and the body paramount? Were there, on this mysterious planet, two co-existing types, each a specialist, one for the physical work and the other for the mental?

I stood with Snap and Grantline in that dark balcony doorway, gazing down to where the giant brain stood braced upon its shriveled arms and legs, and realized why we of Earth and Venus and Mars are all cast in the same mould we call human. It is a little family of planets, here in our solar system; for countless eons we have been close neighbors. The same sunlight, the same general conditions of life, the same seed, were strewn here by a wise Creator. A man from the Orient is different from an Anglo-Saxon; a man of Mars differs a little more. But basically they are the same.

Yet, confronting us now was a new type, from realms of interstellar space, far beyond our solar system.

"For the last time, will you talk?" snapped Brayley.

There was another interval of silence. The eyes of the brain were very watchful. Its gaze roved the hall as though it were seeking for help. It shifted its little arms on the table, seemingly exhausted from the physical effort of supporting itself.

Brayley's voice came again. "Doubtless you can feel pain acutely. We shall see."

With what effort of will to overcome his revulsion we may only guess, he reached forward and pinched the little arm. The result was electrifying. From the upended slit of mouth in that goggling face, came a scream. It pierced the heavy tense silence of the hall, ghastly in its timbre, like nothing any of us had ever heard before. And in it was conveyed agony as though Brayley had not merely pinched that flabby arm, but had thrust a red-hot knife into its vitals.

The brain could feel pain indeed. It crouched with stiffened arms and legs. The membrane of its great head seemed to bulge with greater distension; the knotted blood-vessels were gorged with purple blood. The eyes rolled. Then it closed its mouth. Its gaze steadied upon Brayley's face, so baleful a gaze that as I could see the reflection of its luminous purple glow a shudder of fear and revulsion swept me.

"So you did not like that?" Brayley steadied his voice. "If you don't want more, you had better speak. How did you get here on Earth? What are you trying to do here?"

There seemed an interminable silence; then Nippor took a menacing step forward. "Speak! We will force it from you!"

And then it spoke. "Do—not—touch—me—again."

Indescribable voice! Human, animal or monster no one could say. But the words were clear, precise; and for all their terror, they seemed to hold an infinite command.

A wave of excitement swept the hall, but Brayley's gesture silenced it. He leaped forward and bent low over the palpitating brain.

"So you can talk. You came as an enemy. We have given you every chance today for friendship, and you have refused. What are you trying to do to us?"

It only glared.

"Speak!"

"I will not tell you anything."

"Oh, yes, you will."

"No!"

All the men on the platform were crowding close to it now.

"Speak!" ordered Brayley again. "Here in Greater New York is a hiding place. Where is it?"

No answer.

"Where is it? You are perhaps a leader of your world. I lead ours, and I'm going to master you now. Where is this hiding place?"

The thing suddenly laughed, a gruesome, eerie cackle. "You will know when it is too late. I think it is too late already."

"Too late for what?"

"To save your world. Doomed, your three worlds! Don't touch—me!"

It ended with a scream of apprehension as Nippor grasped the crooked little arm. "Tell us!"

"No!" It screamed again. "Let—me—go!"

"Tell us!" Nippor strengthened his squeezing grip. The thing was writhing, the thin ball of membrane palpitating, heaving. And suddenly it burst. Over all its purpled surface, blood came with a gush.

Nippor and Brayley staggered backward. The scream of the brain ended in a choking gurgle. The little legs and tiny body wilted under it; the round ball of membrane sank to the table. It rolled sidewise upon one arm and ear, and in a moment its palpitation ceased. A purple-red mass of blood, it lay deflated and flabby.

It was dead.

CHAPTER FOUR

"But see here," I said, "did they mention the Martian, Molo, at all?"

"They were discussing Molo before you arrived," Grantline told us.

We had drawn back from the doorway. The conference, with the dead thing removed, was proceeding. Snap and I had momentarily forgotten Anita and Venza; but now we were in a panic to get back to the Red Spark.

"But you can't go," said Grantline. "Brayley ordered you here. He'll want to see you in a moment."

"Well, why doesn't he see us now?" Snap protested. "I'm not going to cool myself off sitting here."

"Oh yes, you are."

Grantline sent word to Brayley that we were here. In a moment the answer came. We were to wait a short time; he would want to see us.

We swiftly told Grantline what had happened at the Red Spark, and found that already he knew. Francis had relayed it to the conference, and Halsey was in constant communication with the officials here.

"Then what is happening?" I demanded. "Where are the girls? Has Halsey heard from them?"

Again Grantline went to a nearby room.

"Anita sent a message," he said, when he returned. "They are with Molo. Halsey is ordering a squad of men to be ready."

Grantline told us what had been happening in the Red Spark. Anita and Venza, simulating drunkenness with a skill for acting which I knew both of them possessed, had joined Molo's party. Perhaps if Meka had been there she would have seen through them.

But Molo did not. And they have since told me that the Martian himself was far from sober, although he was probably not aware of it. He yielded to their demands to leave the restaurant with him. He wanted, as we know, to leave unobtrusively; and Venza threatened a scene unless she could go.

He took them, leaving openly in a public fare-car. Doubtless he at first intended to de-rail them somewhere, but they convinced him that he was not being followed. Twice he used his detector, and Anita and Halsey were clever enough to throw off their rays in time to avoid it. Then Halsey lost connection with the fleeing car, and after that Molo changed his mind about ditching the girls.

"But where are they now?" I demanded.

"You," said Grantline sternly, "are out of it. Do you think that Halsey, under Brayley's orders, will neglect any chance to find out where Molo is hiding? Something is about to happen. This conference is wrestling with it. In Grebhar and Ferrok-Shahn they're striving to find out what it is. Something impending *now*. Helios are pouring in here from Venus and Mars. They're mobilizing their spaceships, just as we are."

Grantline at last was letting out all his apprehensions on us, with this burst. "Halsey didn't tell you that the entire resources of his organization are out upon this thing tonight. Here at this conclave there's a room of information-sorters. That's just where I came from a moment ago. Every country on our Earth is making ready—for what, nobody knows!

"He's had two fragmentary calls from Anita. He has a hundred men ready to rush to their aid, and to capture Molo's lair. He expects another message from Anita any moment. This conference here knows every movement that is being made, within ten or twenty seconds of its making. Perhaps upon Anita and Venza the whole outcome of this thing may hang."

We had no answer to that. "Do you know who Molo is? He's an interplanetary pirate; his ship is the *Star-Streak*."

"Good Lord!"

We had heard of him. For five years past, a gray spaceship, with a base supposedly hidden in the Polar deserts of Mars, had been terrorizing interplanetary shipping.

"They think," Grantline went on, "that Molo was cruising with his pirate ship. He has, as you know, a band of criminals drawn from all the three worlds. There are about fifty of them, commanded by his sister and himself. We think that Molo encountered the three ships which that new planet sent out. The *Star-Streak* was captured, perhaps destroyed. Molo and his band, joined with this new enemy, to save themselves, and because they have been promised rewards."

"But why should these brains want their help?" Snap demanded.

"Wouldn't you say it was because, in Ferrok-Shahn, Grebhar and here in Greater New York, simultaneously tonight, something has to be accomplished, something the brains themselves could not do? Molo and his band know all three cities. How they landed here in Greater New York nobody knows; the enemy spaceship is

200,000 miles out. Obviously they came from it, landed secretly with some smaller ship somewhere on Earth and made their way here."

A buzzer sounded beside us. A voice commanded: "Grantline, bring Gregg Haljan and Daniel Dean to room six at once."

IN ROOM six we stood before the War Secretary, who had arrived there a moment ahead of us.

"Ah, Haljan and Dean. I'm glad to see you."

He was still white and shaken. Beads of perspiration stood upon his forehead. He mopped them off.

"I've just had a rather terrible experience." He did not suggest that we sit down. He went on crisply: "Grantline no doubt has told you of what's going on. Disturbing, terrifying. Haljan, we have a ship being rushed into commission tonight. You know her, the *Cometara*."

"I know her," I said.

"Quite so. She is taking off as soon as we can ready her. She will carry about fifty men. Grantline is in charge of the armament and men. You, Dean, we want to handle her radio-helio."

"Right," said Snap.

"And you, Haljan, we can think of no one better to navigate her."

He waved away my appreciation. "Within a brief time we shall have thirty such ships in space. Mars and Venus also are mobilizing."

He stood up. "We feel, Haljan, that if anyone can handle the *Cometara* with skill enough to combat this lurking enemy, it will be you."

"I'll do my best, sir."

"We know that. The ship is leaving from the Tappan Interplanetary Stage shortly after dawn. When have you and Dean last slept?"

"Last night," we both said.

"Quite so. Then you need sleep now. I want you to go at once to the Tappan Fieldhouse. The commander there will make you comfortable. Eat, and sleep if you can. We want you in good shape. You're to keep out of this night's activities here in the city; you understand?"

"Yes sir."

An orderly was approaching behind Brayley. "I'll be back in a moment, Rollins."

He shook hands with us. "I may not see you again before it's over. Good luck, lads. Grantline, they need you for a moment in the hall; something about electronic space weapons, further equipment for the *Cometara*. Then you'd better go to Tappan House too, and get some sleep."

We were dismissed. Snap and I regarded each other hesitantly. I said impulsively, "Mr. Brayley, Detective-Colonel Halsey is using two girls."

"Yes, we're watching that, Haljan."

"They're the girls we're to marry," I added. "May we communicate with Colonel Halsey?"

"Yes. Call him from here." He smiled wanly. "But keep out of it; we need you at dawn."

The Tappan departure-stage was only a few miles up the Hudson; we could get there in half an hour. It was now nearly trinight, halfway between midnight and dawn. I had my portable audiophone and got Halsey at once.

"You Gregg?"

"Yes. They're through with us at the Conclave. Where is Anita?"

"We heard from her twice. I'm expecting..."

We could hear someone interrupting him. Then he came back. "Gregg? Molo took them somewhere. I didn't dare fling after them. He had his detector going, and Anita warned me not to try it. She had to stop connection herself. God knows how she was able to whisper to me at all."

His voice, like Brayley's, had the ring of a man strained to the breaking point. I could appreciate how Halsey must feel, forced to remain at his desk with its encircling banks of instruments; holding all the network of his farflung activities centralized; his decisions, his commands in a hundred places almost simultaneously, while his body sat there inactive.

"Gregg, the girls must have arrived at Molo's place by now. If only they know where they are! I have lookouts throughout the city with intricate and complete connecting equipment. Gregg, I must disconnect."

"Colonel, give me Anita's frequency. Maybe Snap or I can pick up the message."

He named the oscillating frequency, then disconnected.

"Try that frequency," Snap suggested. "We've got to do something."

The door-slide opened suddenly and an orderly appeared. "Haljan?"

"Get the hell away," roared Snap. "We've had our orders; we don't want any from you."

"Gregg Haljan and Daniel Dean are paged on the mirrors."

Someone in the city wanted us; our names were appearing on the various mirror-grids publicly displayed throughout the city in the hope that we would answer.

"That's different," said Snap. "Answer it for us, that's a good fellow. We're busy."

"It must be important," the orderly insisted. "The caller registered a fee at the Search Bureau; that's how they located you here. He paid the highest fee to search you. An emergency call."

It was against the law to invoke the services of the Search Bureau unless based upon actual impending danger. "We'll take it," I said.

"Come with me." He turned to the left and down the corridor.

We hastened with him to a corridor cubby. Upon the audiphone there I was at once connected with a voice, and an anxious man's face with a two-day growth upon it.

"Haljan! Thank God you answered. This is Dud Ardley. Me and Shac are here. Listen, this is the lower cellar corridor, Lateral 3, under Broadway. Me and Shac just have seen your girls down here."

News of Anita and Venza! I could see in the mirror-image, behind Dud's head the outlines of the little public cubby from which he was calling. He and his brother, on some illicit errand of their own in East Side lower Manhattan, had seen figures alighting from a fare-car. They had caught a glimpse of the faces of Anita and Venza. The girls were hooded and cloaked; a hooded man was with them. The fare-car quickly rolled away, and the hooded figures, suddenly becoming invisible within their magnetic cloaks, had vanished.

"S'elp me, we couldn't do nothin'. You know we take no chances with the police by carryin' cylinders. So I paged you in a hurry."

"Dud, that's damn nice of you. Where are you now? Tell me again."

The Ardleys, knowing nothing of the events of this night, supposed that the girls were being abducted, and decided I should be informed.

"Damn right, Dud. We'll come at once. You two wait for us?"

"Sure. If you got instruments, maybe we can track 'em. It wasn't a quarter of a mile from here, over toward the river. Plenty of rotten dumps down there."

"Wait for us, Dud. We'll come in a rush."

I slammed shut the audiphone. Snap, beside me, had heard it all. He shoved the astonished orderly out of the way.

"What's the nearest exit-route out of here?"

"To the city roof, sir. Up this incline."

We dashed up the spiral incline, through a low exit-port, and were in the starlight of the city roof.

"CONNECT IT, Gregg! You can't tell; her message might come over any minute."

I tuned my coils to the seldom used oscillation frequency which Halsey had told us Anita's transmitter was sending.

"Anything, Gregg?"

"No. Dead channel."

The air, in Anita's channel, was bafflingly silent.

We had been challenged by a roof-guard when we appeared from the upper port of the Conclave Hall; the city roof was not open to public traffic. But with our identifications, he found us a single-seat hand-tram, and started us southward on the deserted route.

It was a cloudless night, with stars like thickly-strewn diamonds on purple velvet. The city roof lay glistening in the starlight. In my great-grandfather's time there had been no roof here; the open city was exposed to all the inclement weather. But gradually the arcades and overhead viaducts, cross balconies and catwalks which spanned the canyon street between the giant buildings became a roof. It spread, now terraced and sloped to top the lofty buildings, like a great rumpled sheet propped by the knees of sleeping giants. Some of the roof was of opaque alumite, dark patches, alternating with the great glassite panes which in places admitted the daylight.

Our little tram sped along southward, wending its way over the terraces. Save for the guards and lookouts in their occasional cubbies, and the air-traffic directors in their towers, we were alone up here. The roof was tangled with air-pipes, line-wire conduits, aerials, arterial systems of the ventilating and lighting devices. As far as one could see the ventilators stood fronting the night breeze like listening ears. There were water tanks, great cross-bulkheads and flumes to handle the rain and snow. A few traffic towers maintained order in the overhead air-lanes. Their beacons shot up into the sky when the passing lights marked the thinly-strewn trinight traffic.

We were stopped at intervals, but in each case were passed promptly.

"Nothing yet, Gregg?"

"No."

Anita's channel remained empty. It was, I suppose, no more than ten minutes during which we sped south along the grotesque maze of the roof; but to us it was an eternity. If only some message would come!

"I'll pull up here."

"Yes."

I gathered up my little audiphone, thrust it under my dark flowing cloak. If only our cloaks were magnetic!

We leaped from our car. "In a rush, Haljan?" asked a guard.

"That's us. Orders from Mr. Brayley."

We left him and plunged into a descending automatic lift. A drop of a thousand feet; we shot downward past all the deserted levels, past the ground-level, the undersurface transportation lanes, the sub-river tubes, the sub-cellar, down to the very bottom of the city.

"Come on, Gregg. Two segments from here."

We advanced at a run. At this hour of night, hardly a pedestrian was in evidence. It was an arched vaulted corridor, almost a tunnel, dimly blue-lit with short lengths of fluorescent tubes at intervals on the ceiling. For all the vaunted mechanisms of our time, the air here was heavy and fetid. Moisture dripped from the concrete roof. It lay on the metal pavement of the ground; the smell of it was dank, tomb-like.

There were frequent cross-tunnels. We turned eastward into one of them. For a segment there were the lower entrances to the cellars of the giant buildings overhead. We passed a place where the tunnel-corridor widened into a great underground plaza. The sewerage and wire-pipes lay like tangled pythons on its floor. Half across it, by the glow of temporary lights strung on a cable, a group of repairmen were working. We passed them, headed in to where the tunnel narrowed again and there were now occasional cubby entrances to underground dwellings.

It was a rabbit warren from here to the river, haunted by criminals and by miserable families, many of whom never saw the daylight for weeks at a time. The giant voices of the city hardly carried down here, so that an oppressive silence hung upon everything.

"That next crossing, Gregg. They said they'd wait for us there."

Occasional escalators led upward. In advance of us was a narrow intersection. There were a few lights in the bullseyes of the subterranean dwelling rooms, but most of them were dark.

"Easy, Snap. Not so fast."

I pulled Snap to a walk. We edged over against the tunnel side. We had passed a small lighted audiphone cubby, evidently the one from which Dud and Shac had paged us. They should have been here waiting; but there was nothing but the empty, gloomy tunnels.

"Something is coming!" Snap clutched at me; we drew our cloaks around us and waited in a shadowed recess. Down a side incline, a segment behind us, a small automatic food truck came lurching. It pulled up at an arcade entrance. Its driver slid the portals, deposited his cases of food, locked the panel after him; and in a moment he and his truck were gone up the incline.

We heard, in the ensuing silence, a low groan near at hand; then abruptly it stopped. We saw, within twenty feet of us, two dark figures lying on the pavement grid in a black patch of shadow where the mailtube came down in a curve and disappeared into the tunnel wall.

We bent over the figures of two men. They lay together, one half upon the other, black-garbed figures with white, staring faces. One twitched a little and then lay still.

They were Shac and Dud Ardley.

"Murdered, Gregg! Good Lord!"

Both were dead, but we could see no marks on either of them.

I found my wits. "Snap, we can't stand like this wholly visible."

I pulled Snap away. We darted a few feet. The light of the tunnel intersection was directly over us. "Not here, Snap! Run!"

Under the curving vacuum tube a little further along, we found shelter. Snap murmured: "The girls went past here. But which way, Gregg?"

As though I knew!

I felt at that moment, under the shirt against my skin, the anode of my audiphone tingling. A receiving signal! In the gloom, I could see Snap's white face as he watched me bring it out.

We heard a tiny microphonic voice, Anita's voice.

"Colonel Halsey. Yes I have the location. Lafayette 4—East corridor, lowest level. A descending entrance. Don't you speak again; I've only a minute! Venza safe—but send help. Something we don't understand—a strange mechanism here."

Then Halsey's interrupting voice. "Anita, escape! You and Venza!"

"We can't. They've got us!"

"I'm sending men. They'll be there in ten minutes."

"Ten minutes will be too late. Molo is…"

It seemed that we heard her scream; then the waves blurred and died.

Lafayette 4—East corridor, lowest level. "Snap, that's here! A descending entrance."

We stood back against the great curving side of the postal vacuum tube. Within it I heard the hiss and clank as a mail cylinder flashed past. Halsey's secret orders must be going out now. His men nearest this place would come in a rush. But Anita said that would be too late.

Snap and I were frantically searching. Somewhere here was an entrance to Molo's lair. It seemed in the silence that Anita's scream was still ringing in my ears. Had it been entirely from the instrument, or were we so close that we heard its distant echoes?

"Gregg, help me." Snap was tugging at a horizontal door-slide, like a trap in the tunnel floor, partly under the vacuum tube. "Stuck!" he gasped.

It yielded with our efforts. It slid aside. Steps led downward into blackness. We plunged in, caution gone from us. The steps went down some twenty feet; we were in another smaller corridor. It was vaguely lighted by a glow from somewhere, and as my pupils expanded, I could see this was a shabby alley, opening ahead into a winding passage with the slide-port above us like its back gate. A warren of cubbies was here, a little sequestered segment of disreputable dwellings.

We stood peering, listening. "Shall I try the eavesdropper, Gregg?"

"Yes. No, wait!" I thought I heard distant sounds.

"Voices, Snap. Listen."

More than voices. A thud: footsteps running. A commotion, back in this warren, within a hundred feet of us.

"This way," I murmured.

We plunged into a black gash. There was a glow of light, a glassite pane in a house wall nearby. The commotion was louder, and under it now we heard a vague humming: something electrical. It was an indescribably weird sound, like nothing I had ever heard before.

Snap clutched at me. "In here, but where is the accursed door?"

There was a glassite pane, but we could find no door. In our hands we held small electronic bolt-cylinders, short-range weapons.

The hum and hissing was louder. It seemed to throb within us, as though vibration were communicating to every fiber of our bodies.

Light was streaming through the glassite pane, and we glimpsed the interior of the room. The light now came from a strange mechanism set in the center of the metal cubby. I caught only an instant's glimpse of it, a round thing of coils and wires. The metal floor of the room was cut away, exposing the gray rock of Manhattan Island. And against the rock, in a ten-foot circle, a series of discs were contacted, with wires leading from them to the central coils.

The whole was glowing with opalescent light. It was dazzling, blinding. Within in it the goggled figure of Molo was moving, adjusting the contacts. He stooped. He straightened, drew back from the light.

Only an instant's glimpse, but we saw the girls, crouching with black bandages on their eyes. Meka, goggled like her brother, was holding them. A tall shape carrying a round black box darted through the light and ran. Molo leaped for the girls; the hum had mounted to a wild electrical scream. Molo flung his sister back out of the light.

They all vanished. There was nothing but the light, and the mounting dynamic scream.

Beside me, Snap was pounding on the glassite panel. I joined him. Everything was dreamlike, blurring as though unconsciousness was upon me.

Where was Snap? Gone? Then I saw him nearby. He had found a door, but it wouldn't yield. I saw his arm go up in a gesture to me.

He ran; I found myself running after him, but I stumbled and fell. Then over me the scream burst into a great roar of sound. It seemed so intense, so gigantic a sound that it must ring around the world.

And the light burst with an exploding puff. The black metal cubby walls seemed to melt like phantoms in a dream. A titan's blowtorch, the opalescent light shot upward, a circular ten-foot beam, eating its way through all the city levels as though they were paper, up through the city roof.

Molo's cubby was gone. His mechanism was eaten by the light and destroyed. There was only this motionless, upstanding beam, contacted here with the Earth, streaming like an opalescent sword into the starry sky.

CHAPTER FIVE

I must paint now upon a broader canvas to depict the utter chaos of this most memorable night in the history of the Earth, Venus and Mars.

From that point in the bowels of Greater New York, near the southern tip of Manhattan Island, the mysterious light-beam shot up. It screamed with its weird electrical voice for an hour, so penetrating a sound that it was heard with the unaided ears as far away as Philadelphia. A titan voice it was, shrill as if with triumph. There were millions of people awakened by it this night; awakened and struck with a chill of fear at this nameless siren shrilling its note of danger. The sound gradually subsided; it seemed to reach its peak within a few minutes of the appearance of the light, and within an hour it had ceased.

But the light beam remained. Those who inspected it closely have given a clear description of its aspect; but to this day its real nature has never been determined.

It was a circular beam of about a ten-foot diameter. In color it was vaguely opalescent, rather more brilliant at night than in the day. With the coming of the sun it did not fade, but remained clearly visible, with a spectrum sheen when the sunlight hit it so that it had somewhat the appearance of a titanic, straightened rainbow.

From that contact point with our Earth, the inexplicable beam stood vertically upward. It ate a vertical hole like a chimney up through all the city levels, through the roof and into the sky. It had a tremendous heat, communicable by contact so that it melted the city above it with a clean round hole. But the heat was non-radiant.

I was found lying within fifty feet of the base of the beam. There had been an explosion, so that Molo's metal room was gone; but from where I lay there was only a warmth to be felt from the light.

Halsey's men found me within half an hour. I was unconscious but not injured. I think now that the sound and not the light overcame me. I presently recovered consciousness; for another hour I was blind and deaf, but that quickly wore off. They rushed me through the chaos of the city to the Tappan Headquarters. Grantline was there, but not Snap. I sent them back when once I was fully conscious. They searched all the vicinity at the base of the light. Snap, alive or dead, was not to be found.

Anita and Venza were gone. I had seen Molo and Meka plunge away with them as the light-beam burst forth. They were gone, and Snap was gone.

There was, by now, a turmoil unprecedented throughout all the metropolitan area. The motionless light-beam itself had done little damage, but its appearance brought instant chaos. Within a radius of five miles of its base, the city was plunged into darkness. All power was cut off. Every vehicle, even the aeros passing overhead, and, the ventilating system stopped. Audiphones were wrecked; it subsided within an hour, though, and after that, lights and instruments brought into the area were not affected.

But during that hour, south Manhattan was in panic. A multitude of terrified people awakened in the night to find blackness and that screaming sound. The streets and corridors and traffic levels were jammed with throngs trampling and killing one another in their efforts to escape.

This was in the stricken area; but everywhere else the panic was spreading. Transportation systems were almost all out of commission. The panic spread until by dawn there was a wild exodus of refugees jamming the bridges and viaducts and tunnels, streaming from all the city exits.

This was Greater New York. But from Venus and Mars came similar reports. In Grebhar and in Ferrok-Shahn, doubtless almost simultaneous with Greater New York, similar light-beams appeared.

"But what can it be?" I demanded of Grantline. "Something Molo contacted there? He did it. That was what he was working for, and he accomplished his purpose. But what will the beam do to us?"

"It's doing plenty," said Grantline grimly.

"He didn't intend that. There was something else."

But what? As yet, no one knew. I had already told the authorities what I had seen. I was the only eye-witness to Molo's activities; and heaven knows I had but a brief, confused glimpse.

The beam remained; it streamed upward from the rock. They thought, this night, that Molo's strange current had set up a disintegration of the atoms, and that electronic particles from them were streaming into space.

The light-beam seemed impervious to attack. Within a few hours the authorities were attacking its base with various vibratory weapons but without success.

From where Grantline and I sat, we saw the dawn coming. But the radiance-beam remained unaffected. "Gregg, look there at Venus!"

To the east of us there was a distant line of metal structures surmounting the mid-Westchester hills; above them, in the brightening sky of dawn, Venus was just rising. Mars had already set at our longitude. Venus, fairly close to the Earth now, was the "Morning Star."; it mounted now above that line of metal stages in the distance.

And as Grantline gestured, I saw from Venus the same sword-like beam streaming off almost to cross our own.

Grantline and I, with a mutual thought, ran around the balcony and gazed to where Mars had set. A narrow radiance was streaming up among the stars off there.

Three swinging swords of light in the sky! With the rotation of the planets, they swept the firmament. The mysterious enemy had planted them—but why? What was coming next?

And as though to answer us, from far to the south, over mid-Jersey, came a new manifestation. We saw a speck rising, a distant mounting speck of something dark, with streamers of tiny radiance flowing from it.

"A spaceship, Gregg."

It seemed so. It came slowly from above the maze of distant structures, gathered speed, and in a moment was gone.

But others, better equipped, had observed it. It was a cylindrical projectile, with stream-fluorescence propelling it upward, an unusual form of spaceship. Telescopically it was seen until well after dawn. Speeding out in the direction of the Moon.

Molo and his weird allies had escaped, I thought. With their work done here on Earth, they were off to rejoin the hovering enemy ship 200,000 miles out.

I stood gripping Grantline on that balcony, and gazed with sinking heart. Were Anita and Venza prisoners on that mounting ship? And Snap: I prayed he was there with the girls to lend them the protection I had failed to give.

"Haljan and Grantline wanted below."

The voice of a mechanic on the balcony behind us roused us from our thoughts. We went down through the busy building.

The workshops of Tappan Interplanetary Headquarters had for hours been ringing with busy activity. The *Cometara* rested upon her departure stage outside, with a score of workmen conditioning her. Newly-installed additional armament was aboard, ready to be assembled after the start. The men to handle it were embarked. My half dozen officers and the ten members of the crew I had already briefly met. They were waiting for me.

"On we go, Gregg. Let's wish ourselves luck." From grim, silent abstraction, Grantline had now sprung into his familiar dynamic self.

There was a solemn group of officers and a hundred or so workmen here; they stopped their fevered labors now to watch the *Cometara* get away, first of Earth's ships speeding into space to confront this nameless enemy. Grantline and I went past them with silent handshakes and murmured good-bys. I saw the towering figure of Brayley. He raised an arm for a farewell gesture to us.

We mounted the incline to the *Cometara*. She rested upon her stage, a great, sleek bronze ship, low and rakish, with pointed ends and a flattened, arched turtle-back dome of glassite covering the superstructure and the decks from bow to stern. She lay quiescent, gleaming in the glow of the departure beacons; but there was an aspect of latent power upon her.

My ship! My first command! As we went through the opened port of the domeside and I touched foot upon the deck, I prayed that I might justify the faith reposed in me.

Men crowded the narrow, covered deck. I saw the space-guns at the deck pressure-ports, partly assembled. My chief officer, a young fellow named Drac Davidson, who with his twin brother had been in the Interplanetary Freight Service, rushed up to me.

"We're ready, sir."

"Very good, Drac."

He hurried me to the turret control room. Grantline instantly had plunged into details of assembling the weapons.

"Her ports are all closed," said Drac. He spoke calmly, but his thin face was pale and his dark eyes glowed with excitement. "The interior pressure is set at fifteen pounds. You can ring us up at once."

No formalities to this departure! With pounding heart I entered the small circular turret and mounted its tiny spiral stairs to the upper control room. But as I touched the levers, calmness came to me with these familiar tasks at which I was skilled.

I slid a central-hull gravity-plate. It went smoothly, perfectly operated by the magnets. The vessel trembled, lifted; outside the enclosing dome I could see the dawn-light of the sky and paling floodlights of the stage. Figures of men out there, made silent gestures of farewell, dropping slowly beneath our hull as we lifted.

The bow gravity-plates slid into the repulsive-force positions. The bow lifted. The *Cometara* responded smoothly. We went up, poised at a forty-five degree angle. I saw the outer beacons on the stage swing upward with their warning to passing traffic in the lower lanes.

"Light our bow-beacon, Drac."

We lifted through the lower thousand and two thousand-foot lanes. The lights of Tappen were dwindling beneath us. The interior of the *Cometara* was humming with the whirr of its circulators and air-receivers, mingled with the throb of air pressure pumps. At three thousand feet I started the air-rocket engines. They came on with a gentle purring. The fluorescence from them streamed along our hull and down past the stern, like twin rocket tails.

With gathering speed we slid smoothly upward through the highest traffic lanes, out of the atmosphere, through the stratosphere and into space.

Leaving the stratosphere, I cut off the air-rocket engines, slid the stern gravity-plates for the Earth's repulsion and the bow plates for the attraction of the Moon and Sun. The firmament swung, in a slow arc, and steadied with the Earth behind us and the Sun and Moon in advance of our bow. We were on our course, plunging through space with accelerating velocity toward the unknown enemy ship hovering two hundred thousand miles ahead of us. My orders were to find the ship and maneuver us close to it; and Grantline's orders were to assail it.

I gazed down at the convex North Atlantic with the reddening coastline of North America spread like a map.

What was the nature of this strange enemy whom we sought? That opalescent beam from Greater New York mounted with its radiance into the dome-like starfield; the one from Venus and the other from Mars seemed crossing overhead amid the stars.

Three swords crossing the sky! What did they mean?

"WILL YOU swing east or west of the Moon?"

"We haven't decided."

Drac Davidson and I were alone in the *Cometara's* control turret.

We were some ten hours out from Earth. Over such short astronomical distances it was impossible to attain any great velocity. When once we were clear of the Earth's atmospheric envelope, the rocket-stream engines were useless. The *Cometara* was equipped also with tail-streamers of electronic nature. They exerted a slight pressure, useful for sudden curving and turning; but they had only negligible influence upon the main velocity of the vehicle.

I used the repulsion of the Earth upon our negatively charged stern gravity-plates; and with those of the bow electronified to the positive reaction, we were drawn forward by the Sun and the Moon.

For three or four hours I held to this combination with steady acceleration; but then I had to retard. In close quarters such as this, the retarding velocity must be calculated with a nicety many hours in advance.

We hung now, very nearly poised, within some forty thousand miles of the surface of the Moon. Bleak and cold, sharply black and white, it hung in a gigantic crescent in advance of our bow. The Sun, whose attraction I had ceased using some hours back, was visible sharply to one side now. Its great gas streams of giant flame licked up into the blackness of the firmament. The sunlight caught the lunar mountains with a white glare, and left the valleys black with shadow; moonlight and the mingled sunlight painted our bow. Behind our stem the great disk of Earth hung somber and glowing.

And everywhere else was the great black enclosing firmament. The stars blazed with a new white glory never seen through the haze of an atmosphere. Like a little world in the vastness of this awesome void, we hung poised.

Grantline came into the turret. "I've got everything ready, Gregg. By the gods, once you can lay telescope upon that accursed enemy ship, I'm ready to open fire on it."

"Good," I said.

But the thought of hurling our bolts at this enemy ship had struck terror into my heart for hours past. I was convinced that the three who in all the world were dearest to me—Anita, Venza, and Snap—were upon that enemy vessel.

Grantline asked, "Are you going closer to the Moon?"

"No."

"The ship couldn't be between us and the Moon. Waters and I have been in the helio room for the past hour, searching with the 'scope there. Nothing doing, Gregg. Not a sign."

"I know. Our instruments here show that."

"There might be a way of sighting them," Drac put in.

"I'll try the Zed-ray," I suggested. "Drac and I have it corrected. But I doubt if it would penetrate the sort of invisibility this enemy would use."

Grantline nodded. "Or the Benson curve-light. You think the ship went behind the Moon? Or landed on the Moon?"

"It could have done either. Has Waters still got contact with the Earth? Have they seen it?"

"No."

I made a sudden decision. It would take us two hours at least to make a careful scanning with the Zed-ray; and to take an elaborate series of spectro-heliographs of the Moon's surface, which might show the enemy vessel if it had landed there, was a laborious process.

After brief thought, I discarded the idea. "We'll go to the helio room," I told Grantline. "I'm going to try the Benson curve-light."

Grantline and I left the turret, heading along the catwalk under the glassite dome toward the helio cubby where the rotund, middle-aged Waters was in charge. It made my heart sink to think of the helio room. Snap should have been there.

We crossed the transverse catwalk. The superstructure roof was under us. Farther down, the narrow decks showed with Grantline's men grouped at the firing ports, where his weapons were mounted and ready. As I saw those grouped men loitering on the deck, waiting for me to give them a sighting, I prayed I could do so; and yet there was the shuddering fear that the first blast would bring death to Anita.

Waters met us at the door of his cubby. His face was red; he mopped the perspiration from his bald head. "I'm so glad you came! Will you want the Benson-light? I say, I've lost connection with the Earth. I had the Washington transmitter. Five minutes ago they sent me a flash of the Mars and Venus news. They both sent ships, out."

He gasped for breath, then added in a rush: "Both the Mars and Venus ships were destroyed and the enemy escaped!"

Grantline and I gasped with horror.

"Destroyed?" I said. "How?"

Waters did not know. The news came; then, immediately after, the Washington transmitter changed its wavelength and he lost connection.

"But why, in heaven's name, man, didn't you ring and tell us?" Grantline demanded. "Destroyed—only that! Just destroyed."

"I was afraid to leave my instruments," Waters said. "How could I tell? I might be able to renew connections with Washington any minute. Come on in. Do you want to try the Benson curve-light, Mr. Haljan?"

"Yes," I said. "I do." We entered the dim helio cubby. "See here, Waters, what about the projectile that ascended from Earth last night? Did the Washington observatory report what happened to it?"

"No, not a word. They lost it, evidently."

Our 'scopes on the *Cometara* had not been able to locate the projectile. The large instruments of Earth had lost it. Was that because, with tremendous velocity, it had sped directly for the new planet out beyond Mars?

Or, with some form of invisibility, might it be close to us now, just as the lurking ship might be somewhere around here?

From the little circular helio cubby, perched here under the dome like an eagle's nest, I could see down all the length of the ship, and out the side ports of the dome to the blazing firmament. The Sun, Moon and Earth and all the starfield were silently turning as Drac swung us upon our new course.

Waters bent over the projector of the Benson curve-light, making connections. The cubby was silent and dim, with only a tiny spotlight where Waters was working, and a glow upon his table where his recent messages from Earth were filed. Grantline and I glanced at them.

Panic in Greater New York, Grebhar, and Ferrok-Shahn. The three strange beams which the enemy had planted on Earth, Venus and Mars still remained unchanged. I could see them now plainly from the helio cubby windows, great shafts of radiance sweeping the firmament.

Waters straightened from his task. "That will do it, Mr. Haljan." He met me in the center of the cubby. "When you locate the enemy, do you think they'll destroy us as they did those other ships?"

Grantline laughed grimly. "Maybe so, Waters. But let's hope not."

Fat little Waters was anything but a coward, but being closed up here all these hours with a stream of dire messages from Earth had shaken him.

"What I mean, Mr. Grantline, is that prudence is sometimes better than reckless valor. The *Cometara* is no warship. If Earth had sent an international patrol vessel…"

Grantline did not answer. He joined me at the Benson projector. "Can we operate it from here, Gregg, or will you mount it in the bow?"

"From here. Drac's swinging. When he's on the course I gave him, I can throw the Benson-ray through the bow dome-port. Waters, you're all done in. Go below and sleep awhile."

But he stood his ground. "No, sir; I don't want to sleep."

"We've had ours," said Grantline. "We'll call you if anything shows up."

We sent Waters away. "Ready, Gregg?"

"Yes. I've got the range."

The coils hummed and heated with the current, and in a moment the Benson curve-beam leaped from the projector.

The Benson curve-light was similar to an ordinary white searchlight beam, except that its path, instead of being straight could be bent at will into various curves—hyperbola, parabola, and for its extreme curve, the segment of an ellipse—gradually straightening as it left its source. It was effective for police work, with hand torches for seeing around opaque obstructions. It had also another advantage, especially when used at long range: the enemy, when gazing back at its source, would under normal circumstances conceive it to be a straight beam and thus be misled as to the location of its source. Or even realizing it to be curved, one had no means of judging the angle of the curve.

A narrow white stream of light, it flung through our window-oval, forward under the dome and through the bow dome bullseye, into space. I saw the men on the deck spring into sudden alertness with the realization we were using it. The bow lookout on the forward observation bridge crouched at his 'scope-finder to help us search.

From the control turret came an audiophone buzz, and Drac's voice: "Am I headed right? The swing is almost completed."

"Finish the job and don't bother me now."

I bent over the field-mirror of the projector. On its glowing ten-inch grid the shifting image of my range was visible, a curving, brilliant limb of the Moon, with the sunlight on the jagged mountain peaks; everywhere else was the black firmament and the blazing dots of stars.

Grantline crouched beside me. "I'll work the amplifiers. Going to spread it much, Gregg?"

"Yes. A full spread first. We're in no mood for a detailed narrow search."

I gradually widened the light. Three feet here at its source, it spread in a great widening arc. With the naked eye we could see its white radiance, fan-shaped as an edge of it fell upon the Moon.

And though optically it was not apparent, the elliptical curve of it was rounding the Moon, disclosing the hidden starfield to our instruments.

"Nothing yet?" I murmured.

"No."

"I'll try a narrower spread and less curve."

Grantline was searching the magnified images on the series of amplifier grids. There was nothing. For an hour we worked; then suddenly Grantline cried: "Gregg! Wait! Hold it!"

I tensed, stricken. I held the angle and the spread of light steady.

"Two seconds of arc, east; try that. The damned thing is shifting." He gripped me. "It's at the eastern edge of the field; it shifts off. It must be in rapid motion."

Then I saw it, a mere moving dot of black; but suddenly it clarified. I saw a dot which I could imagine was a shape with discs along its edge, moving with high velocity. Grantline was shifting our field to hold it.

"Got it, Gregg. By God, that's it! Now we'll see."

Then presently we saw that from its bow a very faint radiant beam was streaming. Beside me I heard Grantline gasp, "Gregg, am I crazy or is that bow beacon like the light-beam planted in Greater New York?"

There did seem to be a similarity, but thought of it abruptly was swept from my mind. Our cubby was alive with signals. Both the bow and the stern observers saw the enemy ship now with their 'scopes gazing directly along our Benson-light. And Drac was calling, "I've got the measurement of its velocity. Doubling every ten seconds. God, what acceleration!"

I flung off the Benson-light. The enemy ship had come from behind the limb of the Moon; our straight-light telescopes showed it clearly. It was heading unmistakably in our direction.

Drac was pleading, "We need velocity! Are you coming to the turret?"

"Yes."

Grantline and I rushed out upon the catwalk. Waters was mounting the spiral ladder from the deck. "Into your cubby," I shouted. "Call Earth. Keep calling until you get them."

Grantline rushed for the deck. I gained the control turret, Drac, with his thin face white and set, met me at the door. "We need velocity."

I nodded. "We'll get it, Drac; have no fear of that."

I set the gravity-plates for the greatest possible acceleration forward and added the stern rocket engines for narrow-angle maneuvering.

With gathering speed we plunged directly for the oncoming enemy ship.

CHAPTER SIX

"But there's something wrong, Drac."

"We've got grade five acceleration."

Grantline had joined us in the control turret. "How far would you say, at a rough guess, that ship is from us now?"

"Thirty thousand miles; about that." Drac scanned his page of calculations. "Impossible to gauge with any exactness; they change their pace so often and I can't figure out how large the damn thing is."

"Say they've got a forty thousand velocity; added to our ten, that's fifty."

"And we're accelerating. In half an hour we'll be within range."

"But there's something wrong," I persisted.

For several minutes now I had been aware that the *Cometara* was acting strangely. A sluggish response to the controls, I thought, but when I called engine chief Franklin, he had not noticed it. Yet I was certain.

Grantline stared at me. "Something wrong?"

"Yes. Drac, try orienting us. I did it ten minutes ago." I shoved him at my equations, giving the angles with the Sun, Earth and Moon which we should now have. "There's our flight course as it ought to be. Measure how we're heading, actual position. If it's what it ought to be, with the plate-combinations I'm using, then I'm crazy."

"Oh, you're just naturally apprehensive," Grantline said.

But we were not where we should be. The *Cometara* was off her predetermined course. And then I realized the factor of error.

There was a gravitational force here for which I was not allowing. The error was not within the *Cometara*; she was responding perfectly. But there was a force upon her, and not that of the Sun, Earth, Moon or the distant starfield. I had calculated all of these. It was something else. Some gravitational pull, so that we were not upon the course of flight we should have been on.

"But what could be wrong?" Grantline demanded.

It was Drac who guessed it. "That radiance from the enemy's bow?"

It was that, we felt certain. Even at this thirty thousand mile distance, the bow-beacon seemed streaming upon us. We could not see that it illumined the *Cometara*, nor could our instruments measure any added illumination. Our flight-orbit, if held, would carry us with a swing some ten thousand miles above the South Pole of the Moon. It would cross diagonally in front of the trajectory that the enemy vessel was maintaining. But we were off our predetermined course, with a side-drift toward the enemy. That bow-beacon radiance was exerting a force upon us, a strange gravitational pull.

Grantline gasped when Drac said it. "If it's that now, what will it be when we get closer?"

The minutes were passing. The thirty thousand miles between us and the enemy was cut to ten thousand; to five. The ship was soon visible to the naked eye. Its visual movement, for all this time measurable only as a drift upon the amplified images of our instruments, now was obvious. We could see it plunging forward, could see that probably we would cross its bow. Within fifty miles? We hoped and guessed that would be the result, so that with this first passing we could use our weapons. Fifty miles of distance at combined speeds of some fifty thousand miles an hour: that would be something like three seconds from a collision. The danger of a collision, which both ships would do anything to avert, was negligible; in the immensity of space two objects so small could not strike each other, even with intention, once in a million times.

We could not calculate the passing so closely, but suddenly it seemed that perhaps the enemy could. The bow-beacon radiance, so obviously a miniature of the weird light-beams streaming from Earth, Mars and Venus, now swung away from us and was extinguished. Whatever alteration of our course the enemy had made, they seemed to be satisfied. The passing would be to their liking. Would it be to ours?

Grantline had left the turret. He was down on the deck, ready with his men. The weapons were ready.

We had long since advanced beyond the possibility of mathematical calculations keeping pace with our changing position in relation to the enemy, but it seemed that the passing would be within fifty miles. Grantline's weapons would carry their bolt that far.

It was barely two thousand miles away now. Two minutes of time before the passing. I stared at it, a long, low ship of dark metal, red where the moonlight struck upon it. I estimated its size to be about that of the *Cometara*, but it was much more nearly globular. Upon its top, seeming to project from the terraced dome, was an up-pointing funnel, like the smokestack of an old-fashioned surface steam vessel; or like a great black muzzle of an old-fashioned gun. And in a row along the bulging middle of the hull there was a series of little discs.

The vessel was still a tiny blob, but every instant it was enlarging, doubling its visual size. Drac said tensely, "Fifteen hundred miles! We'll pass in a minute and a half."

I turned the angle of the stern rocket-streams. The firmament slowly began swinging; the enemy ship seemed swaying up over us. I was turning our top to it, so that Grantline might fire directly upward from both sides almost simultaneously. It might be possible, if I could roll us over at just the proper seconds.

But the enemy anticipated us. As they observed our roll, again the bow-beacon flashed on. It visibly struck us, bathed all our length in its spreading opalescent radiance.

It seemed for an instant to do nothing. Our dome did not crack; there was no shock. But our side-roll slowed. The heavens stopped their swing, and then swung back! We were upon an even keel again, the enemy level with our bow. Against the force of my turning rocket-streams this radiation had righted us. It clung a few seconds more, and again vanished.

Grantline's deck audiophone rang with his startled voice: "Gregg, roll us over! Quick! I can only fire from one side."

"I can't."

It was too late now. A few hundred miles of distance! Drac stood clutching me, staring through the port. And I stared, breathless, awaiting the results of these next few seconds.

The ships passed like crossing, speeding meteors. A few seconds of final approach; I saw the enemy vessel as an elongated, flattened globe, with a triple-terraced dome and terraced decks beneath it. That queer stack on top! The round discs, like ten-foot eyes, gleamed along the equator of the bulging hull.

One of Grantline's weapons fired a silent flash. Still out of range. The spit of our electrons leaped from our side. The enemy was untouched.

The thought stabbed at me: *Anita! Not killed by that one.*

Another shot from Grantline.

No result. It seemed that I saw the bolt strike. There was a reddening, a flash upon that bulging hull, but nothing more.

I was aware again of the enemy bow-beam swinging upon us. The beam was pressing us over again so that in a moment we would be hull-bottom to the enemy and Grantline could not fire.

He anticipated it. The ship was broadside to us. In the split second of that passing I saw that it was not fifty miles away, hardly ten. Grantline flung his remaining bolts. The enemy was a streaked blur going by; and all in that second it was past, reddening in the distance. Untouched by our bolts? It seemed so. The bow radiance darted ahead of it. The globular shape, unharmed, dwindled in the distance behind us.

And it had done nothing to us!

The control levers were in my hands. I would shift the gravity-plates, and make the quickest turn we could. We would go around the Moon, probably, and come back within an hour or two. Perhaps our adversary would also turn to encounter us again.

At that second I had not seen the little discs, but I saw them now! They came sailing in a line, ten foot, flat, circular discs of a dark metal; they gleamed reddish where the sunlight painted them. They had been fastened outside the enemy vessel and in our passing they had been discharged. They sailed now like whirling plates. There seemed perhaps twenty of them, heading in a curve toward us.

Grantline's voice came again from the deck audiophone. "Missed them, Gregg. That's what I thought but at least two of our bolts must have struck. But it didn't hurt them."

"No," I replied. "It seemed not. They must have a defensive barrage."

Drac was pulling at me. "Those things out there, those discs..."

Grantline demanded, "Yes, what in hell are they?"

We could not tell. It seemed that their curve would take them behind our stern. Grantline added: "Will you try going back after that ship?"

"Yes."

But I did not. To the naked eye the enemy ship had already disappeared; but with the 'scopes we saw that it seemed to be turning.

I did not attempt to turn us, for we were afraid of those oncoming discs which took all our attention. They passed within five miles astern of us, but in a great curve they swung and now seemed heading across our bow. With what tremendous velocity they had been endowed by their firing mechanisms! Their elliptical curve swung them a mile or so ahead of us.

They were circling us like tiny satellites in a narrowing spiral ellipse. Our attraction, the normal gravity of our close bulk, was drawing them to us.

The men on the *Cometara's* deck stood gazing, surprised but not yet alarmed. The lookout calls sounded with routine notification each time the discs passed across our bow and stern. In the helio cubby, Waters was still trying to raise an Earth station.

Grantline came running to the control turret. "If those cursed things, should strike us, Gregg!"

I had set the gravity-plates into new combinations, turning our course downward, trying to swing us under the plane of the discs' orbit. But they swung downward with us; they were no more than two thousand feet away now.

Grantline said, "At the next broadside passing I'll fire at them."

Drac looked up from his calculating instruments. "Look! A circular rotation: Horribly swift. But I've caught a picture. Look!"

He had a still image of one of the discs. It had saw-teeth at its thin knife-like outer circumference. Whirling at tremendous speed, these saw-toothed metal discs might cut into our dome, or some other part of our ship.

At the next round, Grantline fired. The discs reddened a little, but came on unharmed. From the other side, he fired again. Three of the discs seemed to have been caught full. His bolts, sustained for their fullest ten seconds of duration at this close, thousand-foot range, took effect. The three discs seemed to crumble with a puff of queerly-radiant vacuum spark-glows, then were gone.

But the others came closing in.

The *Cometara* rang now with the excitement and alarm of the men. Grantline could not set his gauges fast enough to fire at every round.

I had a sudden thought. With the rear rockets, I rolled us over. For a moment we were hull-down to the passing discs. From our hull gravity-plates I flung a full repulsion. Would it stave them off, bend their orbit outward? It did not. Their course was unaltered.

Again Grantline was shouting at me, "Roll us back! I must fire!"

It had been an error, that rolling; Grantline lost several shots because of it. I swung us level. The discs passed within a hundred feet; half a dozen of them were still closer. Gleaming, whirling circles, thin as knife-blades; they passed close under our stern, came broadside.

These were tense, horrible seconds. The discs skimmed our bow; one seemed to miss our dome by inches. Grantline's volley annihilated four more, but there were still eight of them. They swung in at our stern.

I was aware of confusion throughout the *Cometara*. The crew and stewards were running up to the bow quarter-deck. My second officer stood there, stricken. The stern lookout screamed his futile warning.

Useless! I saw one of the discs strike our stern dome, then another. Still others. They were silent blows, but it seemed that I could feel them cutting into the dome-plates.

The dome was cracking! Then, after that horrible instant, came the sound: crunch, a rumble; the grind of crushed and breaking metal; then the puff and surge of the outward explosion.

I saw the whole tip of the stern dome cracking, bursting outward, forced by our interior air pressure. And over all the *Cometara* the outgoing air was sucking and whining with a growing rush of wind.

I shouted, "Drac! Close the stern bulkhead!"

I set the word-buttons for the distress siren, and pulled the lever. Its voice screamed over the uproar. *"Keep forward! Take the space-suits! Prepare to abandon ship!"*

CHAPTER SEVEN

In the midst of the chaos I was aware that all the remaining discs struck us upon the port stern quarter. The broken dome of the stern showed a jagged hole, but the up-sliding cross-bulkhead partially shut it off. Two or three of the crew and the stern lookout were gone behind that closing bulkhead. Their bodies in a moment would be blown into space.

"It may hold, Drac. Order Waters out of his cubby. Forward!"

I was calling the engine-room. "Order your men up by the bow, not the stern." But I got no answer from the engine-chief.

I raised Grantline. "Order your men forward: Clear amidships! I want to close the central bulkheads. If the stern one breaks with the pressure..."

"Right, Gregg. Are we lost?"

"God knows! We'll know in a minute or two. Get all your men into their space-suits. Keep in the bow. Prepare the exit-port there."

"Right, Gregg. You coming down?"

"Yes. When I finish." I cut him off. "Drac, get out of here! Did you order Waters forward?"

"He won't leave."

"Why the hell not?"

"He thinks he may be able to get communication with Earth."

"He can't stay where he is; there's no protection up here! When that stern bulkhead goes..."

It was breaking. I could see it bending sternward under the pressure. And at best it was leaking air, so that the decks were a rush of wind. Already Drac and I were gasping with the lowered pressure.

"Drac, get out of here. Go get Waters; bring him forward. The hell with his transmitter: this is life or death!"

"But you?"

"I'm coming down. From the forward deck, call the hull control rooms. Order everybody forward and to the deck."

"What about the pressure pumps?"

"I can keep them going from here."

I set the circulating system to guide the fresh air forward, but it was futile against the sucking rush of wind toward the stern. As the pumps speeded up I saw, with the little added pressure, the great cross panel of the stern bulkhead straining harder. It would go in a moment.

Drac was clinging to me. "Tell me what to do!"

"I've told you what to do!" I shoved him to the catwalk. "Get out of here. Get Waters forward. Get the men out of the hull."

His anguished eyes stared at me; then he turned and ran forward on the catwalk. I saw him forcibly dragging the bald-headed Waters from the helio cubby. It was the last time I ever saw either of them.

A buzzer was ringing in the turret, and I plunged back for it. The exertion put a band of pain across my chest, a panting constriction from the lowering pressure.

Fanning, assistant engineer, was still at the pressure pumps. His voice came up: "Pumps and renewers working. Will you use the gravity shifters?"

"Hell, no! Get out of there, Fanning. We're smashed. Air going. It's a matter of minutes—abandoning ship. Get forward!"

Suddenly the stern bulkhead cracked with a great diagonal rift. I waited a moment to give them all time to get forward; then I slid all the cross 'midship bulkheads.

It was barely in time. The stern bulkhead went out with a gale of wind, but the barrier amidships stemmed it. Half of the vessel sternward was devoid of air, but here in the bow we could last a little longer. Beneath me I could see Grantline's men—some of them, not all—and a few of the stewards, crew and officers, crowding the deck, donning space-suits. The two side chambers were ready; half a dozen men crowded into each of them. The deck doors slid closed. The outer ports opened; helmeted, goggled, bloated figures were blown by the outgoing air from the chamber into space. Then the outer slides went closed. The pumps filled up the chambers; the deck doors opened again. Another batch of men...

I saw Grantline, suited but with his helmet off, dashing from one side of the deck to the other, commanding the abandonment.

The central bulkheads seemed momentarily holding. Then little red lights in the panel board before me showed where in the hull corridors the doors were leaking, cracking, giving away, breaking under the strain. The whole ribbed framework of the vessel was strained and slued. The bulkhead sides no longer set true in the casements. Air was whining everywhere and pulling sternward.

It was the last stand; I was aware that the alarm siren had ceased. There was a sudden stillness, with only the shouts of the remaining men at the exit-ports mingling with the whine of the wind and the roaring in my head. I felt detached, far-away; my senses were reeling.

I staggered to the gauges of the Erentz system, the system whereby an oscillating current, circling within the double-shelled walls of hull and dome, absorbed into negative energy much of the interior pressure. The main walls of the vessel were straining outward. The *Cometara* could collapse at any moment. I started for the catwalk door. The electro-telescope stood near it and I yielded to a vague desire to gaze into the eyepiece. The instrument was still operative. I swept it sternward.

The enemy ship had not vanished. By what strange means, I cannot say, its velocity had been checked. A few thousand miles from us, it was making a narrow, close-angle turn. Coming back? I thought so.

I suddenly realized my intention of having all the gravity-plates in neutral before abandoning the ship. I seized the controls now. An agony of fear was upon me that the shifting valves would fail. But they did not. The plates slid haltingly, reluctantly.

I recall staggering to the catwalk. It seemed that the central bulkhead was breaking. There were fallen figures on the deck beneath me. I stumbled against the body of a man who had tangled himself in the stays of the ladder rail and was hanging there.

I think I fell the last ten feet to the deck. The roaring in my ears, the bands tightening about my chest encompassed all the world.

Then I was on my feet again, and I stumbled over another body. It was garbed in a space-suit, with the helmet beside it. I stripped it of the suit. I was panting, with all the world whirling in a daze, bursting spots of light before my eyes.

Ten feet away down the deck was the opened door of the pressure chamber. A bloated figure came into my dreamlike vista, moving for the pressure door. It turned, saw me, came leaping and bent over me. I saw behind the vizor that it was Grantline. His bloated, gloved hands helped me don my suit.

He helped me with my helmet. The metal tip on Grantline's gloved hand touched the contact-plate on my shoulder. His voice sounded from the tiny audiphone grid within my helmet. "Gregg! Thank God I found you! All right?"

"Yes." My head was clearing.

"I've got the chamber ready. We're the last, Gregg."

I gripped his shoulder. "You're sure there's nobody else?"

"No. I've been everywhere I could reach. The central bulkheads are almost gone."

He pushed me into the pressure chamber. There was hardly need to close the door after us. I stood gripping him as he opened the small outer slides. The abyss was at our feet; the outgoing wind tore at us like a gale, so that we stood gripping the casements.

"Thank God you've got a power-suit, Gregg. So have I. We must keep together."

"Yes."

I could feel the floor grid of the chamber shuddering beneath my feet. The *Cometara* was cracking, bursting outward throughout her length; at any instant she might collapse.

For a moment we stood poised. Beneath us, here at the brink were millions upon millions of miles of emptiness, the remote, unfathomable void. Blazing worlds down there in the black darkness.

"Good-by, Gregg. It may be the end for us."

"Good luck, Johnny."

His bloated figure dropped away from me. I waited just an instant, and then I dove into space.

For a moment there was a chaos of strangeness, the wrench to my sense of the transition. I had been the inhabitant of a little world, the *Cometara*, with a gravity beneath my feet. Now, in a breath, I had no world to inhabit. I was alone in space. No gravity; nothing solid to touch; emptiness.

I was in a world to myself, and the abnormality of it brought a mental shock. But in a moment the adjustment came. I passed the transition, the sense of falling.

The firmament steadied and my senses cleared. My dive from the *Cometara* carried me in a slow arc some three hundred feet away. There had been a sense of falling, but no actual fall. My velocity was retarded, with the mass of the *Cometara* pulling at me. I went like a toy boat in water shoved by a child, quickly slowing. In a few moments, the velocity was gone, and I hung poised. I saw Grantline's bloated form not over fifty feet from me. He waved an arm at me.

Out here in the void I lay weightless, as though upon an infinitely soft feather bed. I could kick, flounder, but not endow myself with motion. I craned my neck, gazed around through the bulging vizor pane.

The Earth and the Sun hung level with the white star-dots strewn everywhere. I could not see that unknown light-beam from Greater New York; it was shafting out now in the other direction, so that the Earth hid it from me. Venus was visible to one side of the Sun. The enemy light-stream from Grebhar was apparent; and as I turned my body and bent double to look behind me, I saw Mars and the sword-like ray from Ferrok-Shahn. The beams streamed off like the radiance of the Milky Way, faintly luminous but seemingly visible for an infinite distance.

The *Cometara* was obviously falling now toward the Moon, drawn irresistibly, and all of us with her, toward the lunar surface. It seemed so close, that black and white mountainous disc. We were, I suppose, some twenty thousand miles from it, gathering speed as it pulled at us. But that motion was not apparent now. Distance dwindled all these celestial motions, so that all the firmament seemed frozen into immobility.

But there was some motion. Twenty or more bloated figures, the survivors from the wreck of the *Cometara*, were encircling it in varying orbits, revolving around it like tiny satellites. Some were closing in, drawn against it. I saw one plunge against the wrecked dome, and begin crawling like a fly. And I found that the forces of the firmament were molding my orbit also. My outward plunge was checked. I poised for an indeterminate instant, and then I took my orbit. I too, was a satellite of the *Cometara*.

I gazed at the wreck of the *Cometara*. My ship! My first command! So smoothly, confidently rising from the Earth only a few hours ago; and she had come to this. She lay askew in the heavens. The dome was cracked throughout all its length and smashed like a shell at the sterntip.

I could see the interior litter beneath the dome, the twisted and strained lines of the hull. A dead ship now, the mechanisms stilled; dead and silent inside, with all the warmth gone out of it. All the air dissipated, so that in every cubby, every dark corridor of that broken hull there was the coldness and silence of interplanetary space.

I suppose these thoughts swept me within a few seconds. I saw myself starting to revolve in my orbit. Perhaps my motion would carry me around indefinitely; or I might be drawn down to the vessel as those other survivors had been drawn.

Grantline, with one of the few power suits, was coming toward me now, with tiny fluorescent streams back along his body from his shoulder blades. I switched on my own mechanism. It moved me toward him, and our gravity attracted us. We shut off the power when twenty feet apart; drifted together; contacted; bounced apart like rubber balls as our inflated suits struck. Then in a moment we had drifted back and clung.

I touched the metal plate of his shoulder. "Working all right?"

"Yes. Thank God for this much, Gregg. I wonder how many are alive."

In the chaos of the abandonment, many of the men's air mechanisms had failed to operate. It is always so in times of disaster. We could see, revolving around the wreck, and motionless against its dome, those horrible flabby, deflated suits where the delicate Erentz mechanism had failed. Within was only a corpse.

"Too many," I said. "And not more than four or five of us with power. What shall we do first? Round them up? We must all get together."

His answering voice was grim. "We can tow them from the wreck. Six or seven of us altogether have power. Do you suppose we can get away, Gregg? Get loose from the ship before she falls?"

Only trying it could tell us that. The *Cometara*, and all of us with her, were plunging for the Moon. We would seek out the men who were alive and tow them in a string. If we could break the gravity pull of the ship, and then struggle upward from the Moon, we could maintain ourselves here in space until some rescue ship from Earth, Venus or Mars would come and pick us up.

"You take one side, Gregg; I'll take the other. Don't go aboard; she might collapse."

"I'll pick up the men without power and alive. The others with power suits will do the same. Then we'll meet out here, about where we are now?"

"Yes. And hurry, Gregg! Every mile toward the Moon makes it that much harder. We're falling fast."

"Good luck!" I shoved away from him. And within a minute, as he went in an arc toward the *Cometara* bow and I toward her stern, I suddenly thought of that returning enemy vessel. My last look through the 'scope had shown that she was returning; and then I had forgotten it.

My gaze swept the firmament now. I had no 'scope instruments within the helmet. With the naked eye the enemy ship was not in sight. But I knew that meant little; within a moment she could come in view and be here if she were going at any great velocity.

There were on the *Cometara*, at the time of the disaster, some sixty-odd men; perhaps forty had gotten away. And I could see very soon that not more than fifteen, or less, out here were alive.

Two with power were ahead of me now, slowly floating past the wrecked dome of the stern. One had picked up two others, found them alive and was towing them out. They went past me, moving very slowly so that I could see that two were all that one of us could tow and attain any velocity at all.

I contacted with the leader. He was one of Grantline's men.

"Two or three hundred feet out," I directed. I gestured. "Grantline said to meet out there. I'll tow others."

"Yes. Around the stern you'll find—God! Haljan, look!"

A mile from us the enemy ship was in view. Passing—no! Stopping! With incredible retardation she had plunged into view, was here, and yet had no great forward velocity. She seemed no more rapid than a great air liner winging past, so close that her reddish-tinged bulging hull length showed clearly. The discs were gone. The funnel set on top of her was sloped diagonally toward us as she rolled on her side, so that momentarily I could see down into it. There was some mechanism down there. The bow radiance was a narrow opalescent beam in advance of the bow.

"Slowing, Haljan!"

"Yes, stopping. Don't try to meet Grantline. Tow your men away!"

"Or should we board the *Cometara* and hide?"

"No. They've come back to bombard her."

I kicked at him violently. With his two drifting figures clinging behind, he swung past me. I headed behind the stern. Upon its dangling framework several of our men were glued, lying there inert. I caught a glimpse of the interior of the stern, the littered deck; men lying there had been stricken before they had time to get into their suits.

On the outside, forward, I saw Grantline come rounding the bow, towing a figure and heading for another. On the outside of the bow-peak a group of others were perched, gesticulating for help. I started that way; then I saw another, and nearer figure in a power suit heading for them. I swung back. There were two figures on the outside of the under-hull whom I could more quickly reach. Inverted flies. Their feet were on the keel. They stooped and waved toward me.

I took a swoop. Passing close down the hull, my rocket-streams struck the hull plates and gave me sudden downward velocity. I shot down, out past the keel. And again I saw the enemy ship. She hung poised, no more than two miles away. And as I looped over, with all the black, star-strewn firmament in a dizzy whirl, the great Moon-disc, first above, and then below me, I saw the bow-beam of the enemy swinging. It came to the *Cometara*, and there it clung.

I had gone perhaps fifty feet below the keel with my dive when I righted. I was mounting. I saw the opalescent ten-foot circle of the beam moving along the *Cometara* hull. It seemed to do no damage; then suddenly it darted down and clung to me.

I felt nothing save the impact of a gentle push, something shoving with a ponderable force against me.

I saw the *Cometara* receding, the heavens swinging as I turned over. The red disc of the distant Earth swooped. The Moon surface momentarily seemed rotating and lifting above me.

I was helpless, rolling, then whirling end-over-end. Then again I steadied. The beam was gone from me.

I saw the *Cometara*, a full mile away from me! The enemy ship was again in motion, moving toward me, and between the *Cometara* and the Earth. And the beam was steady upon the *Cometara's* mid-section.

The *Cometara* had a new velocity now. I could not miss it. She was dwindling rapidly in visual size; relative to me, she was receding, falling upon the Moon. More than that she was being pushed downward by the repulsive force of the strange enemy beam upon her. I stared, as with all the little dots which were our men around and upon her, she went down into the void.

I found myself presently alone up here, with the enemy ship hovering nearby. Its maneuvering to thrust the wrecked *Cometara* toward the Moon had brought it within a mile of me. The bow-beam was still on the *Cometara*; and then abruptly it vanished.

The *Cometara* had almost dwindled beyond the sight of my unaided vision. By chance, undoubtedly, the beam had fallen upon me and thrust me from the wreck. I was alone up here now with the enemy, but they may not have noticed me, or cared. I found my power mechanism intact. I turned it on; slowly, like a log in water, I began moving away.

A minute. Five minutes. The *Cometara* was lost. Grantline, all the men, were lost; with that added downward thrust they could never free themselves from the falling wreck.

I was jerked out of my thoughts by the sight of an oncoming red blob. Something was coming from the enemy ship, red with the sunlight and earthlight, silvered by the Moon and the stars. It took form. It was a disc, another of those cursed whirling discs, sent to annihilate me!

Then, when it was a quarter of a mile away, I saw that it was a disc which was turning slowly. Rocket radiances came from its rotating circumference; it came sailing directly at me, so swiftly that my own velocity was futile.

Another minute and I was caught. I saw that the disc was some fifteen feet in diameter, and that it bulged, so that within its convex floor and ceiling was a space of several feet.

I cut off my power and with pounding heart lay waiting. The space-suit had no weapons for equipment save a knife hung in the belt. I drew it out, held it in my gloved fingers.

The disc sailed upon its level, vertical axis. Its rotation slowed; I saw little windows set around its convex middle. It came up and bumped me with its metal side. I kicked away, shoved off. Shapes were moving in a dim interior light behind the port-panes. Little hand-beams of radiance darted out. They seemed to seize me, draw me.

I found myself glued helplessly to the convex outer surface of the disc. The rotation gathered speed again, but I looked presently only at the gleaming surface to which I was pinned. Had I been a metal bar upon the horns of an electro-magnet, I could not have been more helpless.

An interval passed. With the contact plate of my fingers against this hull it seemed that I could hear voices within, strange, indistinguishable words. I twisted, but could not see into the port.

Again the rotation was slowing. The near shape of the enemy vessel swung close and past; and again and again I saw that we were over it, dropping down into the wide black opening of the funnel-top. It yawned presently like a great black tunnel, into which we fell.

The jar of landing knocked me loose, and no doubt the attraction radiance also released me. I fell another space, bounced up and sank back. I thought that something like a sliding port-door closed over me.

And then, in the dimness, figures were gripping me. I lashed and struck, but the knife was wrenched away.

I was a prisoner in a pressure-port of the enemy ship!

CHAPTER EIGHT

It seemed that the small room had a very faint radiance showing through my vizor pane. Narrow enclosing walls were visible. It was a triangular-shaped space, fifteen feet or so down one side, with a concave ceiling overhead. I was lying on the floor. The darkness at first had been impenetrable. The figures which had flung me down and seized my knife were gone; I had not seen them nor where they went.

For a moment I lay cushioned by my bloated suit. When I struggled to my feet, I was almost weightless. The movement of getting upright flung me upward as though I were a tossed feather. My helmet struck the metal ceiling, so sharp a blow that I feared for an instant I had smashed the helmet.

From the ceiling, with flailing arms and legs, I sank back to the grid-floor; and in a moment I was able to stand upright with so slight a feeling of weight that I could have been a bit of thistle ready to blow away in the least wind.

There was, as I stood there balancing myself, a queer feeling of triumph within me. A triumphant hope; for coming down in the ship's capacious funnel—larger than it had seemed from a distance—I had seen what appeared to be a small projectile, resting in some strange landing gear. The disc bearing me had settled on a stage alongside it. Was that the projectile from Earth?

A growing air pressure was around me; the tiny Erentz dials within my helmet had been immovable, but now they were showing outside pressure. I stood waiting. Whatever sounds were here I could not tell. Then presently the dials stopped. They registered seventeen pounds—whatever that might mean here. I loosed the helmet and took it off.

With the first gasping breath my senses reeled. I sank to the floor, and though I tried to replace the helmet, it was too late. My thoughts were fading. A strange chemical odor was in my nostrils. It was like breathing a thin, perfumed water.

The drifting away was pleasant.

Tortured dreams came with my awakening. I found myself in the same dim room upon the floor. I could breathe better now, and in a few more hours the strangeness had almost gone. I found now that I was not injured, but I was ravenously hungry.

Again, gingerly as before, I stood up and slid my space-suit from me; and now I was aware of movement and sound. The floor-grid vibrations were apparent. And there was a dim, distant, tiny throbbing; it was much like the interior of the *Cometara* while in flight.

And there were other sounds, indescribably faint, yet strangely clear. I thought they might be distant voices.

I took a cautious step. I could see a dim blank wall nearby with what seemed a bowl-like article of furniture on the floor against the wall. For all my caution, I sailed upward; but this time I held my balance. And I found that with my negligible weight, I could almost swim in this strange air! I hit the wall and slid slowly down it to the floor again, like a man sinking to the bottom of a tank.

It suddenly occurred to me to put my ear against the wall. At once the sounds all became incredibly louder. It was a confusion of sound: the mechanisms of the vessel, some of which I thought I could identify, and some not; the strange swish and thump of what might have been people moving; and there were voices.

The voices seemed mingled babble coming from everywhere. The timber of the sound was very strange. It held no suggestion of how far away from me the voices might be. There were so many of them I could only think they were scattered about the ship; and yet they all seemed together. After a moment, the blend was less confusing. Again, very strangely my hearing seemed able to separate one from the other.

I was to learn that the atmosphere handled sound vibrations differently from that of Earth. Voices had a muffled tone, as though they were smothered. There was undoubtedly a vibrational distortion; and a sound-wave speed slower than Earth's normal-pressure rate of 1,050 feet a second, perhaps as slow as 700. Yet sounds remained audible over longer distances than on Earth.

In this instance now, as I listened with my ear to the wall of the ship, I was hearing all its sounds picked up and carried by the metal.

Now I heard a strange tongue: two types of voices, slow, measured, carefully-intoned phrases, and voices of a curiously sepulchral, hollow sound. My mind went back to the Red Spark restaurant room.

And suddenly I realized that amid the babble I was hearing English. A man's voice, talking English. I caught, very clearly the phrase:

"Master, yes. She means well. Can you not see it?"

Molo's voice! Then the girls must be here also.

Another voice: "I am not sure. Perhaps. The Great Intelligence will talk with her when we are arrived." It was the slow measured voice of one of the brains.

"When will that be? Pretty soon now, won't it, Molo?"

Venza! A great wave of thankfulness swept me. And then I heard Anita. "Your two captives, where are they? You're not going to kill them, are you?"

"No," said Molo. "Perhaps not. No one has inspected the new one yet. The other is being cared for. The Great Intelligence will question him when we arrive."

"We are arriving," said Venza. "That's your world, Wandl, down there, isn't it?"

"Yes. We are dropping fast."

The voice of the brain: "Come, Wyk. The instruments are showing events on our captured worlds. Take me to watch. I am tired of movement."

"Yes. Master."

It seemed that the brain was being carried away; Molo and the two girls were being left alone. I had thought at first that they were in the adjacent room to me, but they could have been far distant. They had mentioned two captives. One, obviously, was myself. Was the other Snap?

"Come," Molo was saying, "stand here with me and we will watch this world. Not mine, Venza *chia*, as you just called it, But my adopted world. And it will be yours, until we rule the new Mars."

I heard them moving to gaze through the window-port. Then came Anita's voice: "If it's anything like this ship, it will be very strange."

"Strange indeed, little dove. I was there only once, a month ago, and for a few hours only. The Great Intelligence, as they call him, talked with me, absorbing my knowledge: they call it that. And he was much impressed by me, and made very wonderful promises in exchange for my fidelity. And for my sister, too."

I learned further how Molo and Meka became identified with the Wandlites; it was as we had suspected.

"You will rule Mars?" Venza was saying. "When this is over, you mean you will really be given Mars to rule?"

"I would rather live on the Earth," said Anita. "There was a young man there."

"He will not be there much longer." Molo laughed. "You are very lucky that I fancy you!"

"Lucky indeed," Venza echoed. "No death for me. I'm too young."

"But all those millions dead. It seems so terrible."

"It is, for them!" Molo was in high good humor, pleased with himself and with these girls. "See down there; that blurring is the heavy air. We're almost down into it now."

I heard the sound of someone joining them, and then the hollow voice again: "Molo! Bad tidings come from Mars. One of the Masters was captured there in Ferrok-Shahn. They tortured him as they did the one on Earth. But he did not die unyielding. He spoke and told our plans!"

"Hah! Did I not advise you to keep those helpless things on Wandl?"

"But it is done now. The worlds know our purpose. They are preparing spaceships. Already some are rising from Ferrok-Shahn, from Grebhar and from Greater New York."

"We knew they were doing that."

"But now they know our purpose. The Master Intelligence fears that they will come raiding Wandl. Our vessels are being made ready to go out and repel them."

The hollow voice ceased.

"Your purpose discovered?" asked Anita. "What does that mean? Won't you tell us now? Twin queens for your future Mars, and you treat us like children!"

"That light-beam he so cleverly planted in Greater New York," Venza hinted.

"Yes, I will tell you. Without me in New York and my men who went with these Wandlites to Ferrok-Shahn and Grebhar, the vital gravity beams could never successfully have been planted. The apparatus was complicated; you saw it. You saw the labor I had making the contact?"

"But what are the light-beams for?"

I listened, breathless, as he told them. The electronic beams could not be destroyed; a disintegration of the rock atoms had been set up. With each rotation of the Earth it was sweeping the sky. From a great control station, Wandl was flinging attraction gravity upon that beam, using it as a monstrous lever upon the rotation of Earth. With every daily passage now the force was being exerted. The rotation was slowing. In a few days it would stop, with the end of the beam drawn to Wandl and held there.

And the beams from Grebhar and Ferrok-Shahn were the same. Three giant chains! Then Wandl, traveling of its own gravitational volition, would withdraw from our solar system. The gravitational chains would pull the Earth, Venus and Mars after it!

Titanic tow-ropes! The destruction, not of our worlds, but of all life upon them, for the cold of interstellar space would leave no living organism. Three dead worlds; Wandl would draw them to her own Sun and then free them, send them, with new orbits, around the distant blazing star. Three new worlds brought home triumphantly by Wandl to join the little family of inhabited planets revolving around this other Sun. Three fair and lovely worlds, warmed back by the other sunlight to be green mansions untenanted, ready to receive the new beings who would come and possess them.

CHAPTER NINE

"You, Snap!"

"Gregg! But how...?"

"Hush! They might hear us."

"They can do more than that. They can almost hear you think."

"Anita and Venza are here."

"I know it. I was with them for a time. This accursed gravity! I can't walk."

"Careful," I whispered. "You can crack your head on something with the least false step. Are they taking us ashore?"

"I guess so. How did you happen...?"

"Tell you later."

They had come for me in that dark pressure-port, taken me along a dim corridor of the ship, which evidently had landed a few moments before. Then Snap, with strange figures around him, had been flung at me.

These weird beings! The brains were here, but not many; I saw half a dozen on the ship. They could move easily now. They bounced upon their small arms and legs, hitching with little leaps of a few feet. Close at hand they were gruesome; from a distance they had the aspect of thirty-inch ovoids, bouncing of their own volition. And I saw too that underneath, toward the back, was a shriveled body.

The other figures were wholly different; they seemed at first to be ten-foot, upright insects. The two legs were like stilts, the body narrow but with bulging chest. The neck was thin, holding the small round head, about the size of my own.

Words seem futile to picture this thing which was a man of Wandl. There was no skin, but instead what seemed to be a glossy, hard brown shell. It was laid in scales; and upon the legs was a brown fuzz of stiff hair. There were many joints, both of the legs and the torso. Clothing was worn; a single garment, hanging from a wide belt halfway down the legs seemed incongruous, fantastically aping humanity.

This was the worker, equipped by nature for mechanical tasks. There were not two arms, but at least ten. From what could have been called the shoulders, they were tentacles, half the length of an elephant's trunk, with many-fingered hands at the ends. From the waist depended huge lobster-like pincers; and from the chest and back the arms were smaller, each with a different type finger-claw.

The head and face were most of all a personal mocking of mankind. Wide, upstanding, listening ears were upon the sides of the head, one on the forehead and one on the back. The face was mobile, with tiny brown scales small as a fish. A nose orifice, with two protruding brown eyes above it was set outward on stems, and an upended slit of a mouth. There was an eye in the back of the head.

Probably, over eons of upward development from what was perhaps an original single type, these two specialized forms had developed. The "Masters," as they were known upon Wandl, neglected the body for the brain, and the "Workers," the reverse. There was no separate individual for the female. As is the case with primitive organisms, they were all bi-sexual, the parent dying in the reproduction of offspring.

Of necessity I have been forced into digression. But at the time, Snap and I clung together, whispering, as a group of workers pushed us down a descending incline. Snap, back there in Greater New York when Molo's contact light had burst into existence, had fallen, half unconscious. They picked him up. Molo was going to kill him, but the girls persuaded him to take Snap with them.

"Anita and Venza pretended never to have seen me before," Snap whispered to me now. "You take the same line."

"If we get with them."

"We will."

It was weird, this landing upon Wandl. We had left the vessel's side-port and were descending what seemed a narrow, hundred-foot landing incline. We were outdoors, and it was night. Shafts of colored radiance flashed around us. The ship was poised on a disc-like platform, with skeleton legs. It seemed a hundred feet or more down to the ground level from where the colored lights were darting up. Overhead was a cloudless, purple-red sky of blurred, reddish stars. No doubt the curious atmosphere of Wandl gave the sky and stars this abnormal look.

Later, what a multiplicity of obscure wonders we were to glimpse upon Wandl! The slowing rotation of the Earth caused climatic changes there, volcanic and tidal disturbances, but Wandl rotated and stopped at will. Undoubtedly she was equipped to withstand the shock. Her internal fires could not break into eruption; she had very little fluid surface. And the nature of her atmosphere was such that it was not easily disturbed into storms. Only if there was laxity in the handling of the planet's motion would a storm come.

But now, questions pounded at me. Earth, Venus and Mars were to be towed into interstellar space; all life on our worlds would perish in the cold of that stellar journey. Yet Wandl had made that journey. Was her atmosphere inherently such that it did not transmit rays of heat?

Snap and I had been pushed down the incline with half a dozen figures in advance of us. Without difficulty we could have leapt down that hundred feet, unaided. Figures were leaping into mid-air from several pressure-ports of the ship. They did not fall, but floated, drifted down. I saw one of the insect-like workers drop with motionless outstretched arms. Others came mounting up, using their arms and legs with sweeping strokes, as though swimming. It was like being under water.

It was a strange, weird scene, the vessel wavering above us; the flashing lights; waving beams of radiance. A fantastic structure nearby reared itself several hundred feet with lights on top and outlining its many lateral balconies one above the other. The air was full of the leaping, swimming insect-like figures. The brains, the masters, were not in evidence; then I saw one of them being carried, and others, floating down like distended falling balloons, to be caught by the workers in small nets and thus saved from jarring contact.

Snap was suddenly whispering: "That fellow back of us is our guard. I can feel his ray. Some form of attraction; it's pulling at me."

Snap was a little behind me. I turned and saw the faint radiance of a narrow light-beam upon him. It came from an instrument in an upper shoulder hand of the insect figure following us, no doubt the reverse form of the same ray which had been used to thrust the wrecked *Cometara* toward the Moon.

We reached the bottom. I saw now that the group of workers in advance of us were carrying metal cubes, seemingly of considerable weight; they also had to use the incline.

We stood presently on a smooth ground surface. We had not seen Anita and Venza, nor Molo and his sister. The insect figure who was our guard came forward. "You stand here. Molo comes."

"Where is he?" I demanded. "I want to see him." I stopped myself quickly; I had very nearly mentioned the girls. "And talk with him."

"He comes soon."

"I'm hungry." I gestured to my stomach. "Food. You know what that is?"

The brown scaly face contorted for a smile, a ghastly grimace. "Yes. You shall have food and drink."

It seemed that the hollow voice came not from the neck but from the shell-like, bulging chest. He stood aside, with the globular weapon of the ray in a pincer hand.

We waited, standing gingerly together, wavering with our slight weight. A wind would have blown us away, but there was no wind. Instead, there was a heavy, sultry air, warm as a mid-summer Earth night, warmer even than the Neo-time of Venus.

Snap and I were dressed much the same, wearing heavy boots, for which weight we were thankful, tight, puttee-like trousers, flaring at the top, and high-necked white blouses. Both of us were bare-headed. Doubtless we were as fantastic a sight to these Wandlites as they to us. Some of the workers crowded up, reaching out to pluck at us, but Snap waved them away and our guard dispersed them.

One of the master brains came bouncing up. Upon his little upright body the great head wavered.

"You will wait here." His eyes glowed up at us.

"But listen," Snap began.

"You will wait here for the Martian. He has his orders to take you to the Great Intelligence." The little arm from the side of the head had a hand with a finger pointing for a gesture. "There is a meeting place there. We decided now what to do to destroy the warships of your worlds. I do not like your thoughts; they are black. I will inform the Great Intelligence when he can spare the thought for you."

He added something in the Wandl tongue. A worker came forward; lifted him carefully, held him in the hollow of an encircling tentacle. And with a bound, the worker sailed upward and was gone.

Again we stood through an interval. I noticed now that the towering structure near us, with its storied balconies, was not perpendicular. Its front curved up and back. It was convex, somewhat in the fashion of an irregular globe, a three-hundred foot ball, with a flattened base set here on the ground. The balconies were segments of its front curve. At the top, the roof was as though the ball had been sliced off, like a giant apple with a slice gone for a base and another for the roof. At the bottom was a huge portal with a glow of light from within. And at the terraced balcony levels were lighted windows.

"Is that the meeting place?" Snap whispered.

"Probably. And look to the side of it, Snap."

It was a city. There was a vista of distance to one side of the great globe structure. Now that our eyes were more accustomed to the queerness of this night upon Wandl, we could ignore the colored light-beams of the landing stage and the disembarking palisade upon which we were standing. Gazing into the distance, the curvature of the surface of this little world was immediately apparent. The reddish firmament of stars came down to meet the sharply-curving surface at a horizon line which seemed about a mile away.

Spread upon this near distance were a variety of structures with little roads of open space winding between them. Most of the buildings seemed globular in shape. Some were small, little round mound-shaped individual dwellings. Others were larger. Some were tiered like half a dozen apples speared in a row upon a stick and set upright.

I saw a ribbon of what might be a river in the distance, with the reddish starlight glinting upon it. To our left, half a mile away perhaps, was a row of buttes and rocks which stood like a miniature range of mountains. The city seemed entirely to encompass them; and every little rock-peak had upon its top a globelike dwelling.

Lights were winking everywhere and figures bounded a hundred feet and more, and sailed in an arc, coming down to the ground to bound again. A row of workers went by overhead, not swimming or leaping but stiffly motionless. Tiny opalescent rays went from them to the ground, as though to give them power.

Five minutes of Earth-time might have passed while Snap and I gazed at this busy night scene in this Wandl city upon the occasion of the landing of their ship so triumphantly returned from its mission to Earth. As I stood, certainly a helpless captive if ever there was one, nevertheless a strange sense of my own power was within me.

This was so small a world; the people were so flimsy. With a poke of my fist I could kill any one of these master brains. The ten-foot workers seemed mere shells, light and fragile; even the buildings were light and flimsy. The little globe-houses on their sticks seemed to waver, almost like nodding flowers. If we ran amuck we could smash everything we saw here on Wandl.

We became aware of Molo approaching. What a solid giant this seven-foot Martian seemed now in the midst of this buoyant, almost weightless city! He was still bare-headed and wearing his garments of ornamented leather, with his brawny legs bare. Upon his feet were strange-looking, wide-soled shoes. His hands and forearms were thrust into loops of small shields. These shields appeared to be constructed of a heart-shaped flexible framework, covered with an opaque membrane. They were about two feet long and half as wide. With a hand and forearm thrust into fabric loops, the shield appeared to serve as wings so that the arms had more thrust against the air. He came at us with a sort of swimming stroke. He landed somewhat awkwardly, half-stumbled and almost fell, but gathered himself up and confronted us.

He gained his balance and waved our guard aside. His gaze went to me.

"You are the new prisoner taken from that wrecked Earth-ship?"

"Yes."

"What is your name? You are an Earthman, evidently."

"Yes." I hesitated. I had seen Molo and heard him talk, back there in Greater New York; but he had not seen me nor heard of me probably.

"Gregg Haljan." I added, "I am a skilled navigator; perhaps it was fortunate you saved me."

He flung me a look and there was a tinge of amusement in it. "You would save your own skin now?"

"Why not? You're a Martian, and this is a war also against Mars."

His look darkened, but then again sardonic amusement struck him.

"We shall see what the Great Master says. There will be a few of our type humans, men and women, wanted when the worlds begin anew. The Great Master said so. He wants to study life on Earth as it was before the destruction."

Molo's glance swept behind us. I turned to see three figures approaching. My heart pounded. They were Anita, Venza and Molo's sister, Meka. They came slowly, trying to walk, with balancing outstretched arms. With a dozen curious Wandl workers crowding them, they came and joined Molo before us. My heart was pounding, but I flung them a curious, impersonal stare.

"You are here," said Molo. "Good. We go now." He bent over Snap and me. "I advise you make no effort to leap away, though it may look easy."

"Not me," said Snap. "Where would I go alone in this damned world? I can't very well leap back to Earth, can I?"

"True enough," said Molo. "You have sense, little fellow. But I just warn you: the guard who will watch you always is very sharp of eye. And the weapons here bring very swift death."

I could feel Anita's gaze upon me, but I did not dare look her way.

"Let's go," I said, "You will have no trouble with me."

With Molo leading us, and the giant insect-like guard following close behind, we made our slow, awkward way across the esplanade portals of the huge globular building.

And within, we traversed a cylinder-like, padded corridor and came presently upon the strangest interior scene I had ever beheld.

CHAPTER TEN

The room was so large that it seemed almost the entire interior of the building. It was a globular room, a hundred and fifty feet or more in diameter. The inner surface was crowded with people. It was a huge, hollow interior of a ball; and upon its concave surface a throng of the brown-shelled workers were gathered. They sat on low seats at the curved bottom of the room, where we entered, and up the sides and upon the slopes and the top, like flies in a globe, hanging head downward. There was no up or down here; the slight gravity made little difference.

I gazed up amazed to where, a hundred and fifty feet above me, head downward, the crowd of figures were calmly seated. These were clinging, of course; the pound-weight of each would drop them down if they let loose. But it required only a slight effort.

Between the tiers, there were narrow open aisles bearing glowlights at intervals. With Molo leading us, we stared up the curving incline of one of these aisles.

"Gregg! Good Lord, it's weird!" Snap said. "Where are we going to sit? Don't speak to the girls yet."

"Have you spoken to them?"

"Yes. A little, on the ship. They're watching for an opportunity but we have to be cautious. Gregg, I've got so much to tell you, but no chance. The brains can just about hear your thoughts."

We went only a short distance up the incline. There were vacant seats seemingly held ready for us. Our passage created a commotion among the figures. Some leaped up and over us to get a better look. I found that we were clinging to the mound-like convex surface of a small half-globe. It raised us some ten feet above the floor. There were low seats with arms against the side-pull of gravity. I found Anita close beside me. Her hand touched me, but she did not turn her head or speak.

Molo was on my other side. I chanced to see his feet. They were planted firmly on the floor. He wore wide-soled shoes equipped with suction pads, no doubt, which would enable him, like the Wandlites, to walk and stand upon the upper inner surfaces of buildings.

As during the moments when Snap and I stood on the landing esplanade, there was so much here that at first I could not encompass it. But now I began to grasp other details of the strange scene.

Poised in mid-air, almost exactly in the center of the huge globular room, was a metal globe of some thirty feet in diameter. It was held, not by any solid girders, but by four narrow beams of light which mounted to it from widespread points of the convex room.

Upon the entire surface of this thirty-foot globe, a group of masters were seated, in little, cup-like seats upon resilient stems. They swayed and nodded with movement. There seemed to be glowing wires and grids and thread-like beams of light carrying current. Light-threads shot from the mechanisms to the heads of the seated brains. All the devices were evidently in operation; and upon this poised central globe the attention of the audience was directed.

Molo bent over me. "The Great Intelligence soon will see you."

Snap, from the other side of Molo, whispered: "What are they doing up there?"

The faint hiss and throb of the devices were audible. I stared, trying to understand. Images, and sounds, invisible and inaudible were being received from across the millions of miles of space, and they were being transmuted within the brains themselves. I saw that discs were fastened upon the bulging foreheads of the brains, upon which the tiny light-beams carrying the vibrations impinged.

These brains, receiving "waves" of some unknown variety were, within the mechanism of the brain-cell, transmuting, translating the vibrations into things knowable. They were not seeing, not hearing, but *knowing* what went on millions of miles across space!

Again Molo bent over me. "They are about to show this audience what is happening on the three worlds."

Upon the thirty-foot globe I saw now a dozen or so balls of about three-foot diameter. These had been dark and I had not noticed them. Now they began glowing, not from wires carrying the current, but from the little hands of the brains touching them.

I stared at the brain nearest me. His flabby little arm was extended; his hand touched the image-ball; gave it light and color, like a fortune-teller of Earth with a crystal before her.

Even though I was some sixty feet from it, I could see the moving images clearly, and recognized the scene. The Tappan Interplanetary Stage. Ships were rising; two of our spaceships mounting.

And all in an instant the scene blurred, took form again. The red-green spires and minarets of Ferrok-Shahn. The Central Canal extended like a gash across the foreground; the "Mushroom Mountains" were in a line upon the horizon. Three Martian space-flyers slid up while we watched.

And now Grebhar. The silver forest in all its shining beauty, where Venza was born. The sunlight sparkled on the river. A spaceship was rising in the distant sky over the shining forest.

Beyond Anita, I heard Venza murmuring, "Home! If only we were there."

I could feel Anita move to silence her.

Molo was whispering: "They come. But we will be ready for them."

Another image: mid-space. The allied ships gathering, waiting for others to arrive. A group here of about ten of our ships from the three worlds: poised, waiting.

I was aware that upon the mound-like protuberance of the room-floor where we were sitting, a door was opening. It slid, or melted away. At our feet was an opening downward into the small interior of the mound.

Molo whispered, "The great Master. Sit quiet! He will talk to us."

Over us now a barrage came with a hiss, a circular curtain of insulation. The huge globular room faded. We were alone on the mound, Snap, Molo, myself, Anita, Venza and Meka upon the end of our bench. Behind us stood our single Wandlite guard, with a weapon in his shoulder hand.

At our feet an opening yawned into the mound-interior. It was a tiny, lighted room. In a cup-like seat a brain was perched, just below the level of our feet: the great Master Brain of Wandl. He was alone here. Not attended by retinue; no pomp and ceremony to usher us into his presence; no underlings obsequiously bowing to mark him for a great ruler.

We stared down, and the great brain stared up at us, seemingly equally curious. His head was a full four feet in diameter; the little body sat in the cup, with dangling legs. The clothes were ornamented: there was a glowing device on the chest.

He spoke with a measured rumble, in Martian. "You are Molo, of Ferrok-Shahn."

"Yes," said Molo.

"You must say, 'Yes, Great Master.'"

"Yes, Great Master."

"I know about you. I know that we trust you."

The huge round eyes next fastened upon me. Then to Snap, and back to me. The words were English this time. "Men of Earth, are you decided, like the Martian, to join with us?"

I tried with sudden vehemence to still my thoughts, or to change them so that they lied. Fear surged upon me. Could this vast mechanism of human mind here at my feet interpret the vibrations of my thoughts? Could this Great Master of Wandl see into my mind?

The brain said, "You are uncertain. You do not want to die?"

"No Great Master," we both answered.

"You shall not, unless you attempt to cause us trouble. Your thoughts are black." He addressed Molo. "Have they ever been read?"

"No, Great Master."

"When opportunity comes, have them read." He added to Snap and me: "I plan to take prisoners. My Supreme Rulers, rulers of a neighboring more powerful planet, which sent Wandl upon her mission of conquest, ordered it. When your worlds are vacant of life, those who command me will want some of you left alive to be studied. Your thoughts are very black, Earthman. I think when they are carefully read you will prove no great advantage to us."

There was irony in the voice, and upon the monstrous bulging face came the horrible travesty of a grin.

The grin on the brain's face faded. His interest went again to Molo. "That is your sister." The eyes swung to Meka and back.

"Yes, Great Master."

"She is caring for this Earth-girl and this girl from Venus?"

"Yes, Great Master. I am fond of them. I have plans."

"They are in your charge, Martian; I will not interfere with you. But guard them well. I trust you and your sister. These others…"

"The Earth and the Venus girl can be of help to me, Master."

"How?"

"They knew young men who were in the Spaceship Service. They can tell me the armament of men and weapons on most of the spaceships which Earth will send against us."

Did Molo really believe that? Probably not, but he wanted the girls with him. Again came that grotesque smile. "Let them not bother you, Martian. You have work to do. Listen carefully. There will be a battle. Earth, Mars, and Venus may perhaps have a hundred ships. I cannot bring destruction upon those three worlds in a day. We soon will make contact with the light-beam you placed on Earth. That I will show you. But the rotation cannot be stopped at once. It will take time.

"The enemy ships might dare to come to Wandl, but I shall not wait for that. All my spaceships are very nearly ready. If there is to be a battle, it shall be far from here, in the neighborhood of the enemy worlds. We are at this time about sixty-two million of your miles from the Earth, a third less than that from Mars, and about a third more from Venus. I understand, Martian, that you are skilled in space warfare."

The brain went on, "I have given you a vessel to command. You will be surprised to know its name: the *Star-Streak*."

Meka gasped, "But you destroyed it, Great Master!"

"Only wrecked it, Martian girl. It is repaired now. You, Molo—and your sister to help you—who could command it to more advantage? All your own weapons, and ours of Wandl have been added. You may select your crew. Is it to your liking?"

"Yes, Great Master."

"You will be housed in this city, Wor, in the dwelling-globe you occupied before. Keep your prisoners with you, if you like."

"These two Earthmen…" began Molo, but he was interrupted.

"Settle that later. I do not want the annoyance."

I was dimly conscious of a great clanging, coming through the curtain of barrage which was over us.

The brain added, "Keep Wyk with you, to guard the prisoners; he will also attend your needs. In the battle, Martian, I expect great things of you and your *Star-Streak.*"

"Great Master, you will not be disappointed."

"And prisoners, but not too many. Bring me a few young specimens like these, representative of Venus, Mars and the Earth. I want both of the sexes, an equal number of each."

"Yes, Great Master."

"The warning signal is coming. You will now see our first contact."

The light at our feet was fading. It clung last by the gruesome face of the huge brain; the goggling eyes shone green, and as the light in the little mound-room dimmed there was in a moment nothing left but those lurid green pools of the brain's eyes.

Then I was aware that the aperture at our feet had closed. Over us, the barrage curtain was dissipating, sight and sound coming in to us. The huge ball-shaped conclave room again became visible, the audience crowding its entire inner surface.

I suddenly felt Anita's fingers twitching at my sleeve.

"Gregg, darling, can you hear me?"

"Yes. Be careful."

But Molo was gazing up over our heads. The crowd was shifting, bending so that they all seemed gazing at their feet. A dim white radiance, seeming to come from down here somewhere near us, lay in a splotch on a segment of the throng overhead. Molo was watching.

I whispered, "All right, Anita. Quick, what is it?"

"The great control station is not far from here. Venza and I have been trying to find out where it is exactly."

She stopped, evidently fearful of Meka. Then she added:

"Gregg, we haven't been guarded very closely; they're not suspicious of us."

"Later, Anita. Can't talk now."

"No. Watch our chance. Later."

I turned toward Molo. "What's that up there?"

"The transparent ray is opening the top of the globe."

The clanging signal gong had stilled. The audience was hushed and expectant. The white patch of light overhead spread until it encompassed all the top of the globe. The whole area was glowing. The people were white, spectral shapes, transparent! And the top of the globe was transparent; I saw the night sky, with the gleaming reddish stars.

It was, in a moment, as though we were staring up at a huge square window orifice cut in the top of the room. A broad vista of cloudless sky and stars was visible. Across it, like a shining sword, was a narrow, opalescent beam.

"The Earth-beam I planted," Molo whispered triumphantly. "Our control station will contact with it now. The first contact!"

Earth was below our angle of vision, but the beam from Greater New York, sweeping the sky with the Earth's rotation, was passing now comparatively close to Wandl.

There was an expectant moment. Then into the sky leaped another ray, narrow, luridly green. It swung up from Wandl and darted into space. The hissing, agonized electrical scream from it as it burst through the Wandl atmosphere was deafening. I saw it strike the Earth-beam, grip it with a blinding burst of radiance up there in the sky, clinging, pulling against the rotation of the Earth with a lever sixty million miles long.

A moment of screaming sound in the atmosphere around us, and that conflict of light in the sky. Then the screaming suddenly stilled. The Wandl beam vanished.

The Earth-beam still swept the heavens like a stiff, upstanding sword. But in that moment when Wandl gripped it, the axis of the Earth had been changed a little. The rotation was slowed. By a few minutes, the day and the night on Earth were lengthened.

It was the beginning of Earth's desolation.

CHAPTER ELEVEN

"But when do we eat?" Snap demanded.

"Soon," said Molo.

"I hope so."

We were leaving the great room as we had come. Walking? I can only call it that, though the word is futile to describe our progress as we made our way to the lighted esplanade, across its side and into what might have been called a street. Globular houses, single, or one set upon another, or half a dozen swaying on a stick, gardens of vegetables and flowers. I saw what seemed to be a round patch of hundred-foot tree-stalks, like a thick batch of bamboo. It was laced and latticed thick with vines.

"A house," Snap murmured. "That's a house."

Another type of dwelling. This patch of vegetable growth, so flimsy it was all stirring with the movement of the night breeze, was woven into circular thatched rooms, birds' nests of little dwellings. Staring up, I seemed to see a hundred of them. Rope-vine ladders; flimsy vine platforms; tiny lights winking up there in the trees.

On a platform twenty feet above us a group of tiny infant brains sat in a gruesome row, goggling down on us.

We passed the tree patch; again the city seemed all a thin, flexible metal. The ground was like a smooth rock surface, alternating with small patches of soil where things were growing.

We walked in a slow, unsteady line. Molo led. Behind Snap and me came the girls, ignoring us; and at the rear, the brown-shelled giant guard stalked after us.

Molo stopped at a large globe-dwelling. "We rest here. I will go see that our rooms are ready." He gestured to his sister. "Meka, you come with me. Wyk will guard them."

We stood at an oval doorway. A worker came out, stared at us, then went back. On an upper balcony, a brain was gazing down at us.

I caught Molo's brawny arm. "Won't you tell us what's going on?"

"Rest here with Wyk."

"What are you going to do?" asked Snap.

"I am going to select my men for battle."

"When do you go?"

"In a few hours, Earth-time."

"And you're taking us on the ship, Molo? Where is your *Star-Streak?*"

"That I must find out." He, gazed at us with a slow, faint smile. "Not far. Nothing is far on Wandl. I do not know if I will take you on my ship. You might be of help, or you might be troublesome. The Great Master wants prisoners, or I would have killed you long ago."

He took his sister and left us. There was a brief moment when Wyk, standing aside incuriously, gave us opportunity for swift whispers.

Again Anita clutched me. "Gregg, we'll be separated now. But with Molo gone, Venza and I can get away from Meka."

Venza whirled on us. "Gregg, listen! Snap, be quiet! If we're ever going to escape, now is the time. You get away from Wyk. We'll handle Meka."

"And do what?" Snap demanded.

"The control station! We'll find it!"

Anita whispered, "We've got to wreck it, Gregg. Stop those contacts. It'll mean the end of Earth if we don't."

I protested. "Better try for Molo's vessel. We might be able to navigate it, escape from this world."

"The control station first," Anita insisted. "Gregg, we know something about it. You and Snap, with your strength, can demolish it. And then, if we can locate the *Star-Streak*..."

It was a desperate, mad plan, but there seemed nothing better. The girls insisted now that though they did not know where the control station was located, they knew the details of its interior; its physical layout; its human operators.

"In an hour," whispered Snap. "Have you got a timer? Is it going?"

The little timers we still had with us were undoubtedly operating differently from on Earth; but they were in agreement.

"An hour by our timers," I whispered. "We'll make the break then, try to find you inside. Anita, if you get free of Meka, don't come out."

"All right."

We had only a moment to try and plan it. "Anita, in an hour, with Molo gone..."

He came suddenly with a driving leap from the doorway and dropped among us. "All is ready. Come."

We ignored the girls. Snap again protested that he was hungry, which indeed, for me at least, was certainly the truth. And I was parched with thirst. I felt that this vaunted strength of my Earth body would not last long without food and drink.

We entered the globular interior. There were narrow corridors; triangular rooms; a slatted, ladder-like incline leading upward to a higher level.

The girls followed Meka up the incline. Molo and Wyk herded us into a nearby room. "You will have your food and drink here. Cause Wyk no trouble and you will be quite safe."

He turned, but Snap plucked at him. "When are you coming back?"

"Not too long."

I said, "We will cause you no trouble. Take us on the ship."

"I will see."

He murmured to Wyk in Martian, then left us.

THE SMALL triangular room had no windows and only the single door. Wyk touched a mechanism and it slid closed. The place was a queer apartment indeed. The floor was convex, curving upward to the walls. The light radiance dimly glowed, as though inherent to the metal ceiling. There was strange metal furniture: a table and chairs, high and large; bunks of a size evidently for the ten-foot workers.

The door opened, and a worker brought us food and drink. Wyk sat apart and watched us while we consumed the meal. I noticed that he seldom let himself get close to us. He sat stiffly upright, with his jointed legs bent double under him, his many arms and pincers hanging inert, save the one short shoulder-arm with flexible fingers gripping his weapon. At his waist, and upon several hook-like protuberances of his chest, other weapons and devices were hanging.

Snap gazed up from where, on the floor, we were ravenously eating and drinking. "Aren't you hungry?" he asked Wyk.

"No."

"You eat often?"

"No."

An incurious, taciturn creature, this insect-like being. Snap whispered, "Got to talk to him; make him let us get close. That weapon..."

How the weapon operated, we did not know; but that a flash from it would bring instant death we well imagined.

Half of that hour of waiting was past.

I said to Wyk, "You would call this night on your world; the sun obviously is on the other hemisphere. When will it be day?"

His gaze swung on me. His hollow voice, deep from the capacious shell of chest, echoed and blurred in the room.

"I think Wandl has no rotation now. Or almost none."

He was not as taciturn, as he had seemed, and presently we had him talking. We learned several things regarding the gravity-controls of Wandl, by which at will the planet could be rotated on its axis; and by which also it could navigate space. We learned that the great control station contained these gravitational mechanisms, as well as the mechanism by which the Earth had been attacked. But we could not discover where on Wandl that station was located.

Then, with our meal finished, Snap rose to his feet. "Those arms of yours, seem very strange to us. But they must be mighty useful."

Snap had taken a cautious, shoving step. It wafted him directly toward the guard.

The weird, brown-scaled face of Wyk, with its popping eyes upon stems and its upended mouth, contorted with surprise.

"Back! Don't come near me!"

He flung himself back, but struck the wall of the room. All his arms were writhing. Alarm was in his voice. It was the first time either Snap or I had made an unexpected move, and it startled Wyk.

"Wait! Let me go!" Snap cried.

Wyk's longest arms were around Snap, like the tentacles of an octopus, and Snap was struggling, fighting. We had not intended this at this time, but the opportunity was here.

I scrambled from the floor. Now, with the need for powerful action, the lack of gravity was a tremendous handicap. I went up with flailing arms into the air. Wyk fired his weapon, but it missed me, a soundless, dimly-white bolt. It hissed along the curving wall of the room. The smell of it was a stench in my nostrils.

I hit the concave ceiling, shoved down, and like a swimmer in water struck against the struggling bodies of Snap and the guard. The waving little shoulder arm with the weapon came at me.

Snap shouted, "Gregg, look out!"

I seized the little arm; it felt like the shell of a huge crab. For a moment we were all three entangled, floundering, unable to find a foothold. Then suddenly I felt Snap pulling me loose.

"We've got him!"

The brown-shelled body of Wyk sank away from us, hit the floor and lay still. I felt the floor under me, and Snap clutching at me.

In my hand I was clutching Wyk's little shoulder arm, with fingers still gripping the weapon. I had jerked it out of his shoulder socket. With a shudder I cast the noisome thing away. Whether Wyk was dead or not we did not know. He lay on his back; the hideous face stared upward.

"I cracked the shell," Snap gasped. "We've got to get out of here. Better try and get the girls loose now."

We wasted no further time on Wyk. Snap snatched several of his weapons and mechanical devices. We stowed them hastily in our pockets. One was like another to us; we could only guess at their uses.

"His shoes, Gregg. I can't get the damn things off him."

"Here are shoes."

A small pile of shoes was in a corner of the room; wide, resilient suction soles, built like sandals. They were very large, but the things were so placed that it seemed we could fasten them to our boots.

"But not now, Snap."

We snatched up four pairs of the shoes.

There seemed nothing else to do. Could we get the door open? Snap was already fumbling at it. "Accursed thing! It won't give."

Then it slid open. The dim corridor was visible. No one, nothing, out there. "Come on, Gregg! In a rush!"

We went like bouncing rubber figures up the incline ladder.

"Snap, watch out!" He all but cracked his head with an upward leap. Every instant we expected to be set upon. There was a terraced upper hall, black with shadow; dark ovals of doorways led into rooms.

No one here. As yet we were not discovered.

We stood at the intersection of two corridors. One went almost vertically up, like a chimney extending into the dome peak of the globe. Its sides were latticed; we could go up it hand over hand, like monkeys. The other sloped at an angle downward.

"Which way?" Snap whispered. "What do you think? Got to find them."

It still lacked about five minutes of our designated time, but it would not do to burst in upon the girls, perhaps to find Molo and guards there.

"Let's wait a minute, listen, see if we can't get some idea."

We were backed against the corridor wall, almost in darkness. From the dark length of the descending corridor came a thump, the sound of a struggle, and then a muffled scream. Venza! And we heard her words: "Anita! Look out for her! She's got a knife!"

As though diving into water, Snap and I plunged head first into the blackness of the corridor.

CHAPTER TWELVE

Later, we learned that Anita and Venza had tried much the same tactics on Meka that we had used on Wyk, but their task was more difficult. She was suspicious of them. Venza asked her where the control station was, but she wouldn't answer.

"Your brother said it was just beyond the dark forest," Anita said. "What is the dark forest?"

"A place with trees where no one lives."

"Off that way." Venza gestured. "That's what Molo said. Will it be day soon, or will the night keep on?"

"If they cause Wandl to rotate, it will soon be day." An ironic look crossed Meka's face. "I am in no mood for answering more of your silly questions. Save the breath."

"Well, if that's they way you feel about it," replied Venza laughing, "we will. There's not much air in here." She shoved herself across the floor toward the closed window.

"Get back!"

"Oh, all right—all right!"

Perhaps Meka herself felt there was not enough air. She stood waveringly upright, and pushed herself with a slow leap for the window. Her back for that moment was to Anita and Venza. They shoved from the floor, whirled through the air and were upon her.

It was a brief struggle, and instantly they knew that they had lost. The huge Martian whirled and flung them off. Her upflung fist, with a blow like a man's, caught Anita's thigh and knocked her toward the ceiling. She sank in a heap on the floor, saw that Venza had shoved back, but was standing upright.

Anita bent double, with her feet braced against a chair, tensed to shove forward again. At the still unopened window, Meka crouched. Anita heard Venza's warning outcry. "Anita, look out for her! She's got a knife!"

Upon this scene, in a moment, Snap and I came with a rush. The closed door was not barred. We slid it down and catapulted through the opening. Meka sailed over us. I swam up at her; seized her. The knife ripped my blouse and slit the flesh of my upper arm with a glancing blow. Then Snap came and struck against us; we sank to the floor.

Meka had fought silently, but now she was shouting. I twisted her wrist, seized the knife handle and flung the knife away. I was aware of Anita lunging to retrieve it. And over us Venza appeared, waving a metal chair as though it were a huge feather.

Snap gasped, "Gregg get your hand over her mouth. Shut her up!"

We had her subdued in a moment, but it seemed almost too late. Outside the opened door a distant shout sounded.

I shoved Meka toward the door. "If you don't do what I say, I'll kill you," I whispered into her ear.

"What shall I do?"

There came another shout, closer, now. Someone was coming.

"Call out in Martian. Say there's no trouble, nothing wrong. You were arguing with these girls."

She did as I commanded. The voice down the corridor answered, and then subsided.

Snap slid the door closed. "Hurry! We'll go by the window. I dropped those damn shoes."

Anita and Venza tore their dark coats into strips. We bound and gagged Meka, laid her in a corner of the room. We had dropped the shoes as we came plunging through the door oval. We found that we could all fasten their things to our feet. I put Meka's knife in my belt.

"Hurry, all of you!" Snap was saying. "Got to get out of here; jump by the window."

"Say, look at these wing-shields!" From a recess in a corner of the room Venza appeared with an armful of the small shields. We thrust our hands and forearms into their loops. The shields extended from a few inches beyond our fingers to the elbow.

Snap had slid the window blind. I bent over the prone form of Meka. "Don't try to move. Molo will release you when he comes back."

We gathered on the starlit balcony. The city stretched around us. There was as yet no alarm. No swimming figures near here; but a distance away we saw the towering conclave globe, with its audience just beginning to emerge, like bees coming from a hive.

"Let me go first." I held Anita and Venza at the rail. "It's like swimming. I suppose we'll get the way of it pretty quickly."

I balanced on the rail, and then leaped off. With the others after me, we swam awkwardly upward into the reddish starlight.

The city structures dropped away, showing in a dark blur with winking lights. Over us were the stars and the cloudless night sky. Behind, the flashing light beams of radiance at the landing stage, the figures fluttering, the great globe, all dropped swiftly beneath a sharply curving horizon.

We had passed the city. A thousand feet below us, a dark forest stretched. It was beyond this that the control station was located.

The swimming flight became less awkward, but it was an effort in this abnormal Wandl air. Snap and Venza were behind me. Anita was leading, a strange, bird-like little figure. White blouse; long parted dark skirt from which her gray-sheathed legs kicked out as she swam, sometimes half upon one side, or with a breast stroke. The braids of her dark hair fell forward over her shoulders.

She was tiring: I could not miss it. How far had we gone? Ten miles, perhaps. There was only a small vista of this little world visible at once, it was so sharply convex. A line of distant mountains was to our left. We had crossed a river at the forest edge.

I suppose we had been half an hour swimming those ten-miles. Was daylight coming? It seemed that the sideline of mountain-tops had a little light on them. The opalescent beam from Earth had swept this portion of the sky and was gone below the horizon.

Apparently there was no pursuit from the city. Behind me, Venza panted, "Say, I'm about finished. Can't we rest?"

With this altitude we could cease our efforts and drift down. It would take several minutes.

We gathered together, falling with a slow drift toward the dark forest under us. The trees seemed huge and spindly, a porous growth something on the Martian style, with huge leaves and a tangle of matter vines. They came mounting up at us as we fell with slowly gathering speed.

"Shall we go on?" I suggested.

"Yes." But she was tired, and Anita as well.

"Girls," I asked, "where is the *Star-Streak*?"

They did not know.

Anita said, "Perhaps we can land in the trees, and examine what devices we have here."

The girls had carefully watched Molo upon several occasions. They thought we might find we had a hand-globe or a couple of the repulsive rays. With these we could attain rapid flight without effort.

We sank, fluttering, into a dark and tangled mass of the forest tree-top growth. I had understood that Wandl was crowded with its human population, yet this dark and silent forest evidently was uninhabited. We clung, like awkward birds, to a swaying limb of a tree-top. The trees were close together.

"Let's see what you've got," Venza demanded.

We handed the girls the various devices we had taken from Wyk. Most of them were the size of my fist: globular metallic projectors like hand bombs; ray cylinders; a device with multiple barrels the size of one's finger, set in a small circumference of a circular grid of wires.

Anita said, "I saw Molo with one of these. He killed an unwilling worker on the ship."

"I'll take a look around," Snap said anxiously. "Suppose we're being followed? Give me that weapon."

There was vegetation partly over us, so that the sky was half obscured. Snap took the weapon, and like a monkey swaying precariously, he ran and leaped among the upper branches, crashing his way until he could see back toward the horizon beyond which lay the city of Wor.

We heard his voice. "All clear. Nothing in sight. You coming up? Better get started."

I put the weapons in my pocket. Snap had one now in the branches over us. I was examining an electronic bolt, when suddenly there came Snap's call. "Gregg! Look out!"

We heard the hiss and saw the flash of his bolt.

Anita swung at me. "Gregg, see there!"

I followed her gesture, and then I knew why this forest was shunned by humans!

CHAPTER THIRTEEN

The forest swarmed with living things. Here in the dark they had been crawling upon us. Every branch of this leafy tree-top angle had something staring at us; the darkness was suddenly glowing with a myriad little green torches which were their eyes. They all winked on in an instant, as though at a signal, or at the sound of Snap's shout and the hiss of his bolt.

Insects? I suppose I should call them that. With a glance I saw that they were of many sizes and shapes; tiny little things with eyes like lanterns; things of many legs, finger-length, hand-length, and some as long as my forearm. Brown-shelled things, with eyes glowing on stems. There was one quite near us, a smooth, brown-shelled body; a round head on top, as big as my fist. And these things had heads like little distended brains.

What horrible jest of nature this was, with miniatures of the Wandl workers, crawling here, unable to stand erect, groping with little pincers. And miniature brains with naked, shriveled bodies.

It seemed that the eyes of that little brain were fixed on me with a baleful green glare in the darkness. Anita and Venza were floundering to their feet in horror. They all but slipped from the limb. The weapons and devices they had arranged there slid off and went down into the darkness unheeded. From above us came Snap's horrified shouts and the hiss of his bolts.

"Here!" I gasped. "My hand—Anita, Venza, jump!"

I shoved Anita upward. The little eyes suddenly were all in movement, advancing upon us. Anita floundered, fluttered, got into the air and mounted toward Snap. Again Venza slipped off the limb. I lunged and drew her up. Green eyes nearest us came swooping. I did not dare fire a bolt; it was too close to Venza. I flung the entire weapon at the green eyes, but I missed.

The little thing bit Venza's arm. She screamed and her flailing hand hit the tiny distended head. Its hideous little scream mingled with hers. It floated downward, massed and purple-red with gushing blood.

I struggled upward with the inert form of Venza under one arm. Anita was mounting, free. Snap came lunging down.

"Fired every bolt in the damn weapon!" He saw the unconscious Venza. "Good God, Gregg!"

Never have I heard such anguish in his tone. "Gregg, she isn't…"

"One of them bit her. Help me."

He floundered up with her, a hundred feet above the tree-tops of that horrible forest. The little lanterns of eyes down there had all winked out. The open starlight was over us.

Anita came swimming, then Venza stirred. She murmured, "…all right."

She had fainted. It seemed nothing more; but I found her upper arm swelling. She tried to bend her body and sit up; but it threw us all out of balance.

"Lie straight," Snap murmured. "Venza, are you all right?"

"Yes. Why not?" And then she laughed. It sent a shuddering chill over me. "What's the fuss about? Let's get away from here. Somebody will be coming."

She was swimming now and we let her loose, but stayed close by her. The reddish firmament was like an inverted bowl. The curving Wandl surface gave us a narrow little vista, the forest rolling up from the horizon in front. Then we saw where the forest seemed to end. Water was beyond it: a ribbon like a broad river, and beyond that, frowning mountains, terraced and spired with jagged peaks.

Snap and I suddenly recalled the gravity ray projectors. We tried them; found that they would fling little beams of two varieties. Pencil points of radiance, they seemed to have an effective range of no more than a few hundred feet.

I let myself drift downward, experimenting. The tiny beam struck the forest-top. I felt the projector pulling violently downward in my hand. I clung to it. I was being drawn swiftly down by the attractive gravity force of the ray. The forest rose rapidly under me: I was all but flung upon it before I could find the other controls.

Then the ray altered its nature; the projector in my hand pulled me steadily up. But after a few hundred feet, I felt I was mounting only of my own momentum, with gravity and air-friction retarding me.

Snap had tried similar experiments. We rejoined the swimming girls. I stared into Venza's face; it was pale but she did not seem distressed. She winked at me.

"How's your arm, Venza?"

"It hurts, but I guess it's all right."

I turned to Snap. "I guess we can work these things. Get Venza to cling to you."

Our progress now was far less difficult. Venza clung to Snap's ankles and Anita to mine. With the repulsing rays directed downward, we had a strong upward and forward thrust. We went forward with great thousand-foot bounds. The forest rolled back under us. We came over the gleaming river. It seemed several miles broad. It appeared to have a swift current.

I saw sunlight upon the mountain ahead. The darkness had been paling. Now day suddenly burst upon us. The sun, smaller than on Earth, mounted swiftly up. It was a flattened, distorted, dull-red disc, blurred by Wandl's strange atmosphere. We were in a dim red daylight.

Anita twitched at my ankles. "Look back of us!"

We were going up. Venza and Snap, behind us, were in a descending arc. Above them, far back in the direction from which they had come, two blobs were visible up against the reddish day sky.

Pursuit? It seemed so. The blobs went down, but came up again, traveling with rays, like ourselves.

I called to Snap, "Someone after us! Two figures back there!"

He was shouting, "Gregg! Gregg, help!"

My gaze had been on the distant figures. I saw now that at the bottom of his arc, and starting upward again, Snap had lost Venza. The impulse of his ray had twitched his ankle from her grasp. Or had she let loose? He was about a hundred feet above the river, and Venza, with acceleration downward unchecked, was falling into it.

"Gregg, help! Venza, swim up!" His frenzied call reached me as I used the attractive ray and Anita and I whirled over and lunged downward.

"Gregg, help! Venza use your arms! Swim!"

She was lying inert, making no effort to keep from falling. Her body turned slowly, end-over-end. She struck the swiftly-flowing river surface but did not sink; instead, she half emerged, came up and lay in a crumpled heap; and with its rapid current, the river carried her away.

It was several minutes before we could reach Venza. Snap was already there, floundering on the water, awkwardly maintaining his balance, bending over Venza. "Gregg, she's unconscious. Fainted again."

The bite of that insect! The thought of it turned me cold.

The river surface was like a very soft rubber mattress. The water clung to us, wet us. We could not kneel or stand erect; but in sitting down only a few inches of our bodies were submerged. We floated like corks, we were so light, and so little water did we displace.

We struggled with Venza across the gluey river surface. She had fallen near the further shore. Rocks, crags and strewn boulders were passing as the current swept us along at a speed of about ten miles an hour. She lay in our arms, eyes closed, her face pallid but calm. She seemed to breathe rapidly; but that on Wandl was normal.

We landed on the rocky shore. It was still daylight. The blurred sun was winging across the zenith so swiftly that its movement was visible. Wandl had been suddenly endowed with axial rotation. Even in these few minutes, the day was past its noon. On the distant mountain peaks looming above the nearby horizon; it seemed that the sheen of coming night was mingled with the red sunlight.

Anita and Snap laid Venza on the rocks. I suddenly remembered the two blobs in the sky behind us, which had seemed to be following. I stood gazing across the river. The red sky there seemed empty.

"Thank God, she's reviving!" Snap called at me and I joined them. Venza was stirring. Color was coming into her cheeks. Her lips were murmuring as though she were talking in her sleep.

Then she opened her eyes. Her gaze fixed on us as we bent over her. "Why, what's the matter? Where are we? I thought we were in the tree-tops. Snap, don't look at me like that, dear. I'm all right—only confused."

She could remember nothing since that gruesome thing bit into her arm, but the attack of its poison in her veins seemed definitely over. We sat with her, soothing her, explaining what had happened. And she was wholly rational. Her strength came back; her mind cleared.

The brief red day came to its close. The sun plunged below the horizon; the stars winked into being. The red-purple Wandl night again was here. And now we saw that the whole firmament was swinging, the rotation made visible.

The darkness leaped around us. Shadows filled the rock hollows. The caves and recesses of this rocky shore turned black with darkness. And in the sky now we saw another of those familiar opalescent beams. This was the one from Mars: we could identify the red disc of the planet.

And then, from the mountains ahead of us but still below our horizon, the Wandl control station shot its attacking beam upward. Again there was that conflict in the sky. The axis of Mars was being altered, its rotation slowed.

We could see now that we were much nearer than before to the control station. It seemed only about twenty miles ahead of us. The scream from it was deafening.

The Wandl beam died presently. The electrical scream from the control station was stilled.

The Earth's axis had been altered. Now Mars; and next would be Venus. A few more of these gravitational attacks and then the helpless planets, with rotation checked, would be towed away by Wandl, out into the deadly cold of interstellar space.

Anita abruptly gave a startled outcry. The four of us, sitting in a group, had no time to rise. From behind a dark crag nearby, two figures appeared. The starlight showed them clearly.

Molo and Wyk! They lunged forward at us.

CHAPTER FOURTEEN

We were unarmed. I had flung my weapon at the thing in the forest; and Snap had exhausted all his bolts firing at the multitude of green eyes. Molo and Wyk came with a dive through the air. Two tiny flashes leaped from them to the rocks behind them, and flung them forward.

Snap and I seized Venza and Anita. It was a second of confusion; then I saw we would not be able to rise in time. The driving, oncoming figures were no more than twenty feet away.

"Protect Venza, Snap! Get her behind you!"

Snap shoved Venza behind him; I got myself in front of Anita. We had almost gained our feet. I tried to thrust Anita and myself violently upward. We rose, but only a few feet. And then we were struck by the oncoming body of Wyk, like a huge, light-shelled, three-pound insect lunging in mid-air against us. The two longest tentacle arms wrapped around us. Anita twisted and kicked. The gruesome, goggling face of Wyk thrust itself almost into mine. The hollow voice panted, "I have you fast."

One of my arms was free and I struck with my fist at the gaping, upended mouth. There was a crack. My fist sank through the shell; a cold, sticky ooze spurted out.

Wyk screamed. His encircling arms fell away. The grisly smashed face was white with ooze and pulp where my fist had gone in.

We had sunk back to the rocks. I kicked the dead body of Wyk away.

"Anita! Swim up!"

"No!"

Sinking beside us were the flailing bodies of Molo, Snap and Venza were drifting down. They seemed intermingled. Snap was shouting: "No you don't! Drop that!"

I leaped for them. Something long and thin and glowing was dangling from Molo's hand. He broke loose from the struggling Snap and Venza; his feet struck the rocks and he shoved himself backward. My leap had carried me too high. I saw that in his hand was a six-foot length of glowing wire. He whirled it. The weight on its end described an arc, and then he flung the handle. The weighted wire struck Venza and Snap just as their repulsive ray shot down against the rocks and shoved them upward. The whirling wire wrapped itself around them, bound them together. Its glow vanished. Snap had been shouting, "Gregg, come up." But it died in his throat.

All this while, in those few seconds, I was vaulting over Molo, trying to get back to the ground to leap again. I saw that Anita was crawling on the rocks. My gravity cylinder was at my belt. I had jammed it there to leave my hands free just as Wyk struck me.

I saw that Snap and Venza, wrapped together by the wire, had dropped their gravity projector. Their entwined figures went up some fifty feet and stopped; then began drifting down.

Molo was shouting, "You, Gregg Haljan! Now for you!"

I struck the rocks and fell twenty feet beyond him. I jerked out my gravity projector, but I did not know what I wanted to do with it. And in that second I saw that the standing Molo was aiming at me. Directly over my head the inert bound bodies of Venza and Snap were falling.

A flash leaped over the dark rocks from Molo. There was a split-second when I thought it was the end of me. But I was still alive. The bodies of Venza and Snap struck my head and shoulders; knocked me down. I felt Molo's ray upon me. Not death, but only his gravity ray, like a giant hand pulling me. Apparently he wanted us alive. I was scrambling on the rocks, entangled with Venza and Snap. Molo's radiance clung. All three of us went tumbling forward toward him. I flashed my own ray, but I was rolling end over end, and it went wild.

I dropped it, saw Molo's beam vanish, saw his upright standing figure towering above me. Snap, Venza and I were in a heap at his feet. He leaned down and seized me. "Now, Gregg Haljan, I will teach you not to try escaping like this!"

With the huge, muscular Martian gripping me, his fist striking for my face but missing and hitting my shoulder, this was a semblance of normality. I could understand fighting like this. I wrapped my legs around him; my fingers reached for his brawny throat as he kicked us into the air free of the entangling bodies of Snap and Venza.

We rose a few feet and sank back, gripping each other, lunging and striking. He was very powerful, this Martian. I caught the round pillar of his throat with my hands. For an instant I shut off his wind, but I could not hold the grip. He struck me a glancing blow in the face, then the heel of his hand was under my chin. It forced back my head, broke my hold on his throat. With returning breath, he gasped an inhalation. And I heard his exulting words: "You are not strong enough!"

We rolled and bumped over the rocks. I caught a blow from his fists full in my face. It was almost the end; I felt my strength going. He laughed as he struck away my answering swing. I was on my back against the rocks, with his body on top of me. Then beyond and behind his hulking shoulder, silhouetted against the sky, I saw Anita rise up. She was lifting a jagged gray mass of stone, full four feet in diameter. She poised it, then crashed it down on Molo's head. He sank away from me; his arms relaxed. The boulder rolled beside him.

It was over now. Wyk was dead; his gruesome body with its smashed face lay near us. Molo was unconscious, breathing heavily, lying motionless, with a wound on the back of his head, the blood welling out, matting his hair.

Anita and I were uninjured, victorious—but what a hollow victory. On the rocks here, bound together by that strange wire, Snap and Venza lay inert. We bent over them. The wire was cold to the touch now. It resisted our efforts to untwine it. We pulled frantically as we pleaded: "Snap, speak to us! Venza, can't you speak?"

Their eyes were open. I was aware that there was no starlight above us, but instead, a lurid sky of flying clouds, shot with a greenish cast. The darkness here was green. The glow of it struck upon the wide-open staring eyes of Venza and Snap. It seemed that there was intelligence in those eyes.

"Snap, can't you hear us?"

His eyelids came down and up again, slowly, as though by a horrible effort. "Can you move, Snap?"

His right eyelid moved. Was his answer, no?

Anita and I had never felt so horrible a sense of aloneness as that which swept us in those succeeding minutes. A breeze was springing up in the lurid green night. It came from the mountains. It wafted across the nearby river, rippling the surface which was now green and sullen. We did not know where to go, what to do.

We found at last that we could untwist the stiffly clinging wire. We laid Venza and Snap on the rocks side-by-side, about thirty feet back from the river. The glowing wire had burned their clothes only a little, as the current was absorbed by the contact with their bodies.

"Snap, are you in pain?"

His eyes seemed to be trying to talk to me. Anita rose from Venza: "Oh, Gregg, what shall we do? Can't we carry them?"

But where? To what purpose? Wild thoughts thronged me: Wandl's control station, bringing chaos and death upon Earth. Mars and Venus. What was that now to me? I thought of Molo's ship.

"Anita, if we can get to the *Star-Streak*, seize it and escape from this world..."

"Carry Snap and Venza there now? But we don't know where it is. Can we make Molo lead us?"

But Molo lay unconscious. I could not rouse him.

Anita and I were so alone! We clung together.

"Gregg, look at that sky!"

The mounting wind was tugging at us. It whined through the dark mountain defiles, surged out over the river where the water now was beginning to toss with waves crossing the swift current. The sky was shot with green shafts of radiance. Over us, the lowering, leaden clouds were scudding, riding the wind.

It burst now upon us; I found suddenly that Anita and I were bracing against it. A puff dislodged us, so that we were blown a dozen feet, bringing up against a crag, as though we were balloons.

"Anita—this wind—we can't maintain ourselves here. We..."

Horror checked me at the thought of Venza and Snap, lying there on the rocks. We saw the body of Wyk, like a great dried insect, lifted by the wind, whirled like a brown leaf over and over, and carried away.

A little pebble came hurtling and struck me. Then a rain of pebbles, like hailstones was pelting at us.

The storm was probably caused by the axial rotation of Wandl. The light-beam upon Earth had been attacked by the Wandl control station without axial rotation. But to attack the beam from Mars, a manipulation of Wandl was necessary. The planet's rotation was started; and suddenly checked. It remained night now, here in this hemisphere. Perhaps there were natural storm tendencies here; perhaps the operators of the control station were unduly eager, manipulating the rotation too suddenly.

At all events, it was frightening. I shouted above its whine and the clatter of the pebbles: "Hold onto me! We'll get to Venza and Snap."

We reached the two inert forms, where they had blown into a niche between two boulders. "Can't stay here, Anita."

"No! If it begins again!"

"Over there! A cave!"

We got Venza and Snap into it, just as another gust came, with a rain of dirt and loose stones pelting past outside.

Suddenly I thought of Molo. "Anita, stay here! Must get to Molo."

"Gregg, no!"

"I must. If we can bring him to consciousness, make him tell us where the *Star-Streak* is..."

I flung off her restraining hold. The wind had eased up. I leaped out into it, swimming. The rocks slid by close under me in a swift sidewise drift. In a moment I would be carried out over the river. It was a chaos of green, windswept darkness. But there was bursting light now overhead and rumbling claps, like thunder.

I saw Molo's body where the wind held him pinned against the side of a flat, ten-foot rock butte, and dove for him, swimming down frantically until I struck against the rock with a blow that almost knocked the breath from me. Molo was still obviously unconscious.

How long it took me to get back to Anita, floundering with Molo's body, I do not know. I managed to keep against the ground; was blown back, and struggled forward again. The wind came with strange puffs. In one of the lulls, I hauled Molo through the air and into the cave.

"Gregg!" Anita held to me, her arms around me. "Gregg dear, you were gone so long!"

I was battered and bruised and breathless. The cave's mouth was like a ten-foot tunnel leading downward into blackness.

"Gregg, I put Venza and Snap here."

They lay side by side, like two dead bodies, here in the greenish darkness. We placed Molo with them. Together Anita and I crouched beside them, clinging to each other, listening to the wild sweep of the wind outside. The storm had burst into full fury now. It would whirl us away like feathers, outside there now. The lightning and thunder hissed and crashed. Stones and boulders were being flung like hailstones.

This flimsy, weightless world! It seemed as though the rocks here on which we were crouching would be shifted and carried away.

"Gregg! Gregg, is this the end?"

A mass of rocks fell at the opening, closing it, so that we were buried here in the darkness. "Anita, my darling, I will never stop loving you."

Darkness, with her arms around me and a shuddering world outside. But here, only Anita and her soft arms.

"Gregg!"

Horror was in her voice. Then I saw what she was seeing. It was not just Anita and I buried here in the darkness with the bodies of Snap and Venza and Molo. Something else was here.

From the blackness of the cave, two green, glowing eyes were staring. Their radiance showed me the outlines of a distended head. An insane thing? But it was not another of the forest insects. This seemed to be an animal. The glow of its distended head disclosed a lythe, horizontal body, seemingly solid and muscled. A chattering, insane animal, here in the dark with us! We heard mouthing, mumbling words, and an eerie, cackling laugh as it came padding toward us.

The thing in the cave stared at us as we clung together in the darkness, transfixed for a moment by horror. The distended head, ghastly of face with its green glowing eyes, wobbled upon a long, spindly neck. The eyes seemed luminous of their own internal light. The radiance from them faintly lighted the black cave so we were able to see its tawny, hairy body. It was long sleek, the size of an Earth leopard. A muscled body, with ponderable weight, it was moving toward us, padding on the rocks.

I recovered my wits and shoved Anita behind me. I crouched on one knee. There was no escape, nowhere to run. This tunnel was blocked by a fallen rock mass behind us, with the wild storm raging outside. The thing was some twenty feet away, where the tunnel broadened into a black cave of unknown size. Beside me Snap and Venza lay inert, the still-unconscious Molo with them.

There was nothing to do but crouch here and protect Anita. I waved my arms, shouted above the outside surge of the storm; my voice reverberated with a muffled roar in this subterranean darkness.

"Get back! Back! Back, away from me!"

It stopped. Round ears stood up from the bloated head. Then it laughed again. I felt Anita shoving a rock at my hand, a chunk of rock the size of my head. "Its face, Gregg! Aim for its face!"

The rock felt like a ball of cork. I flung it and hit the thing on the body. Its laughter checked abruptly; it crouched, as though gathering for a spring.

And then I thought of my gravity projector. I flashed on the repulsive ray to its full intensity.

The tawny body leaped. It came hurtling, but my beam met it in mid-air. For a second I thought that I had been too late. The thing was clawing the air; its momentum carried it against the push of my ray. For an instant it hung, snarling, and then laughed that wild laugh.

The ray forced it back. It receded through the air, back across the blackness of the cave, gathering speed until, in a moment it brought up against the opposite wall some forty feet away. There it hung, pinned as I held the ray upon it. The body had struck the rocky wall but the head was uninjured. It was writhing and twisting: the cave was filled with the reverberations of its screams.

Over the screams, I heard another voice: "Oh Gregg, where are you?"

Snap! Behind me, Anita was moving sidewise toward where Snap and Venza were lying. The thing pinned in my light stopped its screaming, with curiosity perhaps at this new sound.

"Snap! We're here, Snap!"

Then Venza's voice: "It's letting me talk. We're better now."

They were recovering, Anita was bending over them. "Gregg, they're all right. The shock is wearing off, thank God."

But I did not dare move to them. My light on the snarling thing across the cave held it, but I did not dare to relax my attention.

I called, "Stay with them, Anita." I moved slowly forward, holding the beam steady. The cave floor was littered with loose stones and boulders. Ten feet from the pinned animal I selected a great chunk of rock. It towered in my hand, but the weight of it was only a few pounds.

The gravity held the animal as though I had pinned it by a pole. From the distance of a few feet I heaved the boulder. The palpitating head mashed against the wall. The body and the pulp of the head and the boulder sank to the floor when I removed the beam.

"Snap, thank God you've recovered! And you, Venza!"

Anita and I sat with them. They had been fully conscious all the while, but they were out of it now.

An hour passed while we sat crouched, listening to the storm.

"It's letting up," Venza said out of a silence.

Anita was sitting over the prone form of Molo. He had stirred and mumbled several times.

"Let's see if we can get out of here," Snap suggested.

Rocks had fallen and blocked the only exit from the cave. But to our strength, even the hugest of the rocks was movable.

"Shall we try it now, Gregg?"

As though we were elephants, heaving and pushing, we struggled with the litter choking the passage. There was a danger that the whole thing would cave in on us; but we were careful of that. We tossed the small rocks aside like pebbles. There was one main mass. Together we pulled and tugged and shifted it. A small opening was disclosed, large enough for our bodies. The wind puffed in through it.

The girls called us. Molo had regained consciousness. The blow from the rock had only stunned him. We bound his wrists with a portion of his belt which we cut into strips.

"What is it you do with me? Is Wyk dead?"

"Yes."

He lay silent and sullen. "Look here, Molo, we're going to get out of this, and you're going to help us. If you don't..." The knife which we had taken from him to cut his belt was in my hand. I drew its blade lightly across his throat. "Will you talk freely and truthfully?"

"Yes, I will talk the truth."

"Do you know where the control station is located?"

"Yes."

"Where?"

"Not far."

"The hell with that!" Snap burst out. "Get it meshed in your mind, Molo, that we're in no mood for talk like that. How far is it?"

"On Earth you would call it ten miles."

"In these mountains?"

"He told us it was," said Anita. "Underground."

"Do you know where your ship is?" I persisted.

He told us that it was some thirty miles in another direction, not in the mountains, but in the outskirts of a city like Wor. It was equipped and ready for flight, all but the assembling of its crew.

And now we had weapons! Molo was carrying several of the gravity projectors; two small searchlight beams, little hand torches; and three electronic ray-guns of short-range size.

Hope filled us. The storm was abating. We could creep upon the single small control room of the gravity station, where usually but two operators were stationed. The delicate mechanisms there could be wrecked.

And then we would seize the *Star-Streak*. No one would be on the lookout for us. The fact that Molo's prisoners had escaped was as yet unknown; he and Wyk had not dared tell it. Meka was back there waiting. Our absence from the globe dwelling might have been discovered; but Meka would say that we were with Molo. She was waiting there, hoping that her brother and Wyk would recapture us. All this we dragged piecemeal from Molo.

Snap and I shared the gravity projectors and the small electronic guns. "Let's get started, Gregg. The storm seems over."

It was. We found the purple-red starry night again outside. The river was lashed white with waves, but they were spent. There was only a mild warm breeze remaining.

Molo's legs were free, but his wrists were lashed behind him. I hooked an arm under his, holding him like a huge, but light, oblong bundle. Snap called, "Ready, Gregg?"

"Yes."

Snap flashed on his gravity ray and mounted, with the girls clinging to his ankles. Then I followed with Molo. By great arching swoops, we swung up into the frowning, tumbled mountains.

CHAPTER FIFTEEN

"This will be the place to land, Gregg Haljan."

We were drifting down upon a barren region of naked crags, dark, frowning rock-masses, broken and tumbled, as though by some great cataclysm of nature. Mountains upon the Moon could not be more desolate of aspect.

We landed on the rocks. The heights here had a purple-red sheen from the starlight. We had seen frequent evidence of the storm; and it showed here. Rocks were abnormally piled in drifts; smooth areas showed, where the pebbles, stones and boulders had been swept away by the wind.

Snap and the girls landed beside us. We spoke softly. None of us, not even Molo, knew how far sound would carry in this air.

"Where is the place from here?" Snap demanded.

"Off there."

Molo spoke with docile, guarded softness. He gestured with his head and shoulder. A quarter of a mile away, over these uplands, the broken land went down in a sharp depression.

"It is there. I think from here we should go on the ground. There is no guard, and I think seldom is anyone on top."

"If I help you now, if we should wreck the gravity controls, then Wandl will be helpless to navigate space, or to interfere with the rotation of Earth, Mars and Venus. The allied worlds might then defeat the Wandl ships in battle. If that happened, perhaps your governments, because of my help here, would forgive what my *Star-Streak* has done."

"Your piracy?" I said.

"Yes. I am outlawed. I might be reinstated if you would speak the good words for me."

"Maybe."

"Maybe even they would reward me. You think so, Gregg Haljan?"

He wanted to be on the winning side; this suited us. "Let's try it and see, Molo. I'll speak plenty of good words for you."

Now, as we landed on the uplands, he said, "You will do best to free my hands."

"Oh, no!" Snap declared.

"But I am a good fighter. Something unexpected might come."

"Too good a fighter," I said. "We trust you because we have to, Molo, but no more than is necessary."

A small recess in the rocks was near us. We put Molo there, with his hands bound, and with Anita and Venza to guard him. Venza held the electronic gun; she knew how to fire it. The girls crouched in a depression about twenty feet away. They could see Molo plainly; if he moved, a flash of the gun would kill him. He knew that.

The girls gazed at us as we were ready to start. "Good-by, Gregg. Good-by, Snap. Good luck!"

"We won't be long. Sit where you are." Snap touched Venza's shoulder for his good-by. "Listen, Venza: Molo has already told us enough to enable us to find the ship. If he tries anything, kill him."

"Right," she said.

We left them. A minute or two, cautiously shoving ourselves along the rocks, and we were crouching there. The cauldron was about two hundred feet broad and fifty feet deep; an irregular circular bowl. The starlight gleamed on it, and there were dots of small artificial light. We saw a group of small metal buildings, very low and squat, like balls mashed down, flattened in a bulging disc-shape; between them were tiny skeleton towers.

The towers, twice the height of a man, were spread at irregular intervals in a hundred-foot circle, with a group of three or four in the center. There seemed some twenty of them. Taut wires connected their tops, each tower with every other, so that the wires were a lacework above the small disc buildings. The bottoms of the towers were grounded with electrical contacts, and every tower had a ground connection with each other by means of cables.

Far to one side, across the bowl from us, was a single globe-dwelling with lighted windows. From its ground doorway, a narrow metal catwalk extended like a sidewalk on the ground, winding and branching among the towers and discs.

This was the exterior of the Wandl gravity station. It lay silent and dark, save for the starlight and the little lights on the towers. No sign of humans. Then we saw movement in the globe-dwelling. A man came to the doorway, gazed at the sky and went back.

I whispered, "Which is the best entrance to the underground rooms?"

We saw where, at several points, the winding catwalk terminated in low, dome-like kiosks, giving ingress downward. One was on our slope of the cauldron. "That's the one we'll try," Snap murmured.

He stopped suddenly. The top of the distant globe-dwelling was glowing. A little round patch there was radiant, like a lighted window. A transparent ray was coming from inside. The operators within this globe were observing the sky, training instruments upon it, no doubt.

And now we saw in the sky the third of those sword-like beams. It had probably been visible there for some time but we had not noticed it. "That's Venus," I murmured.

It seemed so. A blurred star, red in this atmosphere, was close above the horizon. The light-beam stood out from it, sweeping up to the zenith.

The gravity station here was about to make contact with the Venus beam. We heard a muffled siren, a signal echoing from the subterranean control rooms. The current went into all these wires and towers and twenty-foot ground discs. The hissing and throbbing hum of it was audible. The discs and towers were glowing; red at first, then violet. Then that milky, opalescent white. The overhead wire-aerials were snapping with a myriad of tiny jumping sparks.

I saw now that the top of each tower was a grid of radiant wires, a six-foot circular projector with a mirror reflector close beneath it and a series of prisms and lenses just above. It all glowed opalescent in a moment, a dazzling glare.

Then the tower tops were swinging. The lights from them had reached the intensity of an upflung beam, and the projectors were swinging to focus the beam inward. The focal point seemed about a thousand feet overhead. All the beams merged there; and guided by the towers directly underneath, a single shaft was standing into the sky.

The entire cauldron depression was now a blinding mass of opalescent light. We could see nothing but the milk-white inferno of glare. It painted the rocks up here on the rim so that we shrank back, shaded our eyes and gazed into the sky. And from the cauldron, the hum and the hiss of the current, the snapping of sparks, were all lost in a wild electrical screaming turmoil.

Overhead, we saw the Wandl beam from Venus.

Apparently this control station had two functions: the control of the planet's movements, its axial rotation and its orbital flight, and its ability to apply gravitational force to other celestial bodies.

Wandl was controlling her own movements by applying gravity force, attraction and repulsion, to all the celestial starfield; and doubtless also by applying the repulsive beam tangentially against the ether like rocket streams. In this respect, I realized, the planet was probably operated not unlike one of our familiar spaceships. In effect, it was itself a gigantic globular vehicle. Later I learned that it was thought that Wandl's atmosphere could be highly electronized at will, with a resulting aberration of the natural light-ray reflected from her into space. This could have caused the blurring of the image of Wandl when viewed telescopically from other worlds.

Again, for a moment of the contact, there was that bursting light in the sky.

The contact with the Venus beam lasted a minute or two. Snap and I, on the cauldron rim, were engulfed in the blaze of reflected light and the wild scream of sound. Then presently the turmoil subsided. The contact in the sky was broken. The tow-rope of Venus jerked itself away. But on the next Venus rotation it would be attacked again.

Another few minutes passed. The little circular depression beneath us was dim and silent as we had first seen it. Figures were moving within the dwelling structure. From several of the underground entrances figures came up, the ten-foot insect-like shapes of workers. Three or four of the brains came bouncing up, moving along the ground catwalk with little leaps. All the figures entered the distant main dwelling house. The contact was over.

"Probably hardly anyone left down below," Snap whispered. "Now's our chance."

"If we can get into that opening without being seen," I said.

"Shadows, down the rocks to the left. Damnation, Gregg, we can make it in one calculated leap."

"I'll try it first. I'll get in and wait for you."

"Right."

We each had a gravity cylinder at our belt and a ray-gun in our hand. The slope of the depression was dim here, merely starlit; it was a steep, broken and fairly shadowed descent, fifty feet to the little dome-like kiosk which marked the nearest subterranean entrance. I went down it with a swoop, landed in a heap beside the kiosk and ducked into it. Instinct made me fear a guard, but reason told me none would be here; there was only the danger of encountering someone coming up.

I was at the top of a winding, descending passage, a step-terraced floor; there were occasional lights in the ceiling. In a moment Snap joined me. "Got here! I wonder how far down it goes?"

I gripped him. "Snap, no matter what happens, do it with a rush. Keep with me. And if I shout to get out..."

"We go out with a rush!"

"Yes. Back to the girls. Use your ray-gun and the gravity projector in getting back to them and get away without me, if I fall."

"Same for you, Gregg."

We went down the deserted passage. We had had experience in movement on Wandl now; we handled ourselves more deftly. We went down several hundred feet. The passage branched, but there always seemed a main tunnel.

It was all deserted. There were distant, dimly-lighted, silent rooms. Were these factories of the strange forms of electronic gravity currents Wandl used? Some were in operation. A hum issued from them. Workers moved about.

We stopped to consult. The girls, and Molo himself, had described what we would find: a main route leading to the control room where the delicate mechanisms which operated all this were centralized, the nerve center of Wandl. It seemed that we were following that main route.

A worker came with a swimming leap past us. We dropped into a hollowed shadow at a tunnel intersection, and he went swooping by.

"Lord, Snap," I muttered, "that was too close for comfort."

Again we advanced. The tunnel turned sharply. Down a short slope, a glowing room was disclosed, with two or three workmen moving within it.

The main control room! We could not doubt it. Molo, in his enthusiasm, had once described it clearly to the girls, its great skeins of little thread-like wires spread upon the walls, the myriad tiny opalescent discs contacted with the small gray rock surface under the tangled masses of thread-wire, the levers and dials banked on the circular tables: they were unmistakable features.

"There it is, Snap," I whispered in his ear. "In that central rack. Those insulated rods, see them? Anita told us they used them to adjust the discs. Watch out for the current."

"But it's off now, Gregg!"

"There's still danger in it, and you'd short-circuit somewhere. Keep your hands off. Use the rods."

"The operators..."

He got no further. A figure lunged into us from behind, a giant worker! His largest pincer bit into my shoulder; his hollow shout resounded. The control room operators came with leaps at us.

There was a moment of wild confusion. Light, seemingly almost weightless bodies flapped against us. Arms gripped us, but they were flimsy. The huge body-shells cracked gruesomely as we struck with our solid fists.

A moment of turmoil passed. No bolts were fired. The shouts were brief down here in the narrow confines of the tunnel. Panting, bruised more by our collisions against the rocks than by our adversaries, we ceased our wild lunges. We did not look at the scattered, broken and crushed bodies drifting now to the floor.

"Now, Snap! Hurry! Others may come."

We lunged into the glowing control room, seized the long insulated poles from the central rack. They had a grateful feel of weight. I picked one up, jumped with a long leap to the wall.

The wires came down like cobwebs under my sweeping blows; the little discs knocked off as though they were fungus growth.

Sparks flew around us. Shafts of electronic radiance spat out. The wall was hissing over all its length as I ranged up and down it. The tangled broken threads of wire writhed like living things on the floor; then crumpled, fused and turned black.

I swept that wall-segment with frantic haste, lunged around and started another way. Across the room I saw Snap doing the same. A turmoil of electrical sound was reverberating around us, deafening, and the glare was blinding. A belt-shaft shot from the wreckage under my rod. It seared my left arm. My sleeve burned off; the arm hung limp and tingling at my side. I stopped to rub it; in a moment strength came back to its muscles.

Snap was raging like a great heavy bird gone amok. Through the green fumes of electrical gases which were filling the room I saw him lunging at the circular tables, overturning them. They cracked like thin polished stone as they struck the metal floor.

I finished with the wall. There was a twenty-foot square piece of metal apparatus, ramified and intricate; I heaved it over upon its side. A thousand little mirrors and prisms, dislodged from it, came out in a splintering deluge.

I was aware of Snap fighting with a brown-shelled figure. Then he was free of it. I saw it mashed and broken at his feet as I dove past, swimming in the smoke to lunge the length of a great fluorescent tube which was still dimly glowing. My pole pried it over; it crashed with a brief puff of light and the rush of an explosion as air went into its vacuum.

I found Snap panting beside me, clinging to me in mid-air. The glare was dying around us; the din was lessening. We were choking in the chemical fumes of the released, half-burned gases. Turgid darkness was coming to the wrecked room, with little hissing flares spitting through it.

"Enough, Gregg! Listen! Up overhead..."

A great siren from up there was screaming into the night.

Snap panted, "Got to get out of here. Can't breathe."

Together we lunged for the tunnel by which we had entered. I stood a moment, gazing back upon the strewn and scattered room.

The delicate nerve-center of Wandl. Heavy green-black gas fumes swirled in it; darkness and silence closed down.

CHAPTER SIXTEEN

Over us was turmoil, that screaming siren. Then suddenly it was checked and we heard the thump and swish of what on Earth would have been called running footsteps and shouts.

Snap shoved me. "Don't stay there, you fool!"

We lunged up the passage. Figures barred it but they scattered; a bolt hissed at us, but missed. At the kiosk a group of workers and several peering little brains leaped away in terror to let us pass.

We gained the open air. With the small gravity rays darting down with repulsion upon the rocks we mounted like rockets out of the cauldron. The upper plateau lay silent in the starlight, but the cauldron behind us was ringing with alarm, and again the danger siren was blaring.

I changed my way of direction, swung it to the plateau rocks ahead. The arc of my flight was sharply bent as I went hurtling down. Over me, I saw Snap use the same tactics. I tried to aim for where we had left the girls and Molo. I could not see them down there amid the starlit crags; and suddenly a wild apprehension filled me. How had we dared leave them to Molo's trickery?

Then, ahead and below me, I saw the slight figure of one of the girls, standing on a rock with arms outstretched to signal us. I changed my ray to repulsion barely in time to avoid crashing. The landing flung me in a heap. Twenty feet away, Snap came whirling down. We picked ourselves up, saw Anita waving from the rock, and bounded to her.

The girls were safe. Venza sat intent, with unwavering watchful gaze across the intervening space to where Molo had flattened himself against his rock, not daring to move.

"Still got him," Venza exulted. "He wasn't willing to take any chances with us. You did it, Snap?"

"I'm a motor-oiler if we didn't. Come on; got to get out of this. They're after us! We wrecked the whole damn place, Venza. Wandl's a normal planet now. No more of this accursed dislocation of Earth."

We learned later that our hope and our assumption that we had irretrievably wrecked the entire gravity control system of Wandl was proven to be a fact. Wandl was, in effect, a normal celestial body now. The beams planted in Greater New York, Ferrok-Shahn and Grebhar still streamed across space. But there was no giant beam from Wandl to seize them, and Wandl now could not move through space of her own volition. Like Earth, and all other known planets, satellites, comets and asteroids, she was subject now to all the normal natural laws of celestial mechanics. We had done a thorough job of it.

Now I shoved at Snap. "No time to talk. You tow the girls; I'll take Molo. Got to get to the *Star-Streak*."

I lunged over and seized Molo. "We did it. Now for your vessel! It will be ill for you if she is not where you say she is."

"She will be there, Gregg Haljan."

He docilely put himself in position for me to hook my forearm under his crossed, bound wrists and carry him. Snap rose up past us, towing the girls. Over the nearby cauldron a figure mounted to gaze and see the nature of this strange attacking enemy, and then sank back.

With Molo hanging to me, I mounted with my ray, following Snap and the girls into the starlight, with the turmoil of the cauldron receding until in a moment or so it was gone behind our horizon.

We headed now, not toward Wor, whence we had come, but over at an angle to the side. Our great bounding arcs soon left the mountains behind. We crossed the river, another portion of the forest, and came over undulating lowlands.

It was a flight of under half an hour. The pursuit, if indeed anyone followed us, remained below our little segment of curving horizon. Everywhere there was evidence of the storm; the forest trees were laid flat, strewn like driftwood over the area. The river had in several places lashed over its banks. The lowlands were dotted thick with globe-dwellings. Some were hanging awry on their stems; others were pulled from their place, cracked and piled into a litter.

We kept well aloft. The surface scenes were only glimpses of wreckage, moving lights and people. And there were areas which the wind had seemingly spared.

The confusion from the storm was mingled now with the spreading alarm from the gravity station; the sound of the danger siren there was still audible behind us. As we advanced into what now seemed the outskirts of a city like Wor, with a pile of solid-looking metal structures ranging the horizon ahead, I saw a distant spaceship rise up and wing away. Wandl was proceeding with the dispatching of her space navy to oppose the distantly gathering ships of Earth, Venus, and Mars. No doubt with the wrecking of the control station, the masters of Wandl immediately recognized the paramount importance of the coming battle.

The huge, globular, disc-like ship sailed high over us, rotating with the impulse of its rocket-streams. In a moment it was lost in the stars. And then another rose and followed it.

There were many human figures in the air around us now. I mounted higher, and Snap with the girls followed me. The figures, intent upon their own affairs, did not seem to heed us.

Molo's vessel lay alone upon a low metal cradle. No other ship was near it; but half a mile away on both sides we could see others resting on their stages. Lights were moving around and upon them, but the *Star-Streak* was dark and neglected.

We poised a thousand feet over her, and to one side. I saw her as a long, low, pointed vessel, dead gray in color, longer than the *Cometara*, and seemingly narrower, but very similar in aspect.

"Meka and I are supposed to be gathering our crew," said Molo. "No one bothers with my vessel. Will you take me to Wor now to get Meka?"

"I will not."

Snap was drifting down with the girls. They were near us. His arm waved at me with a gesture. And then came the muffled tone of his voice: "Shall we drop down, Gregg?"

"Yes, but cautiously. Have your gun ready."

Molo protested, "I would like to take Meka with us, and a few of my crew. You will have trouble handling the *Star-Streak*, just us three men."

"We'll take our chances."

We dropped swiftly down upon the dark and vacant platform. The gray hull of the *Star-Streak* loomed beside us, her dome arched still higher. An inclined catwalk went up to her opened deck-port.

"I'll go first," I said softly to Snap. "Come quickly after me. Watch out: there might be someone on board."

Venza still clung to her weapon. Mine was in my hand as I lifted Molo. And, ignoring the incline, bounded the thirty feet for the deck-port. I landed safely, and stood Molo upon his feet. "Don't you move," I admonished him sternly.

He stood docilely against the cabin wall of the superstructure. No one here. We had thought there might easily be one or two workers on board.

Snap and the girls came sailing, one after the other, and landed on the deck beside me. We stood silent, alert. No one appeared from within the cabin or from the lengths of the deck. Venza was watching Molo with her weapon upon him. Snap and I had planned this boarding: Anita and Venza to stay here and guard Molo while we searched the ship, and inspected the controls. We started for the cabin door oval.

"Gregg!"

It was all the warning Snap could give. I was within the dim cabin, but he, behind me, was still on the deck. I whirled to see a dozen dark forms leaping from the roof of the cabin superstructure. Snap was all but buried by them. These were not men of Wandl, but Molo's pirate crew, Martians, Earthmen and Venusians. Snap's ray-gun spat as he went down; one of the men dropped away. I saw Venza turn with startled horror, as the huge figure of Meka leaped down upon her and Anita from the roof.

For an instant, weapon in hand, I paused in the doorway. I could not fire into the turmoil of that struggling group, so instead plunged into it, striking with my fists.

Molo was shouting, "Do not kill them! I was ordered not to kill them!"

These men, so different from the insect-like workers and the brains of Wandl, were solid in my grip; but we were all so weightless! I felled one, but others gripped me, pounded me. A struggling mass of bodies, arms and legs, we surged up to the superstructure roof and dropped upon it. My weapon was gone. Half a dozen adversaries had me pinioned.

Down on the deck I saw that Venza had lost her weapon; Molo and Meka were clutching her. Snap was fighting with several antagonists. Anita was loose. She dove for the group in which

Snap was struggling, hit them, kicked and bounded upward, to be seized by two of my own captors.

"Anita, don't fight! They'll kill you!"

I tried to break loose, but four huge Martians were holding me.

"Oh, Gregg!"

There was horror in Anita's voice. Snap had broken away. At the open deck-port he stood, as though undecided what to do. The deck was almost black around him; he was silhouetted against the outside starlight. From almost at his side, in the darkness, a tiny bolt spat upward at his head. His arms went wildly out; he tumbled backward. At the top of the boarding incline his body seemed spasmodically to kick, and the thrust whirled it down into the darkness.

The end of Snap! A pang went through me. Snap, my best friend!

Molo cursed the unknown man of his crew who had fired the shot. But none would admit who did it.

"Get to your posts," Molo roared in Martian. "Enough of you are here. Lash up the prisoners; we're launching away now." He thumped his brawny sister as she passed him. "Well played, Meka!"

These wily Martians! Molo had planned that Meka was to gather the crew and wait here at the ship for him and Wyk. If they returned with us as captives, it would be here that they would come. But if by chance things went adversely, Molo reasoned we would act just as we did; and Meka and her men were lurking here in ambush, waiting for us.

All the many various ports swung shut. Anita, Venza, and I, with arms and legs bound, were taken by Molo to the forward observation and control room.

The ship was resounding with signals. The interior controls in the hull-base raised the gravity-pull within the vessel to a strength comparable to that of Earth. Within a few minutes the *Star-Streak* lifted from the stage. Strange, weird Wandl fell away from us. We slid upward through the atmosphere, following one of the globular Wandl vessels, and headed into space toward the point where, a few million miles distant, the ships of allied Earth, Venus, and Mars were gathering.

CHAPTER SEVENTEEN

"They are visible." Molo turned from the eyepiece of his electro-telescope. "Do you want to see them, Gregg Haljan?"

We were in the forward control and observation turret of the *Star-Streak*, Molo and his sister Meka, Venza, Anita and myself. Unobtrusively squatting on the floor was a small, gray, rat-faced fellow, put there, weapon in hand, to watch us. He was a ruffian from the underworld of Grebhar, a member of the *Star-Streak's* pirate crew.

We were some ten hours out from Wandl. A group of four of the globular Wandl ships were with us, strung in a line some ten thousand miles to our left. We had been heading diagonally toward Mars. Some fifteen other Wandl vessels were ahead and others following.

We were no more than fifteen million miles from Mars when Molo sighted the allied ships. "Will you observe them, Gregg Haljan?"

I moved to take his place at the 'scope-grid, with the gaze of Anita and Venza upon me. They sat huddled together on a low bench against the back curve of the circular turret.

It was dim here, with little spots of instrument lights, and the radiance coming in the glassite plates of the encircling dome. The loss of Snap had put a grim look upon the girls. They were dispirited, docile with Meka. They had hardly had a word with me. I think that all of us had about given up hope during those hours. Molo had consulted me several times with his policies of navigation.

But I saw no chance to trick him. He was indeed, far more experienced than I, and more skillful, in celestial mechanics. I worked with him. I learned the operation and the handling of the *Star-Streak*, which was not greatly different from the *Cometara* or the *Planetara*.

Poor Snap! He and I had planned to capture and navigate this *Star-Streak*. We could have handled her. There were, I gathered, some fifteen men aboard her now, but no more than two or three were engaged at the navigating mechanisms. Even they could be dispensed with at times, for the ship's controls were all automatic, handled directly from the forward turret.

I learned too, something, though not much, of the *Star-Streak's* weapons. They were similar to those of the allied ships, since Molo in equipping his pirate craft had seized upon all the best he could find of the three worlds.

The *Star-Streak*, during this flight toward Mars, was in close communication with the Wandl craft. There was a giant vessel, the Wor, off to our left now. It carried the brain master in command of the Wandl forces. Molo took his orders from the Wor, but since his equipment and his weapons were so wholly different, the *Star-Streak* was set apart.

"I can do what I like," Molo told me. "With my own judgement I can act; you shall see."

"You've had plenty of experience, Molo."

"Have I not! The terror of the starways, your world called me." He chuckled vaingloriously. "I must justify it now."

"Act, do not talk," Meka commented sourly. "Children with toys make speeches like that, and then the toys get broken."

"Fear not, sister. Never again will the *Star-Streak* come to grief."

And now I gazed through the 'scope at the waiting allied ships. They were lying some eight million miles off Mars. I gazed and saw the poised little group. There were perhaps fifty of them. The majority were Martian, long, low and very sharp-ended, and dull red in color. The wider Earth and Venus ships were silvery and drab. I could distinguish the several different types of craft in this hastily assembled fleet: many converted commercials like my ill-starred *Cometara*; a few rakish police ships; and about a dozen of the long, narrow supermodern warships. It was their first voyage into battle. They had only been built these past few years, by peaceful governments that protested there never again would be another war!

The little fleet was lying waiting for us. It was being augmented by occasional other ships from Mars. They saw us coming now. The radiance of a Benson curve-light enveloped them, with a shaft toward us. The image of them shifted over a million miles to one side.

Molo laughed when he saw it. "Protecting themselves already! But we are not going to attack them there."

The first tactics of the Wandl commanders surprised me. We swung away from the course to Mars and headed diagonally toward Earth and Venus. Earth was the nearer to us, with Venus some forty million miles beyond her. For hours we turned in that sweeping curve. Then with our Wandl convoy following, we headed for Earth. I could not help admiring the way the *Star-Streak* was handled. She turned more sharply than the Wandl craft; and before our next meal, we were leading them all.

Would the allied ships follow us? It was immediately apparent they were coming; but from their poised position, hours of attaining velocity would be needed. The other allied vessels approaching from Venus and Earth checked their flight and turned after us. We passed within five or six hundred thousand miles of several of them.

I found now that some twenty other Wandl ships, leaving Wandl after us, had headed directly for Earth. We were all together presently, the *Star-Streak* and nearly fifty Wandl ships, gathered close to one side of the Moon. The allies, about a hundred of them, were strung through space, scattered, with varying velocities and flight direction, but most of them endeavoring to get between the Moon and Earth.

This was the day! I call it that: a routine of meals which Meka grimly served us in the turret, and a little sleep when she took the girls below and I lay on the turret floor. I wondered who was in command of this allied force, and did not learn until afterward that it was Grantline. The *Cometara* had fallen upon the Moon Apennines, not very far from where my old *Planetara* still lay, near the base of Archimedes. But Grantline and a few of his companions, with their powered suits, had struggled free from the gravity pull of the wreckage; and a few hours later, a ship out from Earth picked them up.

Grantline, on one of the Earth police ships, commanded the fleet now, and he afterward told me in detail how he endeavored to conduct his forces in the battle, thus enabling me to describe it from both viewpoints. He had been cruising toward Mars when he saw us make the turn. He thought a landing upon Earth might be planned and hastened all his ships into the area between the Moon and Earth to cut us off.

But that was what Wandl wanted. The Wandl ships, with the *Star-Streak* among them, made a complete slow circuit of the Moon. It took another day. Molo said very little to me in explanation of the Wandl tactics, but I could see that the object was to lure Grantline into following. A few of the allied ships did follow us around, but not many. The rest stayed carefully guarding the line between the Moon and Earth.

There had been no encounter yet between the hostile ships. The huge distances involved in the engagement must be kept in mind. The gravity rays from the Wandl ships were only a slight disturbing element at such a long distance; Grantline's Zed-rays and Benson curve-lights were defensive only. For offence, Grantline's electronic guns and other weapons were of varying range, but none for such distances as these.

Wandl seemed unwilling to begin the battle, and Grantline was cautious as well. He did not know what weapons these strange globular vessels would use; his only experience had been our encounter with the whirling discs.

Then, at the end of the second day, came the first clash. The *Star-Streak*, and all the Wandl ships, were again clustered on the Earth side of the Moon; they were hovering perhaps twenty thousand miles above its surface. Grantline's force was a hundred thousand miles off, toward Earth. One of the Wandl ships came tentatively forward, and Grantline sent one of the new-style warships to meet it.

They encircled each other. Both were cautious, but there was a passing within fifty miles. The Earth ship fired her bolts. The insulated barrage of the Wandl ship withstood them. There was a shower of ether sparks close to the ship, and a reddening of the hull, but nothing more. It seemed that the electro-barrages of the Wandl and allied ships were very similar in nature, an aura of electro-magnetism, enclosing the ship like a curtain fifty feet away, absorbed the electronic stream of the enemy bolt. The Wandl ship flung no bolts; she loosed a score of the whirling discs during the passing. They were of varying sizes, but similar to those which cut and wrecked the *Cometara*; in this instance, the Grantline ship was able to destroy each of them as it came close.

This was the first encounter. The Earth warship went back to its squadron and the Wandl vessel rejoined its fellows. It had fired no bolts. Grantline suspected now what afterward proved to be the fact: these Wandl vessels were not equipped with long-range electronic guns. The Wandl defensive tactics were necessary; they feared a widespread encounter. They were hovering in a compact group, covering a five hundred mile area, over the Moon surface. Their purpose was not yet apparent, but Grantline saw now that one of the Wandl ships was dropping down and landing on the Moon. It skimmed the Apennines and landed not far from Archimedes.

What was that for? Grantline noticed that the lowering, closely-gathered Wandl fleet tried to mask the landing. And their gravity-rays, with repulsive force, darted out to impede the Grantline vessels should they try to advance.

This Earthward hemisphere of the Moon was now largely in shadow, but Grantline's Zed-ray magnifiers showed the vessel on the Moon. Apparatus was being unloaded. It seemed, down there on the rocky Moon plain in the foothills of the Apennines, that some extensive, elaborate base was being prepared.

It was for this the hovering Wandl fleet was waiting, holding off from conflict until this Moon base was ready. When Grantline reached that conclusion, he ordered all his vessels forward to a general attack.

CHAPTER EIGHTEEN

During this time, on the *Star-Streak*, as we and the Wandl fleet made that preliminary circuit of the Moon, an incident occurred which changed everything for me. I had noticed several times as we gathered in the *Star-Streak's* forward turret, that Venza and Anita were eying me. Their expressions were furtive, but I realized that they were trying to attract my attention.

We had no opportunity to speak secretly. Molo or Meka, or that rat-faced guard, were always too near us; and Molo kept me busy with computations of our course.

We rounded the Moon. We gathered with the Wandl fleet some twenty thousand miles above the lunar surface, and I watched that ship descend and land. Like Grantline, I wondered what for. Molo gave me no hint. I saw, through his 'scope, bloated figures in pressure suits unloading mechanisms. They seemed to be placing huge contact-discs in a circle on the lunar rocks. It was reminiscent of the Wandl gravity station, and the contact-beam which Molo had planted in Great-New York.

Then at last the girls had an opportunity to whisper to me. A swift phrase came from Anita. "Gregg! Snap is alive. Hiding on board."

I gasped. Snap alive?

"Planning to rescue us. You and he can capture the *Star-Streak*!"

"Anita! Tell me how."

"No more now! Our room below—he's near it. He spoke to us."

No more. She moved away from me. But it was enough. Snap alive! I recalled that when he fell beside the ship, no one had bothered to go down after the body, and at that time the hull-ports were open.

After a time Meka took the girls below. I sat with Molo, gazing down at the dark and gloomy surface of the Moon. I had finished the mathematical work Molo had given me. My thoughts were with Anita and Venza, down in their cabin now with Meka. Perhaps even now Snap was joining them.

I hardly heard Molo's low, muttered curses, as he set his lenses for a slight alteration of our slow circular course among the Wandl fleet. "That fellow at my gravity-shifts acts like a nitwit. He has them disarranged."

It snapped me to sudden alertness. "Something wrong, Molo? Nonsense!"

"These men of my crew answer my controls too slowly. They should jump when my signals come."

The plates suddenly shifted normally, but there had been an interval of delay. Molo was puzzled and annoyed. My heart pounded as I wondered if he would investigate. But he did not.

"You had better sleep, Haljan. Take advantage now; we shall have action presently. Did you figure our emerging curve?"

I shoved my computations across the table to him. "There."

"You are quick, Haljan."

"We should emerge from the Moon's shadow in about two hours."

"But I will not hold that course. We're staying close near here with the other vessels, but I want some velocity always. Take your sleep, Haljan."

I stretched on the narrow floor mattress. The turret was silent.

I was aroused from a doze by Molo's activities in the turret. The girls and Meka were still below. The ever-silent Venusian, squatting in the turret corner, still had his gun upon me.

I saw that Grantline's ships, over a wide fan-shaped spread, were advancing.

And presently we were engaged in the soundless turmoil of battle. I cannot relate more than fragments, things I saw and experienced, during six or more hours of bursting electronic light and puffs of darkness in that spread of battle area within the Moon-shadow. It was a silent battle of crossing lights, ships a thousand miles apart, gathering velocity with great tangential curves; passing each other in a second; sweeping a thousand miles apart again; turning and coming back. A hundred engagements.

The *Star-Streak* was very fast, very mobile, and, unlike all the other Wandl ships, had the allies' own weapons to use against them. I saw now why they called Molo the terror of the starways!

We swept into the shadowed battle area. Over all its thousand-mile spread were the radiant Wandl gravity-beams, disturbing and impeding the course of Grantline's ships. There was the luminous gleam of projectile rockets, like little comets, soundless, launched by the Wandl craft, and the radiance of the rocket-streams which all the vessels were using now for close maneuvering; the glare of Grantline's searchlight bombs and his white search-beams to disclose the deadly whirling discs which the weapons of his vessel must seek out and destroy. A chaos of silent light, stabbed here and there with Grantline's darkness bombs, bombs of limited local range which exploded in space and which, for a few minutes duration, absorbed all light-rays, giving a temporary effect of darkness.

And then wreckage! Broken, leprous Wandl vessels whose barrage at close range had been smashed by Grantline's guns; torn and littered allied ships, struck by the huge exploding comet-projectiles and the whirling discs; airless hulks, and scattered fragments which no longer resembled a ship at all but only a hull plate or a torn segment of dome. And little drifting blobs, the survivors in pressure suits who had leaped from the wreckage; little blobs ignored, whirled away or drawn forward as by chance the sweeping gravity-beams fell upon them; tiny derelicts, floating stormtossed until the Moon's attraction caught and pulled them down, or a whirling disc cut through them, or the distant aura of a bolt shocked them to a merciful death.

It was a three-dimensional, thousand-mile spread of fantasy infernal. Out of it, after an hour or two, a steady sift of every manner of wreckage was drifting down upon the Moon. The scene began to blur. A haze like glowing star-dust, or the radiance from a comet's tail, was spreading a weirdly luminous mist, blurring, obscuring the scene. This was the released electrons and the dissipating gases of the space guns and exploding projectiles, forming dust which glowed in the mingled starlight and Earthlight.

The *Star-Streak* had plunged, during those six or eight hours, through the battle area. Our several encounters were all characterized by the *Star-Streak's* extreme flexibility, her speed, mobility, and Molo's reckless skill. We came through unscathed. There is a certain advantage for the man who seems not to care for his own life. But there was an encounter, the last one as it chanced, just before we emerged downward out of the fog and found ourselves no more than a thousand miles above the Moon's surface, where our adversary was equally reckless and only Molo's skill saved us.

We came upon a Venus police ship. We plunged, as though seeking a collision, and the Venus ship was willing. For a moment of chaos, both barrages held against the exchange of bolts. Then we rolled over and tilted down from the impulse of the stern rockets. The passing must have been within feet, not miles; and in that second, Molo timed a shot to strike at the enemy bottom. It went through their barrage. Behind us, a second later, there was only strewn wreckage of the ship, so finely powdered that it became a silvery radiance, like moonlight shining on a little patch of fog.

"Not too bad?" Molo gazed around for appreciation. "Not bad, Gregg Haljan? Molo is not too unskillful?"

We hung now close above the Moon's surface, with the battle area over us. Out of the fog up there came the drifting wreckage; and now the Wandl ships were coming down, one by one. Not so many of them now; no more than ten of them emerged.

Grantline did not follow. His ships withdrew the other way. The fog gradually dispersed. Grantline could now take stock of the battle; he had been victorious. One might call it that, since his percentage of strength, numerically, was greater now than when the battle began. Ten remaining Wandl ships, and the allies had about twenty-five.

Another hour passed. Grantline's twenty-five ships were gathered in a close group, ten thousand miles above the Moon's surface. Under them, the ten Wandl vessels and the *Star-Streak* seemed ranging in a five hundred mile circle. Down through it, on the rocks of the Moon in the foothills of the Apennines, the mechanism established there abruptly sprang into action.

It was a giant gravity-beam. Of infinitely greater power than any Wandl vessel could generate, it flung out its spreading, conical ray.

So this had been the purpose of all the Wandl tactics, to manipulate Grantline into his present position. This gravity-beam, though far smaller, was comparable to the one used by the Wandl control station. A rock contact against a huge mass, Wandl, and here, the Moon were necessary to give the ray its power. No ship could generate such a ray, so the Wandlites chose this battleground where they could establish themselves upon our deserted Moon.

The beam had about a hundred foot diameter at its base on the rocks; it passed upward through the circle of Wandl vessels and its spread bathed all of Grantline's ships at once. An attractive beam, so powerful that the ships were helpless; against all their efforts they were pinned and drawn downward. A slight velocity at first, but with a tremendous acceleration.

Within an hour they were hurtling, coming together as they speeded down the narrowing cone of the beam. The ten thousand miles, their distance above the Moon, was cut to five thousand. The Wandl ships drew aside, keeping well out of range to let them pass; in another thirty minutes or so they would crash against the rocks.

I gazed in horror from the *Star-Streak's* turret. We were sidewise to the angle of the beam. Grantline's ships were pulled together now into almost a fifty-mile group. They hung all askew, helplessly pinned, some broadside, some upended. The movement of their fall was so rapid that even with the naked eye it was apparent.

"Got them now," Molo chuckled. "This is the end for them, Gregg Haljan."

There were only three of us in the turret: Molo and I, and my watchful, silent guard who sat cross-legged, with a ray-gun pointed at me.

Meka and the two girls were below during all the engagement.

It was over now.

During this lull Molo had sent the men from the deck gun ports to their hull quarters. Our decks were empty now; the bridges and catwalks up here had momentarily no occupants. The *Star-Streak* had little velocity, only a slow drift downward toward the Moon's surface, which now was only a few hundred miles beneath us.

The lunar disc was a great dark spread of desolation, with only the sunlight topping the distant horizon limb. And from under us, to the side, was the source of the giant gravity-beam. Over us were the watch-Wandl vessels, and, still higher, the helpless knot of Grantline's ships hurtling down.

"Got them now," Molo repeated. "In another..."

He never finished. From the open doorway of the turret a figure rose up. Snap! His aspect, even more than his appearance, transfixed me. Snap, with his clothes torn; grimy and spattered with blood; his face pale and gaunt, with hollow, blazing eyes. And above it, the shock of rumpled red hair. In one hand he clutched a ray-gun, and in the other a blood-stained knife!

My guard squatting on the floor, half-turned. Snap's bolt met him before he could raise his weapon. He tumbled dead almost at

my feet. And mingled with the hiss of the bolt was Snap's shout at
the unarmed Molo.

"Into the corner, you! Back up, you damned traitor, else I'll kill
you as I've killed everyone else on this ship!"

CHAPTER NINETEEN

I had leaped and seized the gun which was still in the hand of
the dead guard. "Snap, the girls!"

"Down below. Free. They've got Meka bound and gagged,
locked and sealed in a bunk-room. You bring them up! I'll hold
this accursed traitor. No need to kill him. By the gods, I've killed
enough!"

He saw for the first time the vast silent drama in the firmament
outside the dome windows. "Gregg, for the love of…"

"No time now, Snap! I'll get the girls."

"Watch out. I might have missed somebody down below."

He had. Three men appeared on the forward deck near the
foot of our turret ladder. My bolt spat down upon them; two of
them fell. The other ran aft, toward where I saw Venza and Anita
appearing from the lounge doorway of the cabin superstructure. I
fired again, and the running man tumbled forward on his face. He
was the last of the pirate crew.

Molo was crouching, half-bending forward over his instrument
table, with Snap's gun upon him. The girls burst upon us. We
armed them. Meka was safely fastened down below. We backed
Molo to the floor in the corner, with Venza and Anita watching
him.

Snap and I were in control of the ship. For temporary periods
the automatics would handle the gravity-shifters. I could operate
them here from the turret. We had a downward velocity toward
the Moon. Five hundred miles below us, no more, was the base of
that diabolical gravity-ray which was so swiftly pulling the twenty-
five Grantline ships to their destruction.

I gripped Snap and told him what we must do. "The forward
gun on the starboard side is almost identical with our Earth guns,
the Francine projectors. With a short range you can handle it and
I'll give you a close mark!"

He dashed for the deck. I set the levers. Gravity-plates with full bow attraction. Stern repulsion to the Earth and the stern rocket-streams at highest power.

The *Star-Streak* responded smoothly; with acceleration such as only Molo's famous terror of the starways could attain, we dove for the Moon.

Breathless minutes! Those Wandl ships up in the firmament behind our stern would probably do nothing; they would not understand this sudden move of their friendly ship. The brain masters, the insect-like Wandlites down on the Moon rocks operating the mechanism of the gravity-ray, would not suspect until too late what the *Star-Streak* was doing.

Uprushing rocks, the Apennines to one side; the dark yawning maw of Archimedes on the other. We were diving parallel with the gravity-ray now, hardly a mile from it, diving for the mechanisms of its source. Twenty thousand feet of altitude. I bent our rocket-streams up for the start of our turning. Bow-hull gravity-plates next. Ten thousand feet. Five thousand.

How close we went I never knew. It was seconds now, not minutes. I shifted all the controls. Our bow lifted as we straightened. The whole spreading lunar surface tilted and dipped. Snap fired. I saw the bolt flash at the tilting landscape and a puff of light down there on the rocks. And an instant later there were vacant rocks where the little cluster of men and mechanisms had been. And the upflung gravity-beam was gone!

The giant towering cliffs of the mountain of Archimedes seemed to rush at our upturning bow. The great dark crater-mouth slid under our hull. But we cleared it; the maw of blackness slid down and away; the whole lunar world tilted down and dwindled as we mounted again into the starlight.

Minutes passed while we mounted. Above our upstanding bow was a new drama. The suddenly-released Grantline ships, almost level with the ten Wandl vessels when the ray vanished, turned sidewise. The poised Wandl craft, devoid of velocity, could not pick up the ray to escape now. Grantline, for those minutes, ignored the frantically flung discs; it was a desperate encounter, all at close quarters. We saw the spitting, puffing lights and the silent turmoil, hidden presently by the spreading clouds of luminous fog.

Then out of it came drifting the wreckage. We plunged through an end of the glowing fog, encountered nothing but two triumphant Venus vessels. With them we mounted into the upper starlight.

This was the end of the battle. The victorious Grantline ships one by one came lunging up: only twelve of them now. No Wandl vessels were left.

The great spreading cloud drifted down like a shroud to hide the wreckage, drifted and settled to the lunar surface, a great, radiant area of fog, gleaming in the Earthlight.

CHAPTER TWENTY

There is very little more, pertinent to this narrative, that I need add of the events on Earth, Venus, and Mars during this momentous summer. The main facts are history now: the wild storms, the damage done by outraged nature and the panic among the people—all of it has been detailed as public news. The strange light-beams planted by Wandl in Greater New York, Grebhar, and Ferrok-Shahn have not yet burned themselves away. But they are lessening and scientists say that they will soon be gone.

The changed calendars call this the New Era. The axis of each of the three worlds was not appreciably altered; the climates are at last restoring to normal. But the axial rotations of all three planets were slowed by that attacking Wandl beam before we wrecked the gravity station. The Earth day has been lengthened, resulting in the new calendar, the New Era. Our year, formerly of approximately 365¼ days, now contains, but 358.7 days.

Molo and Meka have been returned to Ferrok-Shahn. They were tried there for piracy and treason and are imprisoned.

And Wandl? With her gravity-controls wrecked, Wandl became subject to the balancing celestial forces. During those succeeding months of the summer and autumn no other spaceships appeared from her: nor did our world investigate. Her presence here, even a little world one-sixth the size of the Moon, was causing disturbance enough!

Wandl moved with slow velocity, like a dallying, strangely sluggish comet about to round our Sun. What would her final orbit be? By fortunate chance she headed in, far from the Earth and Venus; missed Mercury by a wide margin; went close around the Sun: came out again.

But the pull of the Sun, and Mercury dragged her back. Her velocity was not great enough.

I recall that late autumn afternoon when, with Anita, Snap, and Venza, I sat in the observatory near Washington, gazing at Wandl through the dark glass of the solar-scope. Doomed invader! She showed now as a tiny dark dot over the Sun's giant, blazing surface. This was her final plunge. The dot was presently swallowed and gone. It seemed, amid those giant, licking streamers of blazing gas, that there was an extra puff of light.

And some claim now that for a brief time our sunlight was a trifle warmer, a little pyre to mark the end of Wandl, the Invader.

THE END

If you've enjoyed this book, you will not want to miss these terrific titles...

ARMCHAIR SCI-FI & HORROR DOUBLE NOVELS, $12.95 each

D-121 **THE GENIUS BEASTS** by Frederik Pohl
THIS WORLD IS TABOO by Murray Leinster

D-122 **THE COSMIC LOOTERS** by Edmond Hamilton
WANDL THE INVADER by Ray Cummings

D-123 **ROBOT MEN OF BUBBLE CITY** by Rog Phillips
DRAGON ARMY by William Morrison

D-124 **LAND BEYOND THE LENS** by S. J. Byrne
DIPLOMAT-AT-ARMS by Keith Laumer

D-125 **VOYAGE OF THE ASTEROID, THE** by Laurence Manning
REVOLT OF THE OUTWORLDS by Milton Lesser

D-126 **OUTLAW IN THE SKY** by Chester S. Geier
LEGACY FROM MARS by Raymond Z. Gallun

D-127 **THE GREAT FLYING SAUCER INVASION** by Geoff St. Reynard
THE BIG TIME by Fritz Leiber

D-128 **MIRAGE FOR PLANET X** by Stanley Mullen
POLICE YOUR PLANET by Lester del Rey

D-129 **THE BRAIN SINNERS** by Alan E. Nourse
DEATH FROM THE SKIES by A. Hyatt Verrill

D-139 **CRY CHAOS** by Dwight V. Swain
THE DOOR THROUGH SPACE By Marion Zimmer Bradley

ARMCHAIR SCIENCE FICTION CLASSICS, $12.95 each

C-55 **UNDER THE TRIPLE SUNS**
by Stanton A. Coblentz

C-56 **STONE FROM THE GREEN STAR**
by Jack Williamson

C-57 **ALIEN MINDS**
by E. Everett Evans

ARMCHAIR MASTERS OF SCIENCE FICTION SERIES, $16.95 each

G-13 **SCIENCE FICTION GEMS, Vol. Seven**
Jack Vance and others

G-14 **HORROR GEMS, Vol. Seven**
Robert Bloch and others